DANGER RANGE

Fletcher rode under a vast sky, the clouds so close to the earth he felt he could reach up and grab a handful, then watch it vanish from his fist like smoke.

As a boy he'd loved this land, thrived on its wonder, and now, gradually, that sense of awe, of belonging, was coming back to him.

A ring-necked pheasant, startled, fluttered up between the front legs of Fletcher's stud, and the big horse reared in surprise. An instant later, a gunshot boomed across the afternoon quiet, then another, racketing echoes slamming among the surrounding hills like the fall of shattered glass.

Fletcher reined in his horse, looking around him.

The shots could have been fired by a hunter out after meat to store against the coming of winter.

Or they could mean big trouble.

Ralph Compton

Showdown at Two-Bit Creek

A Ralph Compton Novel
by Joseph A. West

A SIGNET BOOK

SIGNET
Published by New American Library, a division of
Penguin Group (USA) Inc., 375 Hudson Street,
New York, New York 10014, U.S.A.
Penguin Books Ltd, 80 Strand,
London WC2R 0RL, England
Penguin Books Australia Ltd, 250 Camberwell Road,
Camberwell, Victoria 3124, Australia
Penguin Books Canada Ltd, 10 Alcorn Avenue,
Toronto, Ontario, Canada M4V 3B2
Penguin Books (N.Z.) Ltd, Cnr Rosedale and Airborne Roads,
Albany, Auckland 1310, New Zealand

Penguin Books Ltd, Registered Offices:
80 Strand, London WC2R 0RL, England

First published by Signet, an imprint of New American Library,
a division of Penguin Group (USA) Inc.

First Printing, June 2003
10 9 8 7 6 5 4 3 2 1

THE IMMORTAL COWBOY

This is respectfully dedicated to the "American Cowboy." His was the saga sparked by the turmoil that followed the Civil War, and the passing of more than a century has by no means diminished the flame.

True, the old days and the old ways are but treasured memories, and the old trails have grown dim with the ravage of time, but the spirit of the cowboy lives on.

In my travels—to Texas, Oklahoma, Kansas, Nebraska, Colorado, Wyoming, New Mexico, and Arizona—I always find something that reminds me of the Old West. While I am walking these plains and mountains for the first time, there is this feeling that a part of me is eternal, that I have known these old trails before. I believe it is the undying spirit of the frontier calling, allowing me, through the mind's eye, to step back into time. What is the appeal of the Old West of the American frontier?

It has been epitomized by some as the dark and bloody period in American history. Its heroes—Crockett, Bowie, Hickok, Earp—have been reviled and criticized. Yet the Old West lives on, larger than life.

It has become a symbol of freedom, when there was always another mountain to climb and another river to cross; when a dispute between two men was settled not with expensive lawyers, but with fists, knives or guns. Barbaric? Maybe. But some things never change. When the cowboy rode into the pages of American history, he left behind a legacy that lives within the hearts of us all.

—*Ralph Compton*

Historical Note

By the time George Armstrong Custer and the 7th Cavalry surveyed the Black Hills in 1874, rumors of gold had been circulating for more than fifty years. At first the government tried to buy the Black Hills from the Sioux. But Paha Saha, as the Indians called their sacred Black Hills, was not for sale.

What he could not get with money, the white man took by force. By 1876, the year in which this novel is set, there were thirty thousand miners swarming all over the hills.

Deadwood, the epicenter of all this activity, was dubbed "the richest one hundred square miles on earth."

There is still gold in them thar hills. The Homestake Mining Company bought the area's richest deposit in 1877, and it's been producing gold ever since. Now more than a mile deep, it is the United States' longest continually operating underground mine, though I heard recently that after one hundred thirty-six years, the gold is finally showing signs of exhaustion.

Today the real mother lode can be found along Deadwood's Main Street—the casinos where tourists from all over the world try their hand at gambling. But if you still have the gold fever and wish to forego the pleasures of the casino, try panning the tumbling streambeds of the Black Hills.

Find a fast-moving stream and look for places where the current suddenly slows, allowing gold particles to settle out.

In streams that flow over bedrock, the gold is often trapped in holes, pockets and other depressions in the bedrock. When the stream runs through boulders or layered rock, pan the sand and grit you'll find in the crevices.

A beginner can usually process a pan of placer gravel in about ten minutes. Be warned: it's a long ten minutes standing in icy water up to your knees. In 1876, a day's work for a seasoned miner was fifty pans a day, but not every batch of gravel panned out, and often he went to his blankets empty-handed.

If you're lucky and find some color, you can pan enough gold to pay for your grub and gas. If not . . . Well, panning is a marvelous experience and a real, living link to the days of the Old West.

Alan Pinkerton was an equal opportunity employer almost one hundred years before the practice became widely accepted in the United States.

He readily hired female agents and expected them to live by the same strict code of morals he placed on men: namely, to have no "addiction to drink, smoking, card playing, low dives and slang."

Pinkerton hired his first female in 1856, slender, brown-haired Kate Warne, who walked into his Chicago headquarters and asked for a job. She surprised Pinkerton when she said she didn't want to work as a clerk but as an agent.

Kate argued her point of view eloquently," says the official Pinkerton history, "pointing out that women could be most useful in worming out secrets in many places which would be impossible for a male detective."

Kate became the first female detective in the United

States. Pinkerton soon hired many other women at Kate's urging, and he later appointed her Supervisor of Women Agents.

By 1876, the female ranks had grown, Kate having shown Pinkerton the tremendous value of women to his organization.

Pinkerton was a man way ahead of his time. Women were not allowed to join regular police departments until 1891 and did not become detectives until 1903. The term policewoman was not used until 1920.

I don't subscribe to the popular belief that Calamity Jane married Wild Bill Hickok in or around Abilene in 1870. Allegedly, the marriage vows were written in the flyleaf of a Bible, and the Reverends W. K. Sipes and W. F. Warren conducted the ceremony.

It seems highly improbable to me that Hickok—a well-groomed dandy who, like his friend Colorado Charlie Utter, took a bath every day—would be attracted to, much less marry, the smelly, heavy-drinking, tobacco-chewing Calamity.

It should be noted that Hickok's notions of hygiene were so unusual in the malodorous and unwashed West that the famed pistoleer's daily bath became one of the "sights" at the end of the trail.

I am of the opinion that Ralph Compton believed the "flyleaf wedding" was concocted by Hickok as a practical joke, and that's how I have interpreted his notes for that portion of *Showdown At Two-Bit Creek.*

Chapter 1

"Seems to me a man who has so much mought want to spare some for poor folks like us who have so little."

Buck Fletcher sighed, sensing the danger even as he recognized an old, familiar pattern that he'd experienced more times than he cared to remember in the clamorous saloons of dusty cow towns from El Paso to Dodge.

He was being set up, backed against the wall, and only his death in a sudden, roaring blaze of gunfire would satisfy the two men facing him.

The men stood tense and eager in a dugout that passed for a saloon in the Bald Mountain country of the Dakota Territory. They were rough, dirty and bearded, buffalo hunters by the look of them, and Fletcher recognized their stamp. These were men who would rather steal than work, and they would kill without hesitation or a single moment's remorse.

Both wore filthy sheepskin coats that were buttonless and tied around with string, moccasins to their knees and shapeless, battered hats that looked like they'd once belonged to other men. Fletcher figured these two shared maybe six rotten teeth between them, and even at a distance of eight feet he could smell their rank stench.

The man who'd spoken was the younger of the two, a mean-eyed towhead with a Sharps .50 caliber cradled in the crook of his arm, his loose mouth grinning, confident of his gun skills.

The two were on the prod, hungry to take what was Fletcher's: his guns, horses and the three hundred dollars in hard gold coins he carried in his money belt.

Fletcher was well aware that what he had was little enough. It wasn't much for a man to show for four years of war, another four as a ranch hand, two as a cow town marshal and then five rakehell years as a hired gun.

During those years, Fletcher had learned his profession well—the difficult way of the Colt's revolver, the draw and fire that took so much time and patience to master. The years had honed him down to six feet of bone and hard muscle, and he was lean as a lobo wolf and dangerous beyond all measure.

That Fletcher had now and then stepped lightly across the line that separates the lawful from the lawless goes without saying. It was the curious way of the gunfighter, a man who was part outlaw, part honest, upstanding citizen.

He had little enough, to be sure. But still, too much to be so easily parted with. A man should be allowed to keep what is his and not be expected to give it up without a fight.

Buck Fletcher had known men like these two before.

Huge, uncurried and wild, they had the look of dry-gulchers and back-shooters. They were men completely without honor, living by no code except that of the wolf. They were bullies who would meet face to face only the old, the weak, the timid and afraid.

The men didn't know it then, though they should have as their lives ticked down to a few final moments, but Buck Fletcher was none of these things.

But he was a man who had already seen more than his share of killing, and now he tried his best to walk away.

"Boys," he said, "I've been on the trail for a month, and all I want is a bottle to cut the dust in my throat and a quiet hour to drink it in. I've never seen you men before, and I mean you no harm."

He reached in his pocket and laid a gold double eagle on the rough plank that served as a bar. "That's yours. Now, drink up and welcome."

The men grinned, and the younger man shook his head. "You don't get our drift, rube, do you?" he asked. "Let me fill you in—we want it all. Every damn thing you got, including them boots an' fancy jinglebob spurs of yourn."

"Now, there's no need to rush your drink." The older man smiled. "Take your time, feller. Me and my boy here, we'll strip what we want from you after you're dead."

Fletcher turned to the man behind the bar. He was as dirty and unkempt as the other two, his eyes sly and feral.

"Can you do something?" Fletcher asked softly. "I mean, can you make it go away and let a man drink in peace?"

The man shook his head, a gleeful, knowing glint in his eyes. "It ain't my problem, feller," he said. "It's yours."

Fletcher nodded. "Figured you'd say something like that."

He'd been standing belly to the bar. Now he turned slowly and faced the two grinning men. "You two have been pushing me mighty hard," he said wearily. "I'm not a man who likes to be stampeded, not by trash like you. So let's haul iron and get it over with."

Fletcher carried a seven-and-a-half-inch barreled Colt low on his right hip, its mahogany handle worn and polished from much use. Another revolver, its barrel cut back to four inches by an Austrian gunsmith in Dodge, hung in a crossdraw holster to the left of his gunbelt buckle.

In that single sickening instant as Fletcher turned to face him, the older man knew he'd made a big mistake. He looked at Fletcher more closely and thought he saw something—something that ran an icy chill through his body and made him think he'd lost his reason. The tall, hard-eyed man wasn't afraid like others he'd known. He stood calm and ready, as if repeating a ritual he'd gone through many times before.

It came to the older man then that he should back off, call the whole thing an unfortunate misunderstanding and get drunk on the twenty dollars lying on the bar. Besides, there might be a better opportunity later, somewhere on the trail when they could use the Sharps big .50 and get a clean shot at this man's back.

That the young man facing him was a practiced gunfighter there was no doubt, and the realization chilled the older man even deeper, all the way to the bone. There was danger here. Cold death was hovering very close, and he knew as the moments ticked by that he was fast running out of room on the dance floor. Now was the time to walk away from this. Now, before it was too late.

He opened his mouth to speak, planning to smooth things over, make what was happening stop before it went any further.

He never got the chance.

His son, meaner but less intelligent and not so perceptive, brought up the muzzle of his Sharps. He was lightning fast.

Fletcher was faster.

He drew his long-barreled Colt in a blur of motion

that had long since become instinctive to him and slammed a shot into the younger man's chest. The towhead screamed and staggered a couple of steps backward. His father roared, gripped by both fear and anger, and drew from the waistband. His gun never cleared the top of his pants. Fletcher fired, the bullet crashing into the bridge of the man's nose. Blood splashed in a scarlet cloud around his head.

The older man's eyes curled back in his head, showing white, and he fell, shaking the foundations of the dugout.

The towhead, badly hurt, screamed something unintelligible and tried desperately to bring the Sharps into play. Fletcher shot him again. The man's face showed stunned surprise, an utter inability to comprehend that he'd caught a fighting scorpion by the tail and that he was the one doing the dying.

He gasped. "I thought . . . I thought . . ." Then he was falling headlong into black nothingness, the rifle dropping from his lifeless fingers.

Out of the corner of his eye, Fletcher saw the bartender come up with a double-barreled Greener. The man fired, but Fletcher was already diving for the dirt floor. Buckshot hissed like a striking snake past his head. He rolled, then came up on one knee and slammed two shots very fast into the man's chest. The bartender crashed against the sod wall behind him, dislodging a shower of bottles from the shelf, then sank to the floor, the light already fading from his eyes.

The air in the poorly ventilated dugout was thick with acrid, gray powder smoke, and the concussion of the firing guns had extinguished the oil lamp above the bar.

In the gloom, Fletcher thumbed fresh shells into his Colt, then shoved it into the holster. He looked at the two men on the floor. They were both dead, the older man's twisted face revealing the stark horror and disbelief of his last moments.

The bartender was sprawled behind the bar . . . if a rough plank laid across two barrels can be described as such. A framed motto had fallen off the sod wall of the dugout and lay across the dead man's chest. It read:

HAVE YOU WRITTEN TO MOTHER?

Fletcher shook his head. "Mister, she must be right proud o' you."

He left the twenty dollars lying on the bar. It would pay to bury the dead should some charitable soul pass by. Otherwise, they could rot for all he cared.

A sick, bitter emptiness in him, Fletcher took one last look at the three men, then stepped outside, gratefully gulping in drafts of cold, fresh air.

He stepped into the saddle of his big American stud and caught up the rope of his mustang packhorse just as a small black-and-white-speckled pup ran around the corner of the dugout. The pup stopped and looked up at him, whimpering.

"You go on home," Fletcher said. "Find your mama."

The pup, his eyes wide and sad, stayed right where he was and whimpered even more.

Fletcher nodded. "Little feller, I think maybe you don't have a mama."

The pup was obviously a stray who'd been hanging around the saloon. Judging by his slatted ribs, the animal was missing his last six meals and then some.

"Where I'm headed, I got no place for a pup," Fletcher said sternly. "So just go on about your business. I want no truck with you."

He swung his horse around, preparing to ride out. The pup stood and immediately started to howl, then lay down again, resting his head on his oversized front paws, and crying softly.

"Oh hell," Fletcher swore. He dismounted, picked up the pup and sat him on the saddle in front of him. "You piss on me, boy, and you and me will part company right quick."

The pup made happy little yelping noises and began to lick Fletcher's hand. The big man smiled. "Well, maybe not."

He turned his horse again and rode away from the dugout and its three dead men without a single backward glance.

Buck Fletcher was going home, riding north with the long winds that stirred the buffalo grass of the Great Plains into a restless sea of green and brown.

Fifteen years of wandering lay bleak behind him, and ahead . . . he had no idea.

There was little hope in him, no dream of a better life with a wife and tall sons and girls as pretty and fresh as bluebonnets in the spring. Such thoughts were for other men: ranchers, farmers, storekeepers. They were not for the likes of him.

He knew only that he was going home. Like the ragged Vs of the wild geese in the sky over his head, it was an instinctive thing, unplanned, the action of a man who had reached the end of his rope and was now hanging on by a thread.

A rootless, violent past lay dark behind him, and he firmly believed all that was left to him now was to die well. The closing act of a famed gunfighter's life was remembered and remarked upon where men gathered, and Fletcher fervently hoped his final curtain would be drawn with dignity.

Yet he feared that when death came for him, it would come as it so often did for his kind—on the filthy sawdust of a barroom floor, where he would meet it with a gun in hand, hot blood filling his mouth with a taste of woodsmoke.

That fall of 1876, Buck Fletcher was twenty-nine years old, a tall, heavy-shouldered man with a long hatchet blade of a face honed sharp by sun, wind and hard times. Even so, women did not turn away from him, for his features were saved from irretrievable homeliness by a wide, expressive mouth that in times long past had been quick to smile and eyes that some-times revealed a faint, self-mocking humor and a well-hidden but nonetheless inherent kindliness.

But those eyes could change in an instant from blue to a cold, pitiless gray when the six-gun rage rose in him. Now, for eleven men, that gray had been the last thing in this life they ever saw.

Fletcher had ridden out of the Badlands and into the Dakota Territory astride his long-legged stud, leading the mustang packhorse.

Some packhorses pony willingly, keeping up with a rider and his mount so that the lead rope is mostly loose. But the mustang, mouse-colored and evil-tempered, was a reluctant traveler and held back con-stantly, pulling on the rope so that Fletcher feared his arm would be ripped right out of its socket.

He turned in the saddle and yanked on the rope for maybe the hundredth time that morning. The mus-tang, resentful, unforgiving and sly, shook his head indignantly and sidestepped to his right, stretching the rope even tighter.

"I swear, hoss," Fletcher said bitterly, wincing against the wrench on his arm, "keep this up and be-fore too long you and me are going to have a major disagreement."

The mustang, instinctively made wary by the tone of the human's voice, once again dutifully fell into line behind Fletcher's stud. But the big man knew by the crafty look in the pony's one good eye that he was just lying low for the moment, planning further deviltry. As he rode, Fletcher pondered the sheer cussedness of the mustang breed and shook his head more in sorrow than in anger.

Fletcher was tired, tired beyond his years. It was the tiredness he'd seen in men when they were old and full of sleep, seeking only a rocker in the shade where they could doze away the long, empty days.

But such a life was not for him. He had thought to head for Deadwood and the gold fields where mine shafts were boring deep into the Black Hills and the precious orange metal was being ripped from the earth.

Where there was gold, there were miners, and where there were miners, there were those who preyed on them: gamblers, loose women and the sellers of bad whiskey. It was a combustible mixture that led to violence, gunplay and dead men. It was a place for a man like Buck Fletcher.

Somewhere back on the trail from Montana, he'd heard that the Denver gambler Colorado Charlie Utter was in town, and Charlie owed him a favor or three. And Wild Bill was there. If Hickok was in Deadwood, then there was work for top gun hands. Buck Fletcher lacked even the smallest shred of false modesty. The years had taught him that he was one of the best with a gun around, maybe the best there ever was. Deadwood, wide open and roaring, could use a man with his flashing draw and steady nerves in the face of fire.

As he followed the path of the wild geese, Fletcher

didn't know it then, but very soon that rare gun skill was a thing he would have to prove and prove again.

He had embarked on a journey that would take him to the edge of hell—and there would be no going back.

Chapter 2

Keeping War Eagle Hill to his south, Fletcher crossed the East Branch, then headed due west toward False Bottom Creek.

He was only half a dozen miles from Deadwood, yet he felt a strange reluctance to ride into the brawling, booming town where there were free-spending miners and thus money to be made, with the banks said to be handling one hundred thousand dollars in gold every single day.

The only home he had ever known was calling out to him, and he must go there even if only for a very short while.

Long enough to visit the graves of Ma and Pa, he told himself.

Yes, that long and no longer.

Then he would ride on to Deadwood.

Fletcher crossed the False Bottom and then swung north along Sheeptail Gulch, riding through a wide-open country of grassland and rolling hills cut through here and there by shallow creeks running off the slopes of flat-topped buttes, some of them rising six hundred feet above the level.

The Black Hills, so named by the Sioux because the pine, juniper and spruce on their slopes looked black when seen from the plains, rose majestically to Fletcher's east, a fantastic landscape of towering rock formations and deep, blue-shadowed canyons.

Even now, in the early fall, as the chill in the air held the promise of winter, pasqueflowers, lady's slippers and larkspurs still bloomed on the slopes of the foothills. In the distance, Fletcher watched a small herd of mule deer step warily toward water.

All this Buck Fletcher saw without joy.

There was a strange restlessness in him, pushing him on—but why? And to where? He couldn't answer.

He rode on and linked up again with the west bank of False Bottom Creek as it curved gracefully north toward Paradise Gulch.

He found shelter in a stand of cottonwoods and staked out the tired horses on a patch of good grass. Then he built a fire, boiled coffee and sat with his back to a tree, rolling a smoke, a habit he'd picked up a couple of years back from the vaqueros in Texas.

The pup he fed what he had, some beef jerky and stale biscuit, and the little animal ate hungrily.

Fletcher lit his cigarette and smiled. "We're two of a kind, pup," he said. "Hungry and homeless."

On a hillside less than fifty yards away, a pack of wolves led by a huge, shaggy-maned lobo appeared from a stand of aspen like gray ghosts. Each head turned in Fletcher's direction, trying to figure out who he was and what was his business in this place.

The leader lifted his nose and read the tangled writing of the wind, attempting to find the answer. He shook his huge head, the man smell troubling him, then turned and trotted back into the trees. The rest of the pack followed, vanishing like puffs of woodsmoke. A pair of angry jays rustled in the branches, calling rude names after them, brave now that any possible danger had passed.

Fletcher watched the wolves leave, then rolled another smoke and drank the last of his coffee. He stood and poured the dregs over the fire, waiting until the small flames died out in a final wisp of blue smoke.

Mounting again, he shrugged into his ragged woolen mackinaw against the growing chill and buttoned it close.

Huge citadels of black clouds were building to the north, and the air held the raw, iron smell of snow. It was going to be a cold ride.

Fletcher rode his big stud at a fast trot northwest toward Tetro Rock, the mustang packhorse giving him more trouble than before now that his wiry strength was beginning to play out.

About a mile shy of the rock, Fletcher turned due west again, following the route of a dry creek bed.

This was cow country, and the ranchers in the area were growing rich supplying Deadwood's thirty thousand hungry miners with beef. And the army too, out in strength after the Sioux and Cheyenne following the Custer disaster, was a regular—if slow-paying and parsimonious—customer.

Fletcher stopped his horse and rose in the stirrups, looking around at the magnificent country on each side of him.

This had been his home for the first fourteen years of his life.

His father, a good poet but a bad farmer, had eked out a meager living here on one hundred and sixty hardscrabble acres: hard, grinding work with the plow and the hoe that had bent his back and aged him long before his time.

Pa had introduced young Buck to books very early, especially the works of Sir Walter Scott. The boy had listened in rapt attention as his father read a chapter of *Ivanhoe* or *The Talisman* every night after supper, the poet and actor in him making the tales come alive, spinning vivid word pictures in the boy's mind, the scarlet and blue and black of heraldic banners, the gleaming, fish-scale gray of knightly mail.

Pa had given Fletcher a love of books that had never left him. On the packhorse, carefully wrapped in burlap, were his father's copies of *Ivanhoe* and *Julius Caesar,* along with volumes he himself had acquired over the years, the works of Dickens and books by Carlyle, Hume, Voltaire and Cervantes. Fletcher had met men all over the West who shared his interest in literature. They were a varied breed. He'd known bartenders who were Ivy League college graduates and quoted Shakespeare, muleskinners who had attended Oxford and read Cervantes by the light of prairie campfires, Texas punchers who were qualified physicians and passed the time in winterbound line shacks poring over huge medical tomes, and he'd once known a saloon swamper in Abilene who read Plato and Homer in the original Greek and the *Meditations* of Marcus Aurelius in the Latin.

Western men came from all walks of life, and far from being crude and uneducated, many—buffalo hunters, mountain men, army scouts, gamblers, miners and ranchers—were well-read, and there were hundreds who could put letters after their name.

Fletcher's father had been one of these, and though chronically ill-suited to farming, in the end it was not the farm but the Sioux that had killed him.

Buck had been out hunting when the war party struck.

Pa had been caught out in the open field behind his plow, and when he made a move for the rifle strapped to the handle, the Indians had shot him down. Ma, shaking with the fever in her sickbed, had been tomahawked and scalped where she lay, her auburn hair, thick and wavy and reaching all the way down to her waist, a valuable prize for any warrior.

Fletcher had washed the bodies with his own hands, that being the way of the frontier, and had buried them both behind the cabin on Two-Bit Creek, saying over them the prayers he remembered.

When it was over, and he had laid them to rest the best way he could, he had taken up his Sharps Model of 1848 rifle and, a terrible rage in him, prepared to descend upon the Sioux.

Fletcher's father had known Christian Sharps in Philadelphia, both men sharing an interest in poetry and literature, and Pa told him the .52 caliber Model of 1848 had been a gift.

Sitting in his office on 30th Street, Sharps had told Pa: "Nathan, I am satisfied from many trials and personal experience that the Sharps carbine you now hold in your hands is the best weapon yet known to our country. Its range and accuracy are greater than the muskatoon, and it can be loaded at full speed.

"Dear friend, armed as you are with my carbine, you will need no pistol and can confidently face the many trials and hazards that await you in the wild Western lands."

Now young Buck Fletcher was about to put Christian Sharps' proud boast to the test.

Back in the Dark Ages, the boy's Anglo-Saxon ancestors had been huscarls, professional fighting men who lived in their lord's smoky hall, their coats of ring mail chiming like silver bells when they sat at his table. The gold their lord gave them (if he was a generous lord and who among them could afford to be otherwise?) they wore on their fingers or on the hilts of their broad-bladed swords or on their great, boar-crested helmets.

Such men lived by a code: a hard, unforgiving code of vengeance called the wergild.

It was the blood price.

Any man, no matter how high or low his rank, who killed the kin of one of these men, was subject to the wergild. It was a steep price, most often paid in gold or cattle, but sometimes in blood.

The philosophy and law behind the blood price was simple: It was a reckoning. In later years, this would be known as settling the score. But though the term changed, the principle would remain the same—as would the philosophy behind it.

In its simplest terms, as far as the Huscarl was concerned, it was the law of an eye for an eye, a tooth for a tooth.

Now, separated though he was from those ancient times by fifty generations, the spirit of the Huscarls still stirred within Buck Fletcher. His kin had been killed, and the boy demanded vengeance as once his ancestors had done.

He would exact the wergild, harsh and unforgiving though that code was.

The blood price.

He would bring about the reckoning.

The Sioux numbered four, all warriors of name and reputation, mighty in battle and with many coups to their credit.

Fletcher, a skilled tracker despite his youth, rode after them through the long day and into the night, his rage a dull fire in the belly.

When full darkness came, the sky was bright with stars, and the soft spring wind stirred the buffalo grass into restless waves and carried with it the scent of early-blooming bluebells and larkspur.

The boy rode his father's horse, a twelve-year-old buckskin mare. But despite her years, the little horse stepped out smartly, and it was she that first reacted to the presence of humans as she caught the smell of woodsmoke in the air, and with it the sharper odor of burning buffalo chips.

Made uneasy by the Indian smell, Fletcher felt the mare tense between his knees as she sidestepped to her right with a toss of her head, unwilling to get any closer.

The boy whispered a few words to the horse that quieted her some. He slid from the buckskin's bare back and, crouching low, went forward on foot, his Sharps at the ready.

He was wearing moccasins and made no sound as he entered a stand of aspen and scattered spruce, the underbrush thick underfoot.

Somewhere very close an owl blinked at the moon and patiently asked his eternal question of the night; farther away, Fletcher heard the sharp, sudden yelp of a hunting coyote.

The Indians' fire had burned down to a dull red glow surrounded by a circle of gray ash. All four were asleep in a narrow clearing among the trees, secure in the knowledge that they had nothing to fear since only the pale and unmoving dead lay behind them.

After the attack, the Indians had unharnessed Pa's big Missouri mule from the plow, and the warriors had driven it off along with the milk cow.

They had already eaten the mule, it being the most desirable of all meat. Unlike white men, an Indian gorged when he could, knowing that he might starve the next day and maybe the day after that. That was the way of the nomadic hunter, learned from bitter and hungry experience.

The boy crept noiselessly into the camp. The Indians' horses stood off to one side. One of them stamped a hoof and blew through its nose, alarmed by Fletcher's sudden appearance.

Quickly, Fletcher took his pocketknife and slashed the picket ropes of the ponies as they jerked their heads away from him in fear.

The Sioux, full of meat and lulled by the warmth of Pa's jug of sour mash whiskey, soundly slumbered on.

Now was the time. The boy let out a wild war

whoop, and the Indian ponies kicked up their heels and ran headlong into the camp.

A warrior sprang up quickly, a Springfield rifle in his hands. Fletcher shot him, and the man went down, clutching his belly. Having no time to reload, the boy picked up the fallen Springfield and shot another Indian as he rose from the ground.

Then, sprinting for the trees, Fletcher faded into the surrounding night, soundless in his moccasins as a ghost.

At first light, from his vantage point on a low hill, he watched the surviving Sioux leave. Two of them rode upright, their heads turning uneasily this way and that. The two others lay belly-down across the backs of their ponies, their long black hair trailing over the buffalo grass.

Fletcher caught them again as they crossed Rubicon Gulch in the rugged, broken hill country just to the east of Bridal Veil Falls.

He let the Sioux enter the gulch and begin to scramble up the opposite slope. Then he rode out from behind a low, tree-covered butte, drumming his heels into the little buckskin's ribs, urging her into a fast gallop.

Fletcher drew a bead on the warrior nearest him, a tall man with a single eagle feather slanting above his head, and fired. The warrior threw up his hands and went over the back of his horse, scarlet blood blossoming on his chest like an opening flower.

The other Indian shot at the boy, but Fletcher was riding fast, and the warrior missed. The Sioux drew a revolver and fired again, but by now Fletcher was out of effective range, and the ball split the air harmlessly over his head.

Now the surviving warrior, no longer wishing to be burdened, left the dead where they lay.

That night the Sioux made camp on the open prairie under a stunted cottonwood by a swift-moving, bubbling creek. The warrior built a fire and sang his death song. Then he laid his rifle across his knees and waited without fear for what was to come.

Fletcher found him just before midnight.

The boy made no attempt at concealment. He dropped from the buckskin's back and walked toward the fire. The Indian watched him come, black eyes steady and aware. Above them the moon played hide-and-seek behind scudding black clouds driven by a rain-laden wind, and the rippling grass sighed and whispered, never remaining still for a single moment.

As Fletcher drew closer, the Sioux rose to his feet and lifted a hand in salute. Then he brought up his Springfield, throwing it quickly to his shoulder. The warrior fired and missed. Fletcher fired at the same instant, and his aim was true.

The boy found his mother's long scalp tied to the dead warrior's rifle. He built up the fire, then threw the scalp into the flames where it would burn to ashes. Kneeling, he took the Indian's steel-bladed tomahawk from his belt. Then, the firelight casting his long, flickering shadow on the ground, the boy raised the ax time and time again and cut off the warrior's hands, first the right and then the left.

This done, Fletcher rose slowly to his feet. He felt sick and empty inside now that the hot anger in him was gone. He looked down at the Sioux's bleeding stumps and found a little comfort in the fact that Ma and Pa were finally avenged.

When he made the long journey to the shadow world that follows death, the warrior would arrive there maimed, unable to draw the bow or hold the lance. He would never be able to make war or hunt or hold a naked woman in the trembling firelight but must wander, lamenting, among the tall, misty lodges of his people, forever an outcast.

The Sioux learned Fletcher's name and remembered it well. In later years, when the Indians recounted his vengeance ride to white men, there were some among the whites who said the dead warrior, whose name was Tall Horse, had been doomed by the boy to endure an eternity of suffering and shame.

Gray beards clucked their tongues and shook their heads and said, "Surely that Indian paid too steep a price. That was an ill-done thing."

But such thoughts had never entered Buck Fletcher's head.

He had exacted the wergild.

The blood price.

He had brought about the reckoning.

Fletcher, only fourteen but already man-grown, had then left Two-Bit Creek and headed east toward where The War Between the States was raging.

He fought under the Stars and Bars in a dozen battles, was wounded three times, and when it all ended at Appomattox, he was a nineteen-year-old brevet major of horse artillery.

Now, for the first time since burying his folks, he'd come home . . . and he still had no clear reason in his mind why he'd done so.

He did not intend to stay. The cabin on Two-Bit Creek was probably long gone anyway, and with it whatever lingering shadows remained of the man and woman who had been his parents.

Fletcher urged his tired horse forward. He trotted along the edge of an ancient buffalo trail, and it was an easy ride. He followed the trail all the way to where Slaughterhouse Gulch met up with Whitewood Creek, then headed south. Fletcher kept to the eastern, pine-covered foothills of Whitewood Peak, riding through

a narrow, pleasant valley until he crossed Boulder
Creek and rode onto flat grassland surrounded by
shallower and more distant hills.

Earlier the gathering clouds had given the promise
of snow, and they didn't disappoint. Fat flakes began
to fall from a sky that looked like sheets of curling
lead. The wind picked up, dropping the temperature
abruptly.

The pup whimpered and buried himself deeper inside Fletcher's mackinaw for warmth, and the big man
patted the squirming little bundle and whispered, "Not
long now, boy, and maybe we'll find us a place where
we can build a fire and shelter for the night."

The snow began to fall harder, and Fletcher bent
his head against the driving wind, flakes frosting his
sweeping dragoon mustache and eyebrows. It was cold
and getting colder by the minute. Fletcher's breath
smoked in the air, and the thin cloth of his mackinaw
provided little warmth.

Behind him the mustang balked, eager to get away
from this open plain and find a sheltered place out of
the snow.

Fletcher turned in the saddle and yanked on the
lead rope, pulling the little horse closer. He kicked
his stud into a weary lope, and the mustang followed,
trusting that the man knew where he was going and
that shelter must be close at hand.

Despite the cold, Fletcher was stunned by the savage beauty of the land around him, made even more
magnificent by the falling snow.

The Black Hills rose in peaks and spires so tall they
vanished into the lowering clouds, and the pine and
aspen on their slopes were slowly dressing themselves
in mantles of white. The canyons and gorges were
deep-shadowed, full of mystery, and here and there
cattle moved like gray ghosts in the distance.

Fletcher rode under a vast sky, the clouds so close

to the earth he felt he could reach up and grab a handful, then watch it vanish from his fist like smoke.

As a boy he'd loved this land, thrived on its wonder, and now, gradually, that sense of awe, of belonging, was coming back to him.

A ring-necked pheasant, startled, fluttered up between the front legs of Fletcher's stud, and the big horse reared in surprise. An instant later, a gunshot boomed across the afternoon quiet, then another, racketing echoes slamming among the surrounding hills like the fall of shattered glass.

Fletcher reined in his horse, looking around him.

The shots could have been fired by a hunter out after meat to store against the coming of winter.

Or they could mean big trouble.

Chapter 3

Trusting the mustang to stay ground-tied, or at least not to wander too far, Fletcher dropped the lead rope and kneed his stud cautiously forward.

Whatever those shots might portend, they were no business of his. The big man rode reluctantly, unwilling to get involved in another's trouble.

As far as he could tell, the shots had come from the direction of a saddleback hill, its slopes and crest covered in pine and spruce, a thick stand of aspen, each tree identical to the other, on its lower level.

Fletcher considered that this was an out-of-the-way place for a hunter to be, though some of the hands from the surrounding ranches could well ride out this far to check for unbranded strays among the hills and deep, narrow arroyos.

The falling snow drew a white curtain against the day. Once, Fletcher's tired horse slipped on a patch of slushy mud, and he had to fight to keep the stud's head from pecking into the snow.

He drew closer to the saddleback, then reined up, an ingrained habit of caution dictating his every move. His eyes squinting against the falling snow, Fletcher scanned the hill. Nothing. There was no movement but for the leaves of the aspen restlessly trembling in the keening wind.

Fletcher brushed snow off his mustache with the back of a gloved hand, nodded grimly, then kneed the stud forward at a slow walk. Only a fool or a pilgrim rides headlong into gun trouble, if that's what the shots signified.

Above him soared the vast sweep of the cloud-ravaged sky, and around him lay lush grassland butting against the pine-covered hills and their deep, unexpected canyons.

It was country for a man to cross with care and with a wary eye to the hills and the hidden places where a rifleman could lie in wait.

The pup squirmed inside Fletcher's mackinaw, trying in vain to find a warmer spot, and he gently patted the animal into stillness.

A young whitetail buck burst in sudden panic from the aspen, followed by a tiny doe, the animals' hooves kicking up little spurts of snow as they ran.

Immediately a horseman followed, his face muffled by a woolen scarf against the cold. He saw Fletcher and reined up violently, startled. But only for an instant. Without warning, the man threw a rifle to his shoulder and fired.

The bullet split the air an inch above Fletcher's head, and the big man, acting from reflex, jerked his Winchester from the boot under his leg.

He hadn't wanted to get involved in gun trouble, but the unknown rider had dealt the cards, and now Fletcher would play his hand to the end.

The man fired again and missed, the shifting curtain of the snow, driven by the wind, making Fletcher an obscured and uncertain target.

Fletcher raised his rifle to his shoulder and took aim, laying his sights square on the rider's chest. He squeezed the trigger just as the frightened pup jerked his head out from under the mackinaw, nudging the rifle butt.

The shot went wide but the horseman—suddenly deciding he wanted no part of a gun battle in these conditions—swung his horse around and galloped back into the aspen and was soon lost behind the trees and the white veil of the falling snow.

Fletcher swore bitterly. He looked down at the pup and said, "Dog, I'm beginning to think you're going to be a lot more trouble than you're worth."

Unfazed, the pup yelped and, not liking the feel of the cold snow on his nose, burrowed deep inside Fletcher's mackinaw again.

Fletcher shook his head, swore with great sincerity, then rode slowly toward the aspen.

He had no doubt that the mysterious gunman had made good his escape, but he was taking no chances, riding with his Winchester ready to hand across his saddle.

Nothing was stirring in the aspen, and Fletcher's straining ears detected no sound. A sudden, stronger gust of wind spattered snow against his face, and his horse, snow getting into his eyes, jerked his head and sidestepped to his right.

Fletcher stood in the stirrups and glanced around him. Off to his left, about a hundred yards away, something large and black lay in the snow. A rock, maybe? Or something else?

Fletcher rode toward the object. As he got closer, he saw what it was. A dead horse lay on its side, the snow around it stained bright crimson with blood.

A few yards farther on, at first hidden from sight by the bulk of the horse, Fletcher spotted a sprawled body.

He dismounted, holding the pup close to his chest, and stepped beside the still figure. A young woman in a dark gray riding outfit lay on her back, her arms spread wide. The black hair on the left side of her head was thickly clotted with blood. Her face—ex-

tremely pretty, Fletcher noted—was covered in flakes
of snow that frosted the long, dark eyelashes that lay
like fans on her cheekbones.

Quickly Fletcher kneeled by the woman. She was
still breathing. A brief examination revealed that she'd
been grazed by a bullet and was unconscious. Judging
by the stained snow around her head, she'd lost a lot
of blood. She was very pale.

Fletcher picked up the woman easily and lifted her
onto the saddle, mounting behind her. He held the
woman in his arms and swung the stud around, heading back to pick up the packhorse.

The snow was falling more heavily, the gloom of
the afternoon slowly shading into the darkness of a
sullen evening. Around him the landscape was turning
from green to white, the hills and pines casting long
blue shadows on the snow.

"Now I have a homeless puppy and an unconscious
woman to take care of," Fletcher said to himself ruefully. "And neither one of my own choosing."

The mustang hadn't wandered far from where
Fletcher had left him. He took up the lead rope again
and rode on, as yet uncertain of his destination.

He could make camp among the pines and start a
fire, but this woman was in shock and would need
more warmth than a handful of damp twigs could provide. Fletcher thought about the cabin on Two-Bit
Creek.

Pa hadn't been much of a farmer, but he had an
appreciation for good carpenter's tools, and with these
he'd built the cabin solidly of heavy, interlocking logs
and a sturdy roof of seasoned timber.

Could the walls at least still be standing?

It was unlikely. The Indians would have burned the
place down long ago. Or perhaps it had collapsed from
time and weather and the passage of buffalo herds. A

big bull was capable of tumbling any wall, no matter how well built, if he chose to match himself against it.

Yet Fletcher had no other choice. He would head for the Two-Bit and hope a couple of walls still stood. If they did, he could rig a roof of some kind, and the woman would at least be sheltered from the falling snow and the worst of the wind.

"Let's hope Pa really did build to last," Fletcher said to no one but himself, the habit of a man who rides much alone. "Or all three of us are in a heap of trouble."

As he remembered it, the cabin stood on a gentle hill slope, a thick stand of aspen behind it, and higher, toward the crest, a scattering of pine and spruce. Near the cabin ran a stream, and the water was clear and cold and good to drink.

Fletcher rode south. When he met up with the Two-Bit, he headed west along its northern bank. Cottonwoods grew along the bank, and here and there a solitary willow. There were brown trout in the creek, and Fletcher had often caught a mess of them here when he was a boy.

The snow was piling up on the grassland and on the tops of the hills, drifting deep in the arroyos and ravines, and the wind was blowing colder, probing with icy fingers through each buttonhole and tear in Fletcher's worn mackinaw.

In his arms, the woman stirred and softly muttered something he could not make out. Then she was silent as unconsciousness took her again.

They would have to reach shelter soon or find a place to hole up until the blizzard was over, a prospect he did not relish but one that was growing more and more urgent with every passing minute.

Fletcher held the woman closer, trying to share his warmth, such as it was. When he took off a glove and felt her cheek with the back of his fingers, the skin was ice cold.

There was nothing else for it. He would have to find a sheltered place and build a fire. If he didn't, having lost so much blood, the girl could freeze to death. His eyes searching every hill and crevice of the surrounding land, Fletcher rounded the slope of a pine-covered hill—and saw the cabin just a hundred or so yards ahead.

He blinked his snow-crusted eyes in disbelief, unable to comprehend his good luck.

To his relief, the walls still stood, and even the roof, though swaybacked, seemed to be intact. But then he noted something else.

There was a light in the window.

Encumbered as he was by the unconscious woman, Fletcher could not reach his rifle, but he opened his mackinaw, pushed the pup aside, and brought the short-barreled Colt in its crossdraw holster closer to hand.

He rode into the yard in front of the cabin and reined up his horse. The mustang, head hanging low, shambled to a ragged, stumbling halt alongside him.

"Hello the house!" Fletcher yelled.

A few heartbeats of silence. Then a man's voice answered, "What do you want?"

"A place to bed down," Fletcher replied, deciding to stay quiet about the wounded woman limp in the saddle in front of him.

The cabin door opened slowly, and a man—old and grizzled, with a gray beard down to his belt buckle— stood in a rectangle of yellow lamplight, a Henry rifle in his hands aimed right at Fletcher's brisket.

"You best be ridin' on, sonny," the man said, his voice hard and flat. "You ain't driving me out o' my cabin in this blizzard. Not tonight you ain't."

"Old man," Fletcher said evenly, "I have a wounded woman here. Now, lower that rifle before I forget my manners and decide to make this a shooting matter."

"Wounded female woman!" the old man exclaimed. "Why didn't you say so?"

"I thought I just did," Fletcher said wearily.

He stepped out of the saddle and with considerable gentleness for such a rough-living man took the woman in his arms and carried her into the cabin. It was much smaller than he remembered. There were holes in the roof in a few places, but a fire glowed cheerfully in the cast-iron stove that Pa had freighted all the way from Cheyenne. Fletcher laid the woman on a bunk opposite the stove. A stew bubbled in a pot on top of the stove, filling the cabin with a savory beef-and-onion fragrance that made Fletcher's stomach rumble.

As if reading the gunfighter's thoughts, the old man said, "I got coffee a-bilin' too, strong enough to float a Colt's pistol an' black as sin." The old man stepped over to the stove and lifted the lid of the coffee pot. "Well, lookee here. I guess she's almost ready to be saucered an' blowed. Got some for your dog, too."

Fletcher smiled, instantly adding a friendly warmth to the uncompromising hardness of his features. "Later, for me, old man. First I got to take care of the horses." He nodded to the woman lying on the bunk. "You might get me some warm water. I have to bathe that wound."

"Depend on me for that," the old man said. "My own pony's in the barn out back, an' I laid in a mess o' hay an' a sack of oats."

Fletcher stepped to the door. "I appreciate that." He paused. "I won't ask you your name unless you want to give it."

"Coons." The oldster grinned, without a moment's hesitation, revealing only pink gums. "Jeb Coons. Coons by name, Coons by nature, I always tell folks."

"Well, Jeb Coons, see to that water," Fletcher said.

He had not offered his own name, and he knew that Coons, as was the way of Western men, would not press the matter.

For just a moment, Fletcher stood silent and looked around the cabin. He'd expected memories to come flooding back, but there were none. He recalled the sound of his father's laugh, his mother's voice, sweet and high, singing "Brennan on the Moor" as she sat with her sewing basket in the short winter twilight. But their faces were no longer clear to him. They had been dimmed like fading tintypes by the passing of the long years, never to return.

A sudden lump rising unbidden to his throat, Fletcher quickly stepped outside, caught up the horses and led them behind the back of the cabin. The barn, being sod with timber roof, had not fared as well as the cabin. The rear portion of the roof had caved in, but there was still plenty of room in front for Fletcher's horses alongside Coon's buckskin. There was roof enough left to shelter the horses from the worst of the falling snow, and the sod walls were still sturdy and would keep out most of the wind.

Fletcher rubbed down his horses with a piece of sacking, forked some hay into their stalls and fed them each a few handfuls of oats.

When he returned to the cabin, Coons had water warming, and Fletcher used this and a fairly clean towel to bathe the woman's head. The bullet had just grazed her, but it had left a nasty cut that had bled considerably.

"Ain't you gonna take her clothes off?" Coons

asked, bending over Fletcher's shoulder. "You ought to take her clothes off, you know."

The gunfighter turned and glanced into the old-timer's eyes, looking for heat there. But he saw none, just genuine concern.

"Why would I take off her clothes?" Fletcher asked. "It's her head that's hurt."

Coons shrugged. "I figured that's what you do with folks that are feelin' right poorly with a misery."

"Well, I don't know anything about taking off women's fixings," Fletcher said. "Anyway, dressed or undressed, she'll be all right. I got most of the blood off; now we'll just let her sleep. I recollect a doctor telling me one time that sleep is nature's medicine."

"Know her?" Coons asked.

It was Fletcher's turn to shrug. "Never saw her before in my life."

"Me neither," Coons said, "but there's a lot of strangers moving into the country around here. Gun-handlers mostly." A sly look crept across his face. "Like you, Buck."

Fletcher was startled, and it showed. "You know me?"

"Figgered it right off as soon as you walked through the door and into the light. Seen you in Dodge the time you kilt them gunfightin' cousins, Austin Bowen an' Jem Lassiter. Mister, you was hell on wheels that day. Me, I took to studying on things when you was to the barn, and I figger you're here for the war."

"What war?"

"You mean you don't know?" The words came slowly.

"If I knew, I wouldn't be asking."

"Why, the war between the PP Connected an' the Lazy R, of course. Deke Tyrone, the owner of the Lazy R, was shot off his hoss, dead when he hit the ground, by person or persons unknown. An' since then, hands have been killed on both sides, herds rustled and sich, and I reckon this is just the beginning. The way this war is stacking up, I'd say the worst is yet to come."

Coons ladled stew into a bowl for Fletcher and poured him a cup of coffee. He watched the big man eat for a few moments, then said, "Got me a poke from my diggins in Deadwood. It ain't much, but I figgered it was enough to let me winter here in this cabin. I found it abandoned an' all, and pegged it as a right snug place to nurse my rheumatisms until spring.

"But then Pike Prescott came up here with some of his boys day afore yesstidy an' told me to get out. That's why, when you rode up to the cabin, I figgered you was here to run me off."

Fletcher scraped his bowl clean, and Coons refilled it. "For what it's worth, Jeb," the big man said, taking up his spoon again, "I was raised in this cabin. My ma and pa are buried out back, among the aspen. I guess that gives me some kind of claim to the place. So after I ride on out of here, you can stay as long as you like."

"That's mighty civil of you," Coons said, "but I reckon Mr. Prescott will have something to say about that."

Fletcher finished his stew and held up a hand, patting his stomach with the other, when Coons offered more. He fished in his shirt pocket for the makings of a cigarette, and as he rolled it asked, "Who is this Prescott, and why does he cut such a wide path around here?"

"Prescott owns the PP Connected," Coons said. "He's the biggest rancher in these parts, and he wants to be bigger still. He offered to buy out Deke Tyrone, but Tyrone, he ran Pike off his place an' told him he'd see him in hell first.

"Three weeks later, Tyrone was murdered, bush-whacked by someone using a high-powered rifle. An' when I say high-powered, I mean a mighty big gun that clean blowed his head off.

"Now, the war that's about to bust this country wide open will be between ol' Pike and Deke's widow, Judith Tyrone. She's a pretty young filly. She owns the Lazy R now, and folks say Prescott is pushing her hard. There's a lot of money to be made selling beef to the Deadwood miners, an' it seems Prescott wants it all for his ownself.

"I hear tell he plans to run his cows all the way from the Platte north to False Bottom Creek an' as far east as Deadman Gulch an' maybe beyond. "When he does that, he'll have the Lazy R boxed in tight as Dick's hatband. Prescott's claiming some of the best winter range in the Territory, an' Judith Tyrone will have nowhere to go with her herd. She can't move 'em west without bumping into some of the big Montana outfits, and Prescott's claiming all the grass to the east."

Coons shrugged. "Like Deke, she's refusing to sell out. Put it all together, and you got—"

"A casus belli," Fletcher said, finishing it for him.

"A what?"

"It's Latin," Fletcher said, smiling slightly. "It means a cause for war."

The old man nodded. "Yup, that's what it is all right—a real cat's belly." Coons' face wrinkled into a puzzled grin. "Buck, you real sure you ain't here to sell your gun, times being as they are? Ain't like you to sit idly by an' watch it all happen."

Fletcher shook his head at the old man. "I'm headed for Deadwood, maybe as early as first light tomorrow. There's nothing here for me, and now I get to it, I don't recall there ever was."

The woman stirred on the bunk and moaned softly. Fletcher stepped to her side and took her hand. "Can you hear me?" he asked.

Slowly the woman opened her eyes, and Fletcher felt his breath catch in his chest when he saw how green and beautiful they were.

"My . . . my name is Savannah," she whispered.

Fletcher introduced himself and Coons, then asked gently, "Who shot you?"

The girl looked surprised. "Somebody . . . somebody shot me?"

"I'd say somebody was doing his level best to kill you."

Savannah looked at the big, hard-faced man with the clear blue eyes by her side, then at old Coons, who was giving her an embarrassed, toothless grin.

"Where am I?" she asked.

"At a cabin on Two-Bit Creek," Fletcher said. "I found you lying in the snow up near Whitewood Peak. Somebody killed your horse and tried real hard to kill you. Me and him, whoever he was, exchanged shots, but I lost him in the snow."

Savannah's fingers strayed to her head. She winced.

Fletcher nodded. "You were wounded. Whoever the would-be killer was, he came real close."

"What was I doing out there?" the girl asked.

"Ain't no place for a lady like you, an' that's for sure," Coons offered. "Nothing out there but grass an' trees an' maybe the odd wolf or coyote."

"I can't remember a thing," Savannah said, panic rising in her voice. "I remember my name, but the rest is a blank. It's like my memory has been wiped clean."

The girl's purse, a small leather affair closed with a drawstring, had been lying forgotten on the floor. Fletcher picked it up and handed it to her.

"Maybe there's something in there that will jog your memory," he suggested.

"Please go ahead and open it," Savannah said. "I might have identification in there."

Fletcher opened the purse and turned the contents out on the bunk. Apart from a few women's fixings, the small pile on the blanket consisted of five newly minted gold double eagles, some loose change and an elaborately engraved .41 caliber Remington derringer.

Shaking his head in puzzlement, Fletcher picked up the gun. "Odd thing for an obviously well-bred young lady to be carrying," he said. "Why did you feel the need for a belly gun?"

Savannah shook her head.

"Mr. Fletcher," she said, "I only wish I knew."

Chapter 4

The snow ended during the night, leaving a six-inch covering outside the cabin and on the flat grassland. The branches of the surrounding pines were bowed under a frosting of white, and the sun rose bright and cool, touching the snow with a pale golden light.

Fletcher, who had spread his blankets on the floor of the cabin, rose early, fed the fire in the stove and put coffee on to boil.

He checked on Savannah, who was sleeping peacefully, then shrugged into his mackinaw and stepped outside, taking his rifle.

The country lay quiet around him, beautiful in a mantle of white, and Fletcher felt an odd elation, a sense of belonging, of discovering the place where he truly belonged.

He shook his head in sudden irritation.

No, he didn't belong here. A man makes a path, sets a course, and the future course of Fletcher's life lay in the brawling, noisy and violent towns where ambitious men paid highly for gun skills in round, hard coins of silver and gold.

He was no farmer to bend his back to a plow, nor was he a cattleman. Fletcher was what he was, what he'd always been, a man who made a living from a gun, on either side of the law, and to that life he must return. It was the only life he knew, and destiny had ordained that it was the only life he would ever know.

The bright flames of elation he'd felt when he first stepped outside the cabin and gasped at the magnificence and beauty of the land had burned out as quickly as they had come. Now, in their place, were left only the cold ashes of defeat and hopelessness.

Buck Fletcher knew he was shackled to his gun as firmly as a prisoner to a ball and chain—and that realization tasted like bitter gall in his mouth.

His face stiff and bleak, Fletcher made his way behind the cabin and climbed the rise until he reached the aspen. He stood among the trees and glanced around, frowning, trying to remember. It had been a long time ago. So long, it sometimes felt like a hundred years and made a man think that maybe it had all happened in a different lifetime.

He'd dug the graves for his parents among the aspen directly behind the cabin and had made two crosses of tree branches. Of those, after the passage of fifteen years, there was no sign. Nor was there any sign of the graves.

The ground under the aspen looked undisturbed, the mounds smoothed out by rain and wind and snow and the turning of time. Ma and Pa were here somewhere, but in a place now known only to God.

Fletcher took off his hat and bowed his head.

This morning he had no prayers. Those, like the graves, were long since forgotten.

"Just so you know I'm here," he whispered. "I came back to see you."

He stood there for a few long minutes, trying to remember how it had been when he was a boy. It was all gone. Too much hard and dangerous living in the intervening years had made every detail recede into forgetfulness. In trying to remember, he was clutching at a mist always drifting just out of reach of his outstretched hands.

An errant wind stirred the branches above Fletcher's head, and a few flakes of snow fell on his shoulders. He nodded as though it was a signal. "Just so you know I was here," he whispered.

He turned on his heel and walked back down the slope to the cabin. He didn't look back.

He had thought to ride to Deadwood that morning. But he delayed, making the excuse to himself that he could not leave Savannah here alone with just an old man for protection.

Her killer might come searching for her, and even though Jeb was no pilgrim, he was stiff and creaking with the rheumatisms and might be no match for a skilled gunman, especially one that shot from ambush.

This is what Fletcher told himself, but even as he did he knew it was a lie. He did not want to leave. Something was holding him here. But what it was, and the reason for his remaining, he could not even begin to comprehend.

That day and the next he spent with his books, reading outside in the bright sunlight, his back to a tall pine tree.

The speckled pup took his accustomed place at Fletcher's side, snuggling close, his eyes adoring. But when the big man read Voltaire aloud to him, the little pup usually decided adoration had its limits and would run off to chase his tail in the snow or wander into the brush on some doggy exploration.

Slowly, Fletcher felt the tension leave his neck and shoulders. At night, as he and Savannah and Jeb talked in the cozy cabin by the firelight, he even managed to laugh a time or two.

Jeb Coons had a fund of stories about gold mining

and had even prospected with a burro in the Arizona Territory. He regaled Fletcher and Savannah with tales of bloodthirsty Apaches and desperate gun battles among craggy, sun-blasted rocks and giant Saguaro cacti, making much of his own bravery and derring-do.

Fletcher doubted that half the stories the old man told were true, but that didn't matter. For someone like himself who rode long and lonely trails, it was the companionship that mattered. The closeness of other human beings.

For her part, Savannah's memory had not returned, and what had been her past remained hidden behind a thick fog of forgetfulness.

She had a fine singing voice and was somehow able to recall the old songs of the Irish and the Welsh and the folk of the Tennessee hills. As he watched her sing in the firelight of that second evening, her face flushed from the fire, eyes shining, Fletcher felt an odd stirring inside him. Could this woman, young, lovely and poised, ever become a wife to a man like him?

As soon as the thought came to him, he shook his head, dismissing it. No, it would never happen. What had he to offer a woman like Savannah?

The answer was nothing—except maybe a life of restless, incessant wandering, gun violence and, at the end of it all, young widowhood.

Savannah was a wife for another man, maybe a man she was yet to meet. But that man would not and could not be Buck Fletcher.

And what of love? He had no idea what love was, what it felt like. When a man visited the girls on the line, was that love? Was it as simple as that? Just a straightforward contract between two people to stay together for an hour or a lifetime?

Fletcher had no answer to these questions. Nor, he

decided, would he seek them. Why trouble himself with matters that would never concern him?

Next morning, Coons and Savannah busied themselves preparing breakfast while Fletcher, deciding three was a crowd and being of suspect cooking skills, took his book and found his accustomed place with the pup under the pine. He sat reading, enjoying the good smells of coffee boiling and bacon frying.

Today he had left his Winchester inside, but he was wearing his gunbelts. The fact that Savannah's mysterious enemy was still out there somewhere continued to trouble him.

Fletcher heard the sound of cantering horses, and he lifted his head from Voltaire in time to see a party of a dozen horsemen heading toward the cabin. He closed the book and laid it down carefully, then stood, a lone but defiant figure, ready to face whatever it was these horsemen represented. If they professed to be friends, he would greet them as such. If enemies . . . Well, he could accommodate them too.

In the past, men had come at Fletcher in many guises, some hiding their true faces behind a smile or a scowl, but the big man who now reined up, a flurry of snow fanning into the air from his horse's hooves, presented no such facade. He was what he was, and he didn't mind showing it to the world. His face was handsome, arrogant, brutal—the face of a man well used to power and the ruthless, uncaring wielding of it.

The men who were with him seemed tough and capable, but they looked to be ordinary punchers—all of them, that is, but one. That exception was young and blond, with the merciless yellow eyes of a snake. He wore two guns, silver-engraved and ivory-handled, each worth more than a cowhand could make in six months.

But this was no cowhand. Fletcher recognized him for what he was and knew he'd be pure poison with a gun.

"You there, fellow!" the big man yelled. "Who are you?"

"Who are you?" Fletcher shot back, suddenly irritated by this man's brusqueness and high-handed manner.

"My name is Pike Prescott, and this is my land. You're trespassing, and I want you off it now."

Prescott was four inches taller than Fletcher's even six feet and at least fifty pounds heavier than his lean one hundred and eighty. His eyes were as hard and devoid of feeling as blue pebbles at the bottom of a creek, and his mouth was a thin white slash of anger.

"If I find you here tomorrow morning," Prescott continued, flat and slow, "I'll hang you alongside the other squatter who lives here."

Fletcher smiled without warmth, a tall, significant exclamation point of danger against the white of the snow.

"This isn't your land, Prescott," he said. He'd purposely left off the "Mister" this man was no doubt accustomed to hearing from lesser mortals, and he saw that he'd stung him. "My father and mother owned this place and the hundred and sixty acres surrounding. They're buried back of the cabin. I was raised here, and I think maybe I'll stay."

That last surprised Fletcher. Where did the words come from? He had no intention of staying here—or did he?

"Hell, Prescott," he pressed on, "you don't even run cows up here."

The big rancher's face was set and hard, his voice level and expressionless.

"If you can show me, right now, a legal deed for

the land you claim, I'll pay you a dollar an acre. That's one hundred and sixty dollars, more money than you've ever seen in one place in your life. I can't say it any fairer than that. Hell, a saddle tramp like you could stay drunk for months on that kind of money."

"No sale, Prescott," Fletcher snapped. "Now get the hell off my property."

"So be it," Prescott said, unmoved. "You heard what I said, and I won't repeat myself. If I find you here come sunup tomorrow, I'll hang you."

The young man with the yellow eyes urged his horse forward. Without taking his gaze from Fletcher, he said, "Hell, Mr. Prescott, let me have him. It will save you the time and trouble of stringing him up later."

Prescott smiled. It looked like the grimace of a hungry wolf.

"Think you can shade him, Hig?"

Higgy Conroy grinned, showing small, badly spaced teeth. "That tramp ain't never seen the day when I couldn't shade him."

Fletcher stood relaxed and ready. He knew the man called Hig would be fast. The question was, how fast? At least the answer to that might be revealed very soon.

"This here is gonna be on the square."

Jeb Coons stepped from behind the corner of the cabin, the Henry in his hands. "I want Buck Fletcher to have a fair shake."

A flicker of doubt crossed Hig's eyes. "I didn't know you was Buck Fletcher."

Fletcher's smile was thin. "Well, you know now."

"Still want to take him, Hig?" Prescott asked dryly.

One of the cowhands, a tall, thin man with shifty eyes, slowly reached inside his leather coat. Fletcher smiled and said conversationally, "Mister, if you were to come up with a gun out of there, I would take it real hard."

The man jerked his hand away like he'd been stung. "I was just reaching for a chaw."

"Stunt your growth," Fletcher said. "Better for your health you do without."

Behind him, Fletcher heard Jeb's thin cackle. Hig flushed with anger.

"I can still take him, Mr. Prescott," he said. "You just say the word."

Prescott shook his head. "Maybe you·can shade him, Hig. Maybe you can't. But right now isn't the time to find out."

"That's true, Prescott," Fletcher said grimly. "Because no matter how it goes between Hig and me, I'll make sure you're the first to die. Then it won't matter to you one way or the other."

If Prescott was intimidated, he didn't show it. He turned his hard, flat eyes on Fletcher. "You can come work for me. I pay top wages."

"For gun hands?" Fletcher asked. He nodded toward Hig. "Like that."

"I protect what's mine," Prescott said angrily, "any way I can. I've already lost a couple of men, bushwhacked, shot out of the saddle." He pointed a thick finger at Fletcher. "If just one more of my hands is murdered, there will be an all-out war between the PP Connected and Judith Tyrone's Lazy R. I plan to win that war."

Fletcher shook his head. "Then you'll do it without my help, Prescott. I reckon you're trying to run roughshod over Judith Tyrone and force her out of the Territory, maybe because she's young and a woman and an easy mark. But my gun isn't for sale to you or anyone else. And my place isn't either."

Prescott nodded. "Then so be it. Clear off my land by tomorrow morning or hang. The choice is yours."

The cabin door swung open, and Savannah stepped

outside. Her hair hung over her shoulders, and she looked fresh and lovely this morning.

Prescott scowled. "That your woman, Fletcher?"

Fletcher studied the big man's face, trying to see if there was the slightest hint of recognition in his eyes. There was none. Obviously, if Prescott didn't know who Savannah was, he wasn't the one who had ordered her murder.

"She's a friend," Fletcher said, deciding to play his cards close to his chest. "She's visiting for a spell." Then, to again test Prescott's reaction, he added, spacing out the words, "Somebody tried to kill her a few days back. He didn't succeed, but his bullet grazed her head, and she's lost her memory."

Prescott didn't flinch, and Fletcher noticed no shadow of guilt in his eyes. The big man's hard glare slid to Savannah. "Same thing applies to you as the rest of them. Woman or no, lost memory or no, if I find you here tomorrow, I'll hang you alongside the rest."

Without another word, Prescott swung his horse around and galloped away, his hands trailing after him like shadows.

But Higgy Conroy still sat his horse, glaring at Fletcher. There was a craziness in his rattlesnake eyes, and they were fevered with the urge to kill.

"You mind what Mr. Prescott told you. On your way out of the Territory, you can tell your boss Judith Tyrone that you and the rest of her hired guns don't scare me," he said. "Some day, Fletcher, you and me will meet again, and next time you won't have an old man and a woman's skirts to hide behind."

"Two things, boy," Fletcher said evenly. "The first is that I don't work for Judith Tyrone. The second is, don't make me draw. I'm way better than you are, and I'll kill you."

Hig spat. "You're a damned liar, Fletcher. On both counts."

Then he was gone, his paint pony a fast-receding splash of mottled black against the white of the snow.

"You made yourself a powerful-bad enemy in that boy," Jeb said, stepping beside Fletcher and shaking his head as he watched Hig Conroy leave. "He killed a man in Deadwood just last week and another in Cheyenne a month afore that."

Fletcher nodded. "He's poison-mean, and now he'll be on the prod."

"He will that," Jeb agreed. "If'n I was you, Buck, I'd sure start watching my back."

Chapter 5

Prescott's threatened attack did not come the next day or the day after. Both days, trusting Jeb and his rifle to guard the place while he was gone, Fletcher saddled the stud and rode in a wide arc around the cabin as far as Deadman Gulch to the east and Tetro Rock to the west. He saw no sign of Pike Prescott or his riders.

This was a long way from the PP Connected home range, and it seemed that Prescott was planning to lay claim to a lot of territory, much of it to the south and east, prime winter grazing where he could sustain his herds through the winter. The Lazy R would be bottled up with nowhere to graze its herd, and Judith Tyrone might be glad to sell after a winter of heavy losses, especially when the blue northers swept in from Canada, freezing the range. As a boy, Fletcher had seen twenty inches of snow fall on this country in as many hours and the temperature hit forty below.

He didn't know Judith Tyrone, but if Prescott did as he planned, that young lady was in a heap of trouble.

On the second day, as he returned to the cabin on the Two-Bit, Fletcher shot a whitetail buck and packed it home, meat enough to last them for a week at least. Savannah's wound had all but healed, and she busied herself with cleaning the cabin and cooking meals. Meantime, Fletcher and Jeb repaired the holes in the roof and did what they could to weatherproof the logs against the coming winter, filling in the chinks with a mixture of straw and mud from the creek banks.

Fletcher fixed up the barn roof, supporting it with poles from the aspen grove, and then began to add to the supply of kindling and logs for the stove.

Despite what he'd told Prescott, he still had no real plan to stay on here at the Two-Bit.

Yet at the back of his mind was always the thought that here might be a good spot to raise horses. If he could find some mares, he could cross them with his American stud. Big, powerful mounts that could shoulder through snowdrifts were always in demand on the northern ranges, unlike in dry, dusty Texas, where cow ponies were small, some of them barely making eight hundred pounds.

A man could make enough money to live by breeding horses, especially if he had a strong wife by his side. Maybe a woman like Savannah.

But Fletcher recognized all that as a pipe dream, and when it popped unbidden into his mind, he shook his head angrily and cursed himself for a fool.

Three more days passed without incident. Once a huge grizzly, grumpy and irritable as hibernation approached, growled around the cabin for the best part of a morning. The day after that, a small herd of whitetailed deer stepped warily to the creek for a drink.

But of Pike Prescott and his riders, there was no sign.

Savannah was now well enough to ride. At supper on the evening of the fifth day, she suggested that she borrow Jeb's horse the next morning and ride into town.

"Town?" Fletcher asked. "You mean Buffalo City?"

"I guess," she replied. "I have vague memories of a town . . . and a hotel. I just . . . I just can't recall being there."

"The only town around is Buffalo City," Jeb said. "It's located in a narrow valley midway between Boomer Gulch and Bear Butte. It ain't much as towns go, but there are them who live there who say they expect it to go far and make its mark one day."

"Maybe there's somebody there who knows me," Savannah suggested. Then, her eyes slanting to Fletcher, she added shyly, "Who knows, I might even have a husband."

If Fletcher was upset by this observation, he didn't let it show. "Maybe we can learn something at the Exchange Hotel," he said. "You must have been staying somewhere around here, and I guess Buffalo City is as good a place as any to start."

"We?"

"Yes, we. I'm coming with you."

"Buck, you don't have to. Really, you don't."

"I know I don't. But I feel responsible for you. I'm the one who found you in the snow, remember?"

Savannah lightly rested her fingers on the back of Fletcher's hand. "I was just teasing you. Really, I'm glad you're coming with me, Buck," she said. "You make me feel . . . safe."

To his annoyance, Fletcher felt his face color. "Let's turn in," he said abruptly, rising from the table. "We'll make an early start in the morning."

Behind his back, he didn't see Jeb's knowing wink at Savannah or her shy answering smile.

Despite its pretensions, Buffalo City was a typical small cow town huddled within a narrow, muddy gulch. There were around two dozen false-fronted buildings and sod cabins on either side of a main street

wide enough for two wagons to pass, and the boardwalks boasted oil lamps placed at intervals along
their length.

As Fletcher and Savannah rode in, they passed a
bank, three saloons, a general store, a restaurant, the
Exchange Hotel and the sheriff's office.

At the far end of town stood six white-painted gingerbread houses. Beyond those, close to where the
gulch ended in a rugged V of soft sandstone rock, were
the livery stable and corrals.

Fletcher noted that the town had grown some since
he was a boy. Jeb had told him there was even talk
of building a city hall and a church.

But Buffalo City was a town on the edge.

Since the Custer massacre on the Rosebud just
three months before, the Indian threat had become
very real. Now men were dying out on the range, and
there was open talk of a range war.

Fletcher saw strain in the faces of the passersby,
and even the saloons seemed strangely quiet. It was
like Buffalo City was holding its breath—waiting for
what was to happen next.

He and Savannah left their horses at the livery stable and walked along the muddy, crowded boardwalk
to the hotel.

The desk clerk recognized Savannah immediately.

"Why, Miss Jones," the man exclaimed, "I do declare, we were getting quite worried about you. The
mayor was thinking of rounding up a search party."

"You . . . you know me?" Savannah asked.

The desk clerk, a small man wearing wire glasses,
his slicked-down black hair parted in the middle,
looked puzzled. "Well, of course I do. You stayed
here for three days. Indeed, your things are still in
your room. Number 22, straight up the stairs and
down the hall to your left."

Savannah touched a hand to her head and swayed slightly. "I . . . I don't remember anything. I . . . I . . ."

Fletcher put his strong arm around the girl's waist and supported her. "The lady isn't feeling too well," he told the clerk.

"Oh that's too bad, really it is. There is a doctor in town, you know, and quite a good one."

Fletcher nodded. "Maybe later." He turned his cold eyes on the clerk, and the man felt an involuntary shiver run down his spine. "Did Savannah—I mean, did Miss Jones tell you anything else?"

The clerk frowned in concentration. Then his face cleared, and he smiled. "Why, yes; yes, she did. Soon after she arrived on the stage from Rapid City, she told me she was from Back East and might be interested in investing in a ranch.

"'Well,' I said, 'this is a real bad time, what with the terrible murders happening out on the range and all.' But that didn't faze her in the least, and she was quite insistent that she wanted to buy ranchland. Sometimes women take strange notions, you know. Oh dear me, yes. Now, you take my wife for example—"

"Did Miss Jones tell you anything else?" Fletcher asked again, interrupting.

The clerk shook his head. "No, not really. About a week ago, she rented a horse from the livery stable and rode out of town. As I said, we were all getting quite concerned about her."

The man raised an eyebrow. "Did you speak to old man Stamphill down to the livery stable? He's a terrible gossip, you know."

"He wasn't there," Fletcher said. He nodded toward the keys hanging on a board nailed to the wall. "Can we have the key to Miss Jones' room?"

"Ah, well, there we have a wee problem," the clerk

said, spreading his hands wide. "It is hotel policy that gentlemen callers are not allowed in rooms occupied by single ladies."

Fletcher's suddenly icy eyes fastened on the clerk, and the man backed up a step and added hastily, "But of course, there are exceptions to every rule."

Savannah and Fletcher went up to her room. A search of the place revealed only some clothes hanging in the wardrobe, a few personal items like face powder and a hairbrush, and a full box of .40 caliber shells.

"I don't know who you really are, Savannah," Fletcher said dryly, hefting the box in his hand. "But you were surely loaded for bear."

The only physician in town was a man named Dr. Silas Hawthorne, and his office was Savannah and Fletcher's next stop.

He looked to be pushing seventy, but Hawthorne seemed to know his business.

"Amnesia is quite common after any kind of head injury," he told Savannah, after examining her wound. "It doesn't require treatment, though I will give you a mild sedative to help you sleep." The old man smiled. "Your memory should start to return within a few weeks, young lady."

Savannah and Fletcher walked back to the hotel. Soon the gunfighter was standing in the middle of her room again, scowling as he looked around.

"We haven't missed anything, have we?" he asked.

Savannah shook her head at him. "Not a thing. It looks like I didn't have much to begin with."

"I wonder . . ." Fletcher began.

He grabbed a chair and stepped onto it, looking at the top of the wardrobe.

"Anything?" Savannah asked.

"Nothing."

Fletcher stepped down, but the chair skidded out

from under him and hit hard against the thin wall
between Savannah's room and the one adjoining.

A few moments later, someone pounded at the door
angrily and yelled, "What in tarnation is going on in
there? Can't you let a man sleep?"

"I know that voice." Buck smiled. He opened the
door and said to the small, thin man who stood there
holding a long-barreled Colt in his right hand, "How
are you doing, Doc?"

"Buck Fletcher," Doc Holliday said, amazement
pitching his voice an octave higher. "I might have
known it was you making all that racket. What the
hell are you doing here?"

"I could ask you the same question, Doc."

Holliday stepped into the room, irritation plain on
his face. "Hell, Buck, I was on my way to Deadwood
when we had us an Indian scare. I reckon the stage
driver saw a tom turkey in the brush and took it for
a whole tribe of Sioux." Doc shrugged his thin shoulders. "I remonstrated with the man, of course, and
even entertained the idea of shooting him right off the
box, but I thought better of it. The way things are
with me and the law at the moment, I really can't
afford to be involved in another shooting scrape."

"Some men need killing, Doc." Fletcher gave another of his rare smiles. "I don't recall you ever shooting a man who didn't deserve it."

Holliday smiled. "Thank you, Buck. You were always very understanding in matters like that." He
sighed, shaking his head. "Anyway, the upshot is that
we detoured to this godforsaken burg, and the stage
won't be leaving until tomorrow morning. That tom
turkey really scared these rubes to death."

Holliday, his cadaverous face flushed around the
cheekbones by the effects of his morning quart of
whiskey, turned to Savannah and said, "Buck, aren't

you going to introduce me to this lovely young lady? Your wife, perhaps?"

Fletcher smiled. "Not my wife, just an orphan from the storm I adopted."

He made the introductions. Holliday stuck his Colt in the waistband of his pants, bowed over Savannah's hand and declared himself to be "Positively enchanted."

"Where is Kate, Doc?" Fletcher asked after Holliday had straightened up.

"Ah, the fair Kate is still in that malodorous dung heap the Texans call Fort Griffin, a doss-house for herders and hide hunters perched on the ragged edge of nowhere. There she diligently plies her profession." He turned to Savannah. "You understand, of course, that with a lady present, delicacy prevents me from saying exactly what that profession is."

Savannah smiled and dropped a little curtsy. "Your manners do you credit, sir."

Holliday smiled in turn, then said, "If my luck changes and I hit a winning streak, I will send for Kate and have her join me in Deadwood. But if the cards are still against me, I must perforce return to Fort Griffin and the less-than-chaste arms of my beloved."

A sly look crept into Holliday's eyes. "Ah, Buck, perhaps after I've had a few hours' sleep—I was up all night playing nickel-and-dime poker with some sodbusters and other assorted rubes—you might care to join me in a game?" Holliday held up a thin white hand, the blue veins very prominent. "But tired and worn out as I am, I fear you may seek to take unfair advantage of me."

Fletcher shook his head and laughed loudly. "Doc, I went that route with you before, remember, in Dodge. You said you was tired and worn out then. I was lucky to rise from that table still owning my horse and saddle. As I recall, I lost everything else."

Fletcher wondered at that laugh. It was the first time in years he'd done that, and it felt good.

"Well, Doc," he said, "it's been real nice talking to you again, but Savannah and me, we have to fill an order of supplies over to the general store."

Savannah laid the tips of her fingers on Fletcher's arm. "Buck, if you don't mind, I'm feeling very tired. I'd like to lie down here and take a nap for an hour while you get the supplies together."

"Do you think that's wise?" Fletcher asked.

"I'll be just fine. I don't think anyone would try to attack me in town."

Doc Holliday, who had been listening intently to this exchange, tapped the butt of his Colt. "Buck, I'll be right here in the next room. Believe me, if I hear anything untoward, I will dash pell-mell to the lady's rescue." He turned to Savannah. "Be assured, dear lady, you can depend on me."

Fletcher knew Doc from old and respected his ability with a gun, but a niggling doubt was eating at him. Doc Holliday was known for a lot of things, but reliability wasn't one of them. Finally, he took a deep breath and said, "That sounds just fine, Doc. But mind you stay wide awake and keep your ears sharp."

"You can leave it all in my hands, Buck," said Holliday. "Savannah Jones is as safe as a snuff box in granny's apron. I'll protect her as I would my own dear Kate."

After Holliday left, Fletcher told Savannah to put a chair under the doorknob and warned her not to open the door to anyone unless it was him or Doc. Savannah nodded. She stepped toward him and stood very close, so close the sweet, womanish smell of her skin and hair made his head swim.

"Buck," she whispered, "take care. You're . . . I mean, you're . . ." Her words stumbled to a halt. She shook her head. "Just take care."

Fletcher stood there for a moment, confused, a big, rugged-looking man, slightly stooped, with all his weight in his arms and shoulders. Standing there in his weather-faded blue shirt, down-at-heel boots and ragged mackinaw, his was not a figure to be cutting a dash among the ladies, and well he knew it.

He opened his mouth to speak, closed it again, then managed huskily, "I'll take care."

He left then and stood in the hallway until he heard Savannah put the chair under the doorknob.

Fletcher walked down the stairs slowly. The fact that Doc, a man real handy with a Colt, was in the room next to Savannah's helped set his mind at ease, a little anyway.

But what he didn't know as he stepped onto the boardwalk and made his way toward the general store was that Doc Holliday, the effects of the morning's whiskey finally catching up to him, was already sprawled across his bed.

Snoring.

Jeb Coons had given Fletcher a list of the supplies he needed, and the big gunfighter dropped it off at the general store, telling the proprietor to sack them up and that he'd stop by later.

He had time to kill, so he crossed the street to the Hole in the Bucket Saloon. Fletcher wasn't normally a drinking man, but bartenders were a gossipy breed, and it was just possible that this one might know something of Savannah's past and why she was in the Dakota Territory.

Unfortunately, the bartender could offer nothing more than the hotel clerk.

"We don't get ladies like her in this saloon," the man said. "And if she doesn't come in, I don't get a chance to talk to her."

At this early hour, there were only two other people in the saloon. A plump, soft-looking man in a broadcloth suit, a banker by the look of him, who sat in a corner drinking coffee while he read the newspaper, now and then darting disapproving glances at a shabby loafer who sat at another table nursing a beer and a hangover.

The batwing doors swung open, and a small, wiry man with mild blue eyes stepped up to the potbellied stove and spread his hands to the warmth.

"Quite nippy out," he said, smiling at Fletcher.

Fletcher nodded. "Some." Then, deciding to take a small step toward sociability, he added, "Wind's from the north. Might be warning of a hard winter."

The little man's eyes slid off the gunfighter's face then back again like he was trying to make up his mind about something. Finally he said, in a clipped English accent, "Is your name Buck Fletcher by any chance?"

Like the banker, the bartender and the loafer, Fletcher recognized this as a grave breach of Western etiquette. You never asked a man his handle. If he wanted you to have it, he'd give it to you. The man had stepped over an invisible yet rigid line, and it rankled.

"It might be," Fletcher said, fighting down his irritation.

"Well," returned the little man, smiling, "if it is, there are two fellows in the street who told me to ask you to step outside."

"Why?"

The little man shrugged. "I'm very much afraid that they seem quite determined to kill you."

Chapter 6

Fletcher stood in silence for a few moments, then turned to the bartender. "Is there a sheriff in town?"

The man shook his head. "Don't have one. The sheriff we had just up and quit, and the mayor hasn't got around to appointing a new one yet. Not that there are many candidates lining up for the job. The tin star is still sitting on the mayor's desk, and I reckon it will stay there for a spell."

The four men in the saloon watched Fletcher, wanting to see what he'd do next.

The gunfighter nodded toward the little man by the stove, who was opening his long tweed coat to the heat. "Two men, you say?"

"Two. And rough-looking, desperate characters. Ruffians, by the look of them."

"Then I'll talk to them."

"Mr. Fletcher, if that's indeed who you are, I believe you'll find those two rather limited conversation-wise," the little man said. "They're the type who only talk with their guns."

The men were waiting in the street when Fletcher stepped outside. Both wore buffalo-hide coats, and both were dirty and shaggy. Long yellow hair fell over their shoulders, and their beards spilled thick and untrimmed over their chests.

There was no mistaking the hate in their eyes and the desire to kill. The larger of the two held what looked to be a .44–40 Winchester, and, a step behind, the other had a Greener, its twin barrels pointed right at Fletcher's belly.

A shotgun had a way of taking the ginger out of a man fast, and Fletcher had seen even feared gunfighters back down from a Greener in the right hands. And he had no doubt this one was in very capable hands. The man was primed, ready and looked like he knew how to use a gun well.

A sickness growing in him, knowing what was to come, Fletcher stepped to the edge of the boardwalk and asked, "What can I do for you boys?"

The man with the rifle made a sudden motion with his right arm, and Fletcher caught the glint of gold spinning through the air. He made no attempt to catch the coin, but let it fall, ringing, to the boardwalk.

"That's yours," the man said. "You left it in a dugout saloon back to the Bald Mountain country after you killed our paw an' our brother Ezra. See, Ezra was just a boy, scarce twenty year old, an' you shot him down like a dog."

"That Sharps he carried was plenty growed up," Fletcher said. "I wanted no trouble, but they brought it to me. They wanted to kill me and take what was mine."

"It don't matter a damn who was in the right or who was in the wrong," the man with the shotgun said, showing yellow teeth in a feral snarl. "Right or wrong, we avenge our kin. That's our way."

"We been following you for quite a spell," the Winchester man said. "Another of our kin, a yellowbelly who ain't around no more, was out deer huntin' an' told us that after the shootin' was over, he seen you ride away from the dugout, a big man ridin' a sorrel hoss an' dragging a mustang behind.

"We been askin' around, an' we was told you got a woman stashed up on the Two-Bit. Me an' him," the man said, nodding toward his brother, "been watching you mighty close."

"Puzzles me that you haven't bushwhacked me by this time," Fletcher said, trying to postpone the gunfire for as long as he could. "I'd have figured that was more your style."

The man nodded. "Studied on that a time or two, but me and Ephraim here, we decided we wanted to watch you die up close." The man shrugged. "It's a lot more fun that way."

There's a time for talking and a time for shooting, and the time for talking was being used up fast. But Fletcher made one last, desperate try.

"Boys," he said, "you got no call to die in the street. Your paw and Ezra just ain't worth dying for."

"That's what you say," the man with the shotgun said. "Why, you yellowbelly, I—"

The talking time was over.

Fletcher dove off the boardwalk, drawing his gun as he flew through the air. His Colt was already hammering as he hit the ground. He saw his bullets kick up puffs of dust on the Winchester man's chest, then he rolled and swung on his shotgun-toting brother. Too late! Ephraim had the Greener to his shoulder and was taking dead aim, his finger already white on the trigger.

A shot slammed behind him, and Fletcher saw the man stagger backward, the muzzles of his shotgun dropping. He'd been hit square in the middle of his forehead, and blood and brain fanned like a crimson halo around him. But he was still standing. Still dangerous. Fletcher rose on his right knee and fired at Ephraim, saw the hit, then fired again.

Like a felled oak, his shotgun blasting harmlessly into the air, the man crashed backward and hit the street with a dreadful thud, sprawling his full length on the frost-hardened mud.

Both men lay there unmoving, as dead as they were ever going to be. Behind him, Fletcher heard a deep, racking sob. He turned and saw the little man in the tweed coat standing on the boardwalk, a shocked, sick expression on his face. He was holding a smoking Colt in his right hand.

"Oh my God, I just killed a man," he gasped. "I can't believe it. I just killed a man. Oh my God, my God . . ."

Fletcher punched empty shells from the cylinder of his own Colt, reloaded and holstered the gun. "Mister," he said, "I don't know why you dealt yourself a hand in this game, but I surely do thank you, and I owe you one."

A gawking crowd gathered around the dead men, and the bartender stepped onto the boardwalk and quickly summed up the situation.

"You there, Lem Wilkins and Brad Elliot," the man said, "take those two down to the undertaker. Then come back, and I'll buy you a drink."

"What about their rifles an' horses an' sich?" the man called Elliot asked.

"Bring them back here," the bartender said, shaking his head slowly. "Maybe they left widows behind or some other kin."

He turned to Fletcher. "Mister, you gave them boys a chance to step away from a shooting. Studying on it, I'd say you done all you could. Now come inside and I'll buy you a drink, but then be on your way."

The bartender's eyes were hard, and there was no give in them. "My name is Caleb Mills, and I own this saloon. We don't have any law in Buffalo City, but I head up the vigilante committee. Now, come in and drink up and be welcome. Then leave town."

"And if I don't?" Fletcher asked, suddenly angry.

The bartender's face didn't change. "Within ten minutes I can round up a dozen men with shotguns. Do you think even Buck Fletcher can face that many?"

"You're pushing me mighty hard, Mills," Fletcher said. "I won't be buffaloed."

The saloon owner was short and stocky, with huge forearms and wrists. He wore a flowered vest and a gold watch chain across his belly, and he looked strong and capable.

"Fletcher," he said, as he watched the dead being carried away, "those were mountain men, born to the feud. Now, maybe you've killed them all, but if you haven't, their surviving kin will come here seeking revenge. I don't want another street fight. Too many innocent people can be killed when the bullets start flying."

Buck Fletcher bitterly sensed the injustice of it all. He'd killed only in self-defense, and now it rankled that he was being run out of town.

His eyes cold, Fletcher was about to angrily tell the bartender exactly where he could shove his drink, but the voice of the little man in the tweed coat stopped him.

"Gentlemen, I pray you," he said, his English accent very strong, "I need a brandy. I've never killed a man before, and I'm afraid I'm quite undone. Indeed, I feel faint."

The bartender nodded at Fletcher. "That invitation for a drink is still open."

"Please, Mr. Fletcher," the Englishman pleaded, "I really do need a brandy."

Fletcher stood there for a few moments, weighing his options.

He decided that he owed the little Englishman a

favor or three, and having a drink with him would be a small start in balancing the ledger.

The ludicrousness of the situation had finally dawned on Fletcher and tickled the wry humor that always lay just beneath his tough, unsmiling exterior.

"Make that two brandies, Mr. Mills," he grinned, "and you have yourself a deal."

As he was about to step into the saloon, Fletcher was passed by the loafer who'd earlier been nursing the dregs of a warm beer. The man ran, scooped up the fallen double eagle from the boardwalk and bit into it. He grinned hugely, then hightailed it, hallooing as he leaped into the air and clicked his heels together.

Fletcher let him go, shaking his head as he walked through the batwing doors. Buffalo City was shaping up to be a mighty strange town.

Mills produced a dusty bottle of Hennessy cognac and poured a generous glass for Fletcher and the Englishman.

The little man nodded toward a table in the corner. "Shall we?"

Fletcher nodded, and they settled themselves at the table. Fletcher built himself a smoke as the Englishman introduced himself. He gave his name only as Bob, and Fletcher did not press the matter.

"It seems to me," Fletcher said, "that I've seen you somewhere before. I just can't recall a place or time."

"Most unlikely," Bob said. His hand was trembling slightly as he held his glass to his lips. "You see, I'm a landscape painter by profession, just arrived from England a couple of weeks ago. I'd read so much about the glory of the Black Hills that I decided to preserve them on canvas before they're ruined by mining."

For the first time, Fletcher noticed faded paint stains on the little man's hands and down the front of his English tweed jacket and pants.

Bob sipped his brandy and said, "Ah, I'm starting to feel a bit better. I've never killed a man before. It's a dreadful thing."

Fletcher nodded. "Yes, it is. It's not easy to kill a man and walk away from it. Every time you kill, a little piece of you dies. Kill often enough, and though you may still talk and eat and breathe, you're a walking dead man your ownself."

Bob smiled slightly. "How very depressing."

"Maybe so, but I reckon that's the way of it," Fletcher said, his eyes bleak and remote.

The Englishman laid his brandy glass on the table. All his movements were precise and exact, with no wasted motion.

"You know, Buck—may I call you Buck?—I was on my way in here to talk to you when I encountered those ruffians outside."

"Really? Why?"

"Well, it was Judith Tyrone who asked me to speak to you. She owns the Lazy R, you know."

Fletcher nodded. "I've heard of her. They say Pike Prescott is pushing her mighty hard."

Bob spread his slim hands, the nails clean and cut short, and shrugged. "Prescott wants her range. There's a fortune to be made supplying beef to the Deadwood miners, and he needs more grazing. Have you any idea how many cows thirty thousand miners can get through in a week?"

"I've a pretty good idea. Say, how did you know I'd come into town?"

"Well, I didn't. Not really. But the Prescott hands were saying you intended to stay up there on the Two-Bit, and I knew you must eventually come in for supplies. When I'm not out in the wilderness painting, I stay pretty close to the hotel, so I told Mrs. Tyrone I'd watch for you."

Fletcher began to build another smoke. "What did

Judith Tyrone want you to talk to me about? I'm not selling my gun, if that's what she has in mind."

Bob shook his head. "No, nothing like that, though God knows she could use you. She's already had two hands murdered out on the range and another who lies close to death. Prescott is very aware that Mrs. Tyrone's hard-working cowboys are no match for his hired guns, especially that Higgy Conroy. He's a born killer."

"I've met him," Fletcher said dryly, adding nothing more.

"Well, to get to the point, Judith—I mean, Mrs. Tyrone—heard you have a very sick woman at your cabin on the Two-Bit, and she's very concerned for her welfare."

"You mean Savannah Jones?" Fletcher asked. Then, without waiting for a reply, added: "She's over to her room at the hotel right now."

"And the poor creature has completely lost her memory, I'm told."

Puzzled, Fletcher asked, "How did you know that?"

Bob smiled. "Prescott's hired guns. My, how they love to stand around the saloon and talk."

"Well, they're right about one thing. Savannah has lost her memory. Doc Hawthorne says it's pretty common after a head injury, and she should start to remember things in a couple of weeks."

"Head injury?"

"Uh-huh. Somebody took a shot at her. When I got to Savannah, her horse had been shot out from under her, and she was lying on the ground unconscious."

"Did you get a look at the would-be assassin?"

Fletcher shook his head. "No. We traded shots, but there was a blizzard blowing hard, and I lost him."

"Too bad," Bob said. "Only a low-down skunk would try to kill a woman."

"A skunk," Fletcher agreed. "Or a hired killer."

"And that points up Mrs. Tyrone's concern," Bob said. "She says a young woman without a memory shouldn't be left alone out there at your cabin, especially with Pike Prescott making all those threats. She says she should come out to the Lazy R where she can get proper care and be protected. If Savannah is willing, I've been charged to escort her there in the ranch surrey."

"I've got to agree with Mrs. Tyrone," Fletcher said. "My cabin is no place for a woman right now. I believe Savannah also knows this and will take her up on her kind invitation."

"Well," Bob said, rising to his feet. "I'll be right here for the next hour or so if you need me. I feel the need for another brandy and"—he smiled—"I don't think the vigilantes will run me out of town. At least not for a little while yet."

Fletcher rose and stuck out his hand, which Bob took. "You saved my life out there. It's something I won't forget." He stood for a few moments studying the little man's face, then added, "Say, just why did you throw in with me? It wasn't your fight."

The Englishman colored, looking embarrassed. "I think it's what we British call fair play. It was two against one, and I evened the odds, even though I'd never fired a gun in anger before."

"Well, I'm much obliged to you." Fletcher stepped toward the door, then stopped. "I'll speak to Savannah about Mrs. Tyrone's offer," he said, turning. "If she agrees, I'll ride out to the Lazy R with you."

Bob nodded. "That's a first-class plan. Savannah will be well protected."

As he stepped onto the boardwalk and made his way to the general store, Fletcher was very much troubled by two thoughts.

The first was that Bob said he'd never before fired a gun in anger and was visibly upset by the killing. Yet he'd been cool enough when he drilled Ezra's brother right through the middle of the forehead at twenty paces. By any standard, that was good shooting, and it took nerve.

The second was that he was sure he'd seen the mild-eyed little Englishman somewhere before, somewhere back along some misty, half-forgotten trail.

But where?

Chapter 7

Fletcher paid for his supplies and crossed the road to the hotel, carrying a bulging sack that weighed pretty heavy.

When he stepped into the hotel lobby, the clerk wasn't in sight. He took the stairs two at a time and walked to Savannah's door. He rapped with his knuckles and said, "Savannah, open up. It's Buck."

No answer.

Fletcher knocked again. "Open up, sleepyhead. It's me."

Silence.

Alarmed, Fletcher tried the door. It opened easily. He stepped inside the room and looked around.

Savannah was gone.

A single glance told him that the bed hadn't been slept on. When he checked the wardrobe, he found that a suede riding outfit with a split skirt was missing. So was the short, fur-lined jacket that he'd seen hanging there earlier. And so was the box of .41 caliber shells.

There was no sign of a struggle. Whatever had happened here, Savannah had left of her own free will.

Doc!

Fletcher's frustration with the snoring Holliday's lackadaisical guardianship gave him the irresistible urge to charge into his room and throttle his skinny neck. But a man didn't barge into Doc's bedroom unannounced—not unless he was real tired of living.

Fletcher stepped out of Savannah's room and quietly closed the door behind him.

For a few moments, he stood outside Doc Holliday's room. Inside, he could hear the man snoring loudly, the strangled snorts and gasps of a lunger who found breathing, even in sleep, very difficult.

Doc had let him down, and now Fletcher decided it was time to let him know it. He stepped up to Doc's door, braced his arms on the jambs and kicked it hard several times, a thundering BANG! BANG! BANG! that echoed noisily throughout the hotel.

The big man stepped smartly away from the door, out of any line of fire. He smiled when he heard Doc's snores strangle to a halt, followed by a startled: "Wha—wha—wha . . . the hell?"

Still smiling, Fletcher made his way downstairs and stopped at the front desk. The clerk said he hadn't seen Savannah leave, since he was taking a nap himself. "Did you check the livery stable?" he asked. "Is Miss Jones' horse gone?"

"I'm just about to go over there," Fletcher said. He heaved the heavy sack of groceries onto the desk. "Take care of these, will you?"

Without waiting for the startled clerk's reply, Fletcher stepped out of the lobby onto the boardwalk.

And the sky fell on him.

Fletcher never saw the bottle that crashed into the back of his head and dropped him, stunned, to his hands and knees on the boardwalk.

A boot came out of nowhere and thudded into his ribs, and he fell over on his right side, pain spiking savagely at him.

Fletcher half-turned his head and saw Pike Prescott looming over him, a grinning Higgy Conroy standing next to him.

"I warned you to get out of the Territory," Prescott snarled. "Now, by God, you're going to pay the piper."

Prescott's boot swung again and crashed into Fletcher's face, rolling him on his back. Prescott straddled him, then dropped his two-hundred-forty pounds quickly, his knees pinning Fletcher's upper arms to the rough planks of the boardwalk.

Prescott's fists swung, first a right, then a left, smashing time and time again into Fletcher's face, turning the gunfighter's features into a bloody pulp.

Through a haze of blood and pain, Fletcher tried to twist from under the big rancher's knees. But he couldn't move, and again Prescott's fists thudded into his face.

After what seemed to Fletcher an eternity as he battled to hold onto consciousness, Prescott rose to his feet, hauling the gunfighter with him. Prescott grabbed the front of Fletcher's mackinaw and threw him against the false front of the hotel with so much force that the building shook.

Fletcher tried desperately to swing a left, but Prescott easily brushed his fist aside and rammed a right, then another hard right, into Fletcher's unprotected belly.

Gasping, Fletcher doubled up, and Prescott let him fall to the boardwalk. Dimly, as if Prescott were speaking from the other end of a tunnel, Fletcher heard the big man turn to the crowd and roar, "I told this man to get off my land. He chose to ignore me, and now you see him lying there, the big gunfighter Buck Fletcher." Prescott swung a kick into Fletcher's ribs. "Well, he doesn't look so big now, does he?"

Prescott stepped to the edge of the boardwalk. "All

of you out there," he said, "take this as a warning. I won't be run off my range, and from this day forth I'll hang any man I find carrying a gun on the PP Connected."

His voice rose. "My name is Pike Prescott, and I aim to keep what is mine." Without a backward glance at Fletcher, Prescott stepped off the boardwalk and angrily shoved his way through the crowd, the grinning Higgy Conroy swaggering after him.

Pain.

Buck Fletcher was at the center of an exploding universe of pain. Every breath he took stabbed at his sides like a red-hot lance. After several tries, when he got to his hands and knees, he saw blood fall like rubies from his face to the boardwalk.

The crowd, stunned and cowed by Prescott's savage violence, melted away, and Fletcher found himself alone.

The livery stable.

He must try and get to his horse.

Slowly, collapsing on his side time and time again, he crawled along the boardwalk. Behind him lay a trail of bloody handprints, scarlet markers mocking his tedious progress.

He wasn't going to make it.

Fletcher collapsed onto his belly. He could go no farther.

"Easy there, feller. Let me help you."

Through swollen eyes that were mere slits in his battered face, Fletcher watched a slender young man bend over him. The man was dressed in a black shirt, black pants and a low-crowned, flat-brimmed hat. The only splash of color was the worn ivory handle of the Colt in a crossdraw holster at his waist.

"My horse," Fletcher whispered through split and battered lips. "Got to get my horse . . . got to get to my cabin . . . Two-Bit Creek . . ."

"Mister, you're hurt bad, awful bad," the young man said.

"My horse . . . livery . . . my cabin . . ."

The young man shook his head. "Not there. Pike and his boys are on their way to the Two-Bit right now. If there's anyone there, they won't be alive come sundown—Higgy Conroy is with them."

"No!" Fletcher gasped. "I . . . I got to get out there . . ."

"Mister," the man said, "I'd say you've had a busy morning. Right now what you need is rest."

Pain.

Then Fletcher's entire universe exploded, a blinding flash of searing, white-hot light.

He was falling, falling into a starless void, tumbling like a falling leaf into a darkness that had no beginning and no end.

Chapter 8

He woke to sunlight.

Bright rays slanted through the lace curtains of the room where he lay. Around him, fresh flowers bloomed.

Fletcher blinked, trying to get his eyes back into focus.

He saw them clearly now. They were not real flowers, but the pattern of the wallpaper. Yet he smelled their sweet scent. How was that possible?

A woman was bending over him.

She looked to be somewhere in her mid-thirties, a beautiful woman with a slender, shapely figure, a thick, waving mass of auburn hair, and soft hazel eyes.

She must, Fletcher decided, be an angel.

"Where am I?" he whispered.

"You're at the Lazy R," the woman said. "I'm Judith Tyrone."

"How . . . how long . . . ?"

"You've been unconscious for three days."

"Three days!"

Fletcher struggled to rise, but Judith gently pushed him back on the pillow.

"You're not going anywhere. You took a terrible beating from Pike Prescott," she said. "I sent for Doc Hawthorne, and he taped up your broken ribs, three of them." She shook her head, smiling. "Strangely enough, your nose wasn't broken."

Fletcher smiled back weakly, an effort that made his battered face hurt. "It's been broke so many times in the past, I guess it just naturally can't be broke again."

"How do you feel?" Judith asked, her eyes concerned.

"About as good as I look."

"That bad, huh?"

In fact, despite his injuries, Fletcher felt stronger than he had a right to feel—and he was very hungry.

Judith held a bowl of beef broth, and she dipped some and held the spoon to Fletcher's lips.

The big man smiled and sipped what was offered. Then he took the bowl from Judith and said, "I think I can manage this by myself." He spooned some broth. "But what I really need is someone to burn me a thick steak and lay six fried eggs on top of it. Oh, and maybe a loaf of bread."

Judith grinned, her eyes wandering over Fletcher's wide, muscular shoulders and the thick, sunburned column of his neck. "That hungry, huh?" she asked.

Fletcher nodded. "That hungry and then some."

Judith rose. "I'll be right back." She dropped a little curtsy. "Just as soon as I give your order to the chef, sir."

When the woman was gone, Fletcher lay back on the bed, his hands clasped behind his head.

He'd been beaten up by Pike Prescott, that much he could remember. It had happened as he was leaving Savannah's hotel—

Savannah!

Fletcher sat bolt upright, ignoring the sudden stab of pain that shot through his ribs on the right side of his chest.

He had to find her. Had she gone back to the cabin? If she had, she was in terrible danger.

Fletcher recalled a man dressed in black who had helped him. The man, whoever he was, had told him Prescott and his gunmen were riding out to the cabin—and Higgy Conroy was riding with them.

Swinging his legs over the bed, Fletcher struggled to his feet. The room spun around him, and he sat down again, the bedsprings squealing under his weight. Judith stepped into the room, and Fletcher realized for the first time that he was stark naked. He dived back under the sheets as the woman laughed.

"Mr. Fletcher," she said, "I've seen a naked man before."

"Not this one," Fletcher said, his face flushing. He looked wildly around the room. "My clothes? And where the hell are my guns?"

Judith nodded toward a wardrobe set against the wall. "In there. Your guns are there, and so are your clothes. Your rifle and revolvers have been cleaned and oiled, and your clothes washed and pressed, I might add." She paused. "Your money belt is there too. Untouched."

Fletcher realized that this woman had done her best for him, and he'd sounded churlish and ungrateful, like a spoiled child.

"I'm sorry," he said. "It's just that I have to find Savannah and quick."

"She's not at the cabin; at least, I don't think so," Judith said. Then, by way of explanation, she added, "I sent some of my hands up there the day before yesterday, and that crazy old man—"

"Jeb Coons," Fletcher supplied, smiling.

"Is that his name? Well, anyway, he was forted up in an aspen grove and drove my men off with his rifle. It's lucky none of my hands were killed."

"Sounds like Jeb," Fletcher said.

Then Jeb was still alive and by all accounts as feisty as ever. But where was Savannah? Was she out wandering in the hills somewhere, a young, pretty and vulnerable woman who was the target of a mysterious and cold-blooded killer's rifle?

Fletcher looked at Judith pleadingly. "Please, Miss Tyrone, bring me my clothes. I've got to get going. I have to find Savannah."

The woman smiled. Her teeth were even and very white. "It's Mrs. Tyrone," she said. "But to you, Buck, I'm Judith."

"Judith." Fletcher smiled. "My clothes?"

The woman said, "Wait a moment." She stepped to the dresser and returned with a small hand mirror. She held it up to Fletcher and said, "Look. Are you still sure you want to ride?"

Fletcher glanced in the mirror and saw the grotesque face of a stranger. His eyes were mere slits, black and blue and swollen, fading to yellow across his cheekbones. His lips were split and puffed, and his nose, though Judith said it hadn't been broken, looked to be twice its normal size, blood crusted around the nostrils.

Fletcher shook his head. "Maybe it's just as well I wasn't too purty to begin with." His fingers went to his mustache. "Thanks for trimming this."

Judith laid the tips of her fingers on the back of his hand. "I don't want you to ride, Buck. Listen, I know how urgent finding Savannah is. I know she's in great danger. That's why I've had my hands out searching for the past couple of days. Doc Hawthorne told you loss of memory wasn't serious, but I assure you it is. Doc is a nice old man, but he just can't treat something like that. Savannah needs to go Back East, where there are proper physicians."

Fletcher nodded. "I agree with you there. But we have to find her first."

Tears reddened the woman's eyes, and she turned quickly away. "I'm sorry," she said. "Suddenly I'm being a woman."

"What's the matter?" Fletcher asked, his voice concerned.

Judith clasped Fletcher's big hand in hers, the paleness of her fine skin a delicate, feminine contrast against the sun-toughened mahogany brown of his own.

"Buck," she said urgently, "it's just that I don't want to lose this ranch. Since my husband was murdered, it's all I have left. Pike Prescott has already moved part of his herd onto my winter grass, and just yesterday he threatened to burn this house down around my ears if I don't sell out to him by the end of the week."

Judith lifted Fletcher's hand to her mouth and brushed it lightly with her soft lips. "That's just four days from now. I need you, Buck. I need you to stand with me. I have good, steady men, but they're working hands, not hired gunmen like Higgy Conroy and that bunch."

Cursing himself for getting involved in another's troubles, yet moved by the memory of the woman's lips still warm on his hand, Fletcher heard himself say, "Judith, you won't lose your ranch. Prescott and me, we have a showdown coming. First I'm going to beat him to within an inch of his life, and then I'm going to run him clear out of the Territory."

"And Higgy Conroy?" Judith asked, her lips pale.

"Him too."

Fletcher ran his finger down Judith's soft cheek. "Now, young lady, for pete's sake bring me my clothes. I've been loafing in bed too long."

*   *   *

It was only when he dressed and stomped into his boots that Fletcher realized just how weak he was. Doc Hawthorne had taped up his ribs, but it hurt to breathe, and he knew he was no match for Pike Prescott in this condition. Not yet, anyway.

He carried his gunbelts to the kitchen and hung them over the back of his chair. Judith's cook, a grizzled oldster who had once wrangled grub on Charlie Goodnight's cattle drives, set a plate filled with steak, eggs and fried bread in front of him.

"Chaw it or chuck it, boy," the cook said. "It's all the same to me."

Fletcher ate hungrily. The food was good, and he said to Judith, who was sitting opposite him in her sunny kitchen sipping coffee, "What your cook lacks in the social graces, he sure makes up for in culinary skills."

Judith smiled. "Sam has cooked for cowboys too long. It's a thankless task."

Fletcher nodded. "It does tend to make a man tetchy after a spell."

After he'd finished eating, Fletcher sat back in his chair, his hand straying to his shirt pocket. Judith reached into the pocket of her gingham dress and produced the makings, new papers and a full sack of tobacco.

"Looking for this?"

"Judith, you sure do know how to take care of a man." Fletcher smiled.

"I was married once, remember?" She looked away from him quickly, then said, a catch in her voice, "There I go being a woman again."

Fletcher put his hand over hers. "It's all right to grieve, Judith. Nobody's going to fault you for that."

"Thank you, Buck," the woman whispered. "It's just that now and again I . . . remember."

"Nothing wrong with that either."

Sitting back in his chair, Fletcher built a smoke and thumbed a match into flame. As he lit his cigarette, he glanced out the window and saw a rider rein up outside. The man climbed down from the saddle and looped the reins around the hitching post, then stood there, looking around.

"Who's he?" Fletcher asked, turning in his chair so he was closer to his gun.

"That's Matt Baker," Judith replied. "The man who brought you here."

"Do you know him well?"

The rider was still standing outside, glancing around as though he was looking for something.

"I never met him before he brought you here face-down across the saddle of your horse. He's used a gun before, and probably well, that much I could tell just by looking at him."

Baker finally strode to the front door, and Judith rose to answer his knock. Fletcher heard her call out a greeting, and a few moments later Matt Baker walked into the kitchen.

Baker stepped close to Fletcher, stuck out his hand and said, "Well, real nice to see you up and around. And may I say, you look really wonderful."

"You could say that, but you wouldn't mean it," Fletcher said, shaking Baker's hand.

"How are you feeling?" the man asked.

"About as good as I look."

"That bad, huh?"

Fletcher smiled. "You're the second person to tell me that this morning."

He studied the man called Baker. Judith had been right on two counts. This man had used a gun before, and probably he'd used it well. There was the look of the professional about him, the look of a man who sold his gun to the highest bidder and would always do the job he was paid to do. He was dressed in black but for a hip-length sheepskin coat, and he stood, slim, significant and relaxed, a slight smile on his lips.

"I owe you," Fletcher said finally. "Judith told me you brought me here."

Baker nodded. "I couldn't leave you on the street. If I hadn't happened by, I reckon you'd still be there."

"How did you know to bring me here?"

Baker shrugged. "That little Englishman, the landscape painter—he told me this would be the safest place."

At that time in the West, you didn't question a man too closely about his past, or his present either, so Fletcher came at it from an oblique angle, not wishing to be seen as pushing too hard.

"Been in the Territory long?" he asked mildly.

"Passing through," Baker replied.

"Heading for Deadwood?"

"Maybe."

"A gambling man?"

"Not so's you'd notice."

Fletcher let it go. "Well, like I said, I owe you one, Baker. You only have to ask."

Baker smiled. "I'll bear that in mind."

Groaning a little against the pain in his ribs, Fletcher rose to his feet. "Now I got to be going."

"Mr. Baker," Judith said, pouting, "can you talk some sense into him? I've told him he's not fit to ride, but he won't listen to me."

Shaking his head, Baker said, "Fletcher is a grown man, ma'am, and he can make up his own mind about things. Besides, I wouldn't want to be the one who'd try to stop him."

"Men!" Judith exclaimed. "Well, at least I can get one of my hands to saddle your horse, Buck."

She tossed her head and stomped out of the kitchen, both men smiling as they watched her go.

After a few moments, Baker said, "I'd say you were going out after Savannah Jones."

"That's right. I've got to find her before the man that's trying to kill her does."

"Mind if I tag along?"

Fletcher shrugged. "This isn't your fight, Baker, but, like I said, I owe you one. Sure, you can ride with me, and welcome."

One of the Lazy R hands brought Fletcher's sorrel around, and Baker helped him into his mackinaw before they stepped outside.

The day was sunny and clear, though cold. Snow lay several inches thick on the ground, and to the west the pine trees on Strawberry Ridge still wore an overcoat of white.

Fletcher, weakness weighing heavy on him, was about to struggle into the saddle when a party of a dozen men loped into sight. He stood, a hand on the saddle horn, watching them come. Beside him, he was aware that Baker had pushed his sheepskin away from the butt of his Colt. The man stood relaxed, his blue eyes calm, but he seemed alert and ready.

On his coat, the man who led the horsemen wore a five-pointed star enclosed by the downsweeping horns of a crescent. He was a tall, skinny drink of water with a droopy black mustache and sad, hound dog eyes, but the Greener across his saddle bow was worn from much handling and spoke quiet volumes about the man who carried it.

Behind him, Higgy Conroy sat grinning on a paint horse, surrounded by the tough PP Connected hands.

"My name is C. J. Graham, and I'm a deputy United States Marshal for the Dakota Territory," the lawman said by way of introduction. "Which one of you men is Buck Fletcher?"

"That would be me," Fletcher said, stepping away

from his horse. He glanced at the grinning Conroy and the hard, hostile faces of the other hands. "Pike Prescott send you to do his dirty work, Marshal?"

If the lawman was offended, he didn't let it show.

"Well, now," he said affably, "that would take a heap of doing, seeing how he was bushwhacked and murdered just yesterday."

That hit Fletcher hard, coming out of nowhere the way it did. He'd planned to meet Prescott again, this time on even terms, but now the man was dead. Murdered, according to the marshal.

"Damn it, Graham," Higgy Conroy snapped, "enough talk. Arrest Fletcher for the murder of the boss. After he attacked Mr. Prescott in Buffalo City for no reason and got the beating he deserved, Fletcher swore he'd kill him. The whole town heard him."

Conroy kneed his horse forward. "Arrest Fletcher, and we'll take him into custody. We'll hold him in the Buffalo City jail until a judge gets there."

"Do that, Graham, and I guarantee you I'd never get to Buffalo City alive," Fletcher said. "Besides, I never killed Pike Prescott. I was lying here, flat on my back, all day yesterday."

"That's true, Marshal," Judith Tyrone said, stepping from the house. "And Mr. Baker there will tell you the same thing."

Graham looked at Judith appreciatively, his saggy eyes wandering over the swell of her breasts and hips and the tall, female gracefulness of her.

"You must be the widow Tyrone," Graham said, touching his hat brim. "I knew your husband well, ma'am. Deke Tyrone was a fine man."

"Thank you," Judith said quietly. "Thank you kindly."

Then, because he seemed to think it might be expected of him, Graham added, "We're still trying to find his murderer, ma'am. And never fear, we will."

"I think my husband's killer has already gotten his just deserts, Marshal," Judith said. "I believe he was killed by Pike Prescott."

"That's a lie!" Conroy yelled. "Don't you see, Graham, she's trying to protect Fletcher. He's always hiding behind women's skirts." Conroy leered. "Maybe he's keeping the widow real happy now her man is gone."

Suddenly angry, Fletcher opened his mackinaw, pushing it away from his guns. "I'm not hiding behind a woman's skirts now, Conroy," he said. "So draw or shut your dirty mouth."

"Enough!" Graham said, kneeing his horse between Fletcher and Conroy. The marshal turned to the furious gunman. "Now listen here, Hig. Mrs. Tyrone's word is good enough for me. If she says Fletcher was here, then he was here. As far as I can tell, all you've done is drag me out here on a wild goose chase."

He looked down at Judith from the saddle and swept off his hat. "My apologies, ma'am."

Judith smiled sweetly and nodded. "None needed, Marshal."

Graham waved to the PP Connected gun hands. "You boys come with me. There will be no arrests made here today."

With visible reluctance, the Connected hands filed out after Graham, but Higgy Conroy stayed his ground.

"You and I will meet real soon, Fletcher," he said, his yellow snake eyes glittering. "And when we do, you won't have a woman to protect you."

Anger still flaring in him, Fletcher said, "There's no time like the present, Conroy."

But the gunman shook his head. "No, not yet. When

we meet, it will be a time and place of my own choosing. That's when I'll kill you."

Then he turned his horse and galloped after the others.

"Know something, Fletcher?" Baker said. "Some day you're going to have to kill that man or he'll kill you."

Fletcher nodded. "I know it."

"They say he's fast, almighty fast," Baker said absently, as though talking to himself.

"I know that too," Fletcher said.

Baker stood silent and wondered—had he really heard a note of uncertainty in Buck Fletcher's voice?

Chapter 9

Fletcher and Matt Baker rode north from the Lazy R toward Two-Bit Creek.

There was always the chance that Savannah had showed up there, and besides, Jeb Coons had been alone at the cabin for a long time now, and for Fletcher that was a worrisome thing.

They rode without talking, each occupied with his own thoughts, until they crossed Windy Flats and cleared Bear Butte.

The sun, climbing in the sky toward its noonday point, sparkled on the snow and the frosting on the pines. Above their heads the sky was wide and blue, with only a few puffy white clouds. But the wind was from the north, filled with the promise of bitter cold to come.

The two men stopped to give their horses a breather, and Fletcher said, "I guess it was Higgy Conroy who hit me with a bottle as I left the hotel."

Baker nodded. "A bottle of Anderson's Old-Fashioned Rye, to be exact. Empty of course, but still, from what I'm told, it made quite a clunk."

"I know," Fletcher said dryly. He nodded. "So it was Higgy. That's a thing to remember."

This time Baker heard no uncertainty in the gunfighter's voice, and, unaccountably, that fact pleased him.

They rode on, and Fletcher said, "Matt, do you know what happened to Judith's husband? I mean, how it happened?"

Baker shrugged. "I wasn't here then, and I only know what I read in the papers. It seems Deke Tyrone was the first man to die on this range. He was shot off the back of his horse by someone using a mighty big rifle. Evidently the bullet put a hole in his head so big the coroner could put his fist into it."

"Do you think it was Prescott?"

"He had the motive," Baker replied. "He wanted the Lazy R. What better way to get it than kill the owner and leave his widow in charge? Maybe Prescott figured he could do to Judith Tyrone what he couldn't do to her husband—bully her into selling."

Baker bit his bottom lip. "Only thing is, later a couple of Prescott's men were bushwhacked and killed. Would he murder his own hands just to start a range war?"

"It's possible," Fletcher replied. "Ambition and greed can do strange things to a man."

Baker nodded. "Well, Prescott is dead, and all his ambitions have died with him. I don't think his daughter has the same drive."

"Daughter?"

"Yeah, just sixteen years old from what I hear, and real pretty. She inherits the ranch, since her mother died a couple of years ago."

Fletcher was silent for a few moments. Then he said, "It's too bad Deke Tyrone had to die like that. I mean, a young man with everything to live for: a fine ranch and a beautiful wife."

Matt Baker turned to face Fletcher, a strange look in his eyes. "He left a ranch and a lovely wife all right, but he wasn't a young man. Deke Tyrone was pushing eighty-three years old."

That stunned Fletcher. Judith, so young and fresh,

married to an old man? Somehow it didn't fit with his image of her, and it troubled him. But why? Young women married old men all the time, for many reasons. It wasn't that unusual.

"And there's something else strange here," Baker said, as if reading Fletcher's mind. "Doesn't the Lazy R claim range all the way to the Two-Bit?"

Fletcher nodded. "It does, and then east as far as the Cheyenne."

Baker nodded. "Thought so."

"What's eating you, Matt?" Fletcher asked.

"Just that Judith said Prescott was already moving his herds onto her range. I've been looking at the brands on the cows we've passed. All of them were wearing the Lazy R. I haven't seen a single PP Connected yet."

"Maybe Prescott didn't get a chance to move his cows this far north. They could be to the south of here and east of here," Fletcher said. "His home range is south of Judith's ranch; it runs almost clear to the Platte."

"Maybe so," Baker said. "But it makes a man think. I believe maybe there's something odd going on here, something I don't understand. Why did Prescott hold back? In his heart of hearts, did he really want to avoid a range war, but there was someone else involved, someone who was pushing him headlong into it?"

Fletcher smiled, realizing Baker was testing him. "Matt, you've missed your calling. You should have been a detective." His smile broadened. "A pretty skittish detective, if you ask me."

The cabin on the Two-Bit still stood. But no smoke rose from the chimney, and as Fletcher and Baker rode closer, they could see no sign of life. The speckled pup was usually alert for approaching riders and by this time should have bounded up to greet them.

"Something wrong here," Fletcher said, reining in his horse. He eased the thong off the hammer of his Colt, and Baker did the same.

Behind the cabin, the aspens moved restlessly in the breeze, and a couple of jays quarreled noisily in their branches. The snow in front of the cabin had been trampled by the feet of many horses, and the door stood ajar about a foot or so, hanging slightly on its rawhide hinges.

Fletcher kneed his horse forward, every nerve in his body tensed, his senses alert for any sign of danger.

He and Baker rode up to the cabin and dismounted. Fletcher held his gun ready, and Baker moved back and slightly to his left, where he could give him cover.

"Jeb?" Fletcher called.

No answer.

He walked forward and pushed open the cabin door with the muzzle of his Colt. It swung wide, and he walked inside. The broken ribs were slowing his movements, and he stepped with great deliberation, like a man walking on ice. The cabin was undisturbed, but the fire in the stove was cold. An old piece of scrap leather the pup used as a chew toy lay in the middle of the floor, and the remains of a meal still sat on the table.

Fletcher checked the bedroom, but it too was empty. He walked back into the main cabin and looked around again, then stepped outside.

Baker had been studying the aspens behind the cabin. Now his eyes turned to Fletcher. "Anything?"

The gunfighter shook his head. "Nothing, though it looks like Jeb left in an all-fired hurry and took the dog with him."

Baker nodded toward the aspen grove. "Them jays

are pretty worked up over something. Could be a coyote or a bear. But it could be something else."

Fletcher's blue eyes scanned the trees, but he could
see nothing. "Maybe we should go look," he said.
"Keep your gun handy."

"I always do." Baker smiled.

The two men walked behind the cabin and up the
slope toward the aspen. They were about twenty feet
from the nearest tree when a voice stopped them in
midstride.

"You rannies hold it right there. I got me a Henry
rifle gun here, an' I know how to use her."

Fletcher grinned. "Jeb, you old he-coon, it's me,
Buck, and I've got a friend with me."

"You sure it's you, Buck? If'n it ain't you, this here
Henry is pointed plumb at your brisket, an' I'll cut
her loose right quick."

"Why, you old goat, of course it's me! Who else
would be powerful dumb enough to walk up this hill
right into your rifle sights?"

"Only you, Buck," Jeb cackled. "Only you."

The old man stepped out of the aspen, his rifle
hanging loose in his right hand. He grinned at
Fletcher—then the grin slipped, and he sank slowly to
the ground. Fletcher ran to Jeb and kneeled beside
him. Blood crusted the front of the old miner's shirt,
fanning up from just below his pants. He was
wounded, and it was in a bad place.

"How are you, old timer?" Fletcher asked gently,
pushing Jeb's shirt aside so he could see the wound.

"It's no good you fussin', Buck. I been gut-shot, and
it's all up for me," Jeb whispered. "But I stayed alive
for you. Sometimes the pain was real bad, Buck, but
I stayed alive 'cause I needed to tell you something."

"Jeb," Buck said, "who did this to you?"

"Higgy Conroy. Him and his gunmen caught me out

in the open playing with the pup, and he shot me. He didn't even say 'Hi' or nothing, just grinned, then drawed his gun and shot me." The old man grasped the sleeve of Fletcher's mackinaw. "But I fooled him, Buck. I ran into the cabin an' got me my Henry, then I hightailed it out the back door an' into the trees.

"When they came at me all in a rush, I killed one of them an' winged another. Then I heard Higgy say to leave me alone 'cause he'd gut shot me real good and that I'd die soon anyway."

Jeb cackled, his lips flecking with blood. "Fooled 'em again. I stayed alive, knowing you'd eventually come back."

The old miner tried to sit up, and Fletcher cradled his shoulders in his arms.

"Buck," he said, shaking his head like he couldn't believe what he was about to say, "Hig shot the pup. The pup knowed something was going on when I got shot an' ran for the trees. I saw Hig get off his hoss. Then the pup ran over and started into barking at him and biting at his boots.

"Hig, he didn't even look. He just lowered his gun and shot the pup, and he laughed while he was a-doing it. The pup, he just crawled away whimpering, an' I guess he's dead by this time."

Jeb's eyes were bleak. "Buck, why would a man do a thing like that? Why did Hig kill the pup? I mean, he was no bigger'n a nubbin, and them little teeth of his couldn't do Hig no harm. An' why did he kill me? I didn't mean him no harm either. I just wanted a warm place to hole up for the winter on account of my rheumatisms. Ain't nothing wrong with that, is there?"

The old man searched Fletcher's face as though trying to find the answer to his questions in the big man's battered features. "Can you tell me, Buck?" he asked. "It's something I want to know."

Miserably, Fletcher shook his head. "Jeb, I don't know the answer. It's hard to figure what drives a man like Higgy Conroy. Some men are just evil, Jeb. They have a black heart, and the blood it pumps around their body is bad blood. All you can do with a vile thing like that is kill it and rid the earth of its shadow."

Jeb grimaced as a wave of pain hit him, and Fletcher said, "Old timer, I've got to get you into bed."

But the old man held up a weak hand. "No, let me die out here, Buck. I want to see the sky. I never was much of a one for a-lyin' in bed when I had me a misery."

Jeb looked up at the bright blue sky, where the sun had already climbed to its noon position. "Dang me if'n it ain't getting dark already, an' the shadows are deepening. Hell, Buck, I shouldn't be lying here. I should be busy getting your supper ready. You must be mighty hungry."

"You lay still, old timer," Fletcher said softly. "Supper can wait."

Baker stepped up beside Jeb, an odd expression on his face. "Jeb," he asked, "have you seen Savannah?"

Jeb looked at Fletcher. "Friend of yours, Buck?"

The big man nodded. "We're on the same side."

"No, mister, I haven't seen hide nor hair of her," Jeb said. "She hasn't come near the cabin, or I'd a seen her fer sure."

Fletcher noted a look of satisfaction on Baker's face that came and went quickly, and he wondered at it.

Did Matt Baker know Savannah?

Could he be the one who was hunting her?

Fletcher couldn't quite bring himself to believe the latter. But it was a possibility to consider, and it was a worrisome thing.

"Buck," Jeb said urgently, "I got something to tell

you." The old man was going fast, and his eyes were clouded. "My poke . . . it's yours. Look . . . look behind the stove. I put it there, for safety's sake."

He pulled on Fletcher's sleeve. "I got nobody, so I want you to use it. Build yourself a life with it, boy. An' listen, don't let them Deadwood banks tell you there's sand or rotten quartz in there with the gold. It's all dust and nuggets, every last ounce of it."

The old miner smiled. "I got something else to say, Buck."

Fletcher nodded. "What's that, Jeb?"

"Just this. What you've been hunting for all these years was right here at Two-Bit Creek all the time. You just didn't know it."

"What was that, Jeb? What was I hunting?"

"A home, boy. This was the only home you ever knowed, an' it still is. You just wandered afar from it, but now you're back."

Jeb struggled to sit up, but couldn't manage it and fell back into Fletcher's arms. "Look around you, boy." He smiled, uttering the last few words of his long life. "This . . . is . . . home."

Then Jeb Coons was gone, his head suddenly heavy on Fletcher's shoulder.

Fletcher laid Jeb on the ground and with gentle fingers closed his eyes.

"He died well," Baker said quietly. "In the end, that's the true measure of a man."

Fletcher opened his mouth to speak, couldn't find the right words, and said only, "I've got a burying to do."

Buck Fletcher knew nothing of love, how it felt to a man, but he knew well of hate. And now hate curled inside him, a venomous, deadly rattlesnake ready to strike.

And it would strike first at Higgy Conroy.

Chapter 10

Fletcher and Matt Baker buried Jeb among the aspens.

Baker, who knew the words, said the Lord's Prayer over the grave, but even that wasn't much to close a man's life and say farewell. But Fletcher consoled himself with the thought that Jeb lay close to his mother and father, and maybe that was as it should be.

As the two men walked back to the cabin, Baker suddenly stopped and nodded toward a tall pine. "I think I see your dog," he said.

Fletcher looked and saw a small, still bundle at the base of the tree where the pup had often sat and pretended an interest in Voltaire, if only for a few minutes before he got bored and went off sniffing and exploring.

"Yeah," Fletcher said bleakly. "It's the pup, all right."

"I'll do this," Baker said. "I mean, the burying."

Fletcher shook his head. He had been given a bitter cup to drink this day, and now he would drain it to the dregs.

"He's my dog," he said quietly. "I'll bury him."

The men walked over to the tree. The pup was stretched out, blood on his chest and hindquarters, and the snow around him was stained red.

Baker kneeled beside the little animal and put a hand on his side. "Hell, Buck," he said. "He's still alive."

Quickly Fletcher kneeled and ran a hand over the pup's body. The little dog was warm but unconscious. As far as he could see, the bullet had entered the pup's chest and exited near his rear left leg. Both wounds were crawling with maggots, but that was a good thing. The maggots had kept the wounds clean and stopped an infection from getting started.

The pup's breathing was very shallow, and his pink tongue lolled out of his mouth. His eyes were shut. When Fletcher put a hand on his chest, he felt the animal's heart fluttering weakly.

Gently, Fletcher picked up the little dog in his strong hands. The pup whimpered softly and opened his eyes.

"I know, I know, boy; it hurts," Fletcher whispered. "But we're going to fix you up, and it won't hurt anymore, don't worry."

Reassured by the man's voice and the gentle cradle of his strong hands, the pup turned his head and licked Fletcher's fingers.

Fletcher carried the little animal into the cabin. He laid him on a blanket on the floor and made up the fire. The maggots had done their job, and now Fletcher carefully cleaned them from the pup's wounds and laid him closer to the stove.

"Just let him lie there quiet for a while, Matt," he said. "I'm going outside to gather up a few things to help him."

Baker nodded and kneeled beside the pup, stroking his head. "He's a tough little cuss, Buck," he said. "A .45 makes a big hole in a dog this small."

Fletcher nodded. "He's a survivor, Matt. Like the rest of us, I guess."

"Think you can save him?"

"I'm going to do my best."

Fletcher walked around outside, gathering the plants and other things he needed. Even this late in the year, purple coneflowers were still blooming, and these would prevent infection. He gathered juniper bark for pain relief and stripped off some pine bark. The barks he would soften in boiling water and use as a poultice to speed healing.

The Indians had used all these natural medicines to heal wounded warriors, and Fletcher reasoned that if it worked on people, it would work on dogs.

His hands full, he returned to the cabin. While he was gone, Baker had made a broth of beef and onions, then strained it through a cloth. As Fletcher watched, Baker spooned up a little broth and blew on it to cool it down. He then let the pup lick it from the spoon.

Weak as he was, the little dog was starving and eagerly lapped up the broth. Baker's face lit up with a joyous, boyish smile. "Hey, at least he still has an appetite."

Fletcher felt a sharp pang of guilt. He'd entertained the possibility that Matt Baker was the rifleman who'd tried to murder Savannah. But judging by the tender way he cared for the pup, it hardly seemed possible that he was a cold-blooded killer. But if he wasn't the mysterious assassin, then who was he? And why had he showed up here just as a range war was brewing?

Fletcher shook his head. Baker would tip his hand eventually, and then he'd know where he stood. He could wait.

The gunfighter boiled water and made a tea of coneflowers and juniper bark. He then boiled up some of the pine bark and, when it was good and soft, squeezed out the excess water.

He managed to get some of the tea down the pup's

throat, though the little animal protested weakly against the taste. Fletcher spread the soft pine bark on some pieces of cloth torn from his second-best shirt and bound up the pup's wounds.

"The coneflower tea will knock him out," Fletcher told Baker, "and that's good. What he needs right now more than anything else is warmth and plenty of sleep."

"You know," said Baker, "I think he's going to make it. He's breathing easier."

"I sure hope so." Fletcher smiled. "I feel responsible for the little feller."

Baker nodded. "He's just a helpless, hurt little thing, Buck. Right now all he has to depend on is you."

"I know. And do you know something else? I kinda like it."

Later Fletcher looked behind the stove. Jeb's gold was where he said it would be, hidden in a recess in the cabin wall.

Baker hefted the leather bag in his hand and whistled. "This is heavy. There must be twenty pounds of gold in here if there's an ounce. How much do you figure this is worth?"

Fletcher shrugged. "Last I heard, gold was selling for about twenty dollars an ounce in Deadwood."

Baker whistled again. "Hell, then this poke must be worth at least seven thousand dollars." He looked carefully at Fletcher. "What you going to do with all that money?"

"I don't know."

"Jeb said it was to build yourself a life. What did he mean?"

"I don't know that either. Jeb was dying. Sometimes dying men say strange things."

"Or true things," Baker said.

Fletcher looked into the young man's eyes, but he could read nothing there.

"Maybe," he said. "But right now I don't want to think on it."

Over the next few days, Fletcher and Baker scoured the surrounding hills looking for Savannah, returning at regular intervals to the cabin to feed the pup and change the dressing on his wounds.

On the night of the third day, clouds drifted in from the north, and it snowed again. Only a few inches lay on the ground, but day by day it was getting colder, and the promise of a hard winter was in the air.

The pup's wounds were healing, and he was getting stronger. The soft bones of his rear leg had been shattered by Higgy Conroy's bullet, and it was obvious to Fletcher and Baker that the leg was healing crooked.

"He isn't going to chase too many jackrabbits when he grows up, that's for sure," Baker said one night as he held the pup in his lap and fed him scraps of meat.

"He's smart though." Fletcher smiled. "He'll bushwhack 'em."

Fletcher and Baker covered the area from Boulder Pass in the north to Elk Creek in the south, but of Savannah there was no sign. It seemed that she'd dropped off the face of the earth.

Matt Baker did not seem overly concerned about Savannah's disappearance, and Fletcher had the idea that he was helping in the search only out of some sense of duty.

Maybe he felt he owed her that much.

Or—a thought that disturbed the gunfighter greatly—maybe he already knew Savannah was dead.

Matt Baker had no past that he cared to reveal, and Fletcher could not get a read on where he stood. The man was as mysterious as his past, and that made him even more of a puzzle.

Once they met some Lazy R hands camped on the south bank of Lost Gulch. The cowboys were hazing a small herd toward winter grazing closer to the ranch, and they said they'd seen no one on the range for days.

The top hand, a tall, quiet-faced man named Garnett, invited Fletcher and Baker to coffee, and, since he seemed eager to talk, they filled their cups and listened.

"Been no trouble around here since Pike Prescott was killed," Garnett said. "Seems his daughter doesn't share his ambitions, and that's a good thing for all of us, especially Miz Tyrone."

"Have you seen any PP Connected cows on Lazy R range?" Baker asked.

Garnett shook his head. "Nary a one. It looks like Prescott's daughter pulled them all back."

"Seems to me, Mrs. Tyrone and Prescott's daughter could become friends," Fletcher said. "I mean, they're women running ranches, and when you get right down to it, there's enough grass for both of them."

Garnett's lips twisted into a smile under his drooping mustache. "Say, wouldn't that be something? I mean, after all this war talk, Amy Prescott and Miz Tyrone becoming as close as sisters."

Another hand, a young towhead in a sheepskin coat, said, "If Amy Prescott pays off her father's gun hands and gets rid of that snake Higgy Conroy, then things really might settle down around here and become downright peaceful."

Fletcher smiled, but when he looked at Matt Baker, the man's eyes were guarded, and his face was set and grim.

"You boys stay on guard and sleep close to your rifles," Baker said. "I got a feeling there are other forces at work here, and I don't think this range war is ending. I got the feeling it's only beginning."

Again, Fletcher studied the man named Baker. And wondered.

After a week of useless searching for Savannah, Fletcher gave it up. He and Baker rode back to the cabin. After supper that night, Fletcher rolled a smoke and said, "Matt, we've been all over this range and haven't found Savannah." He lit his cigarette, then added, "I reckon there's only one place we haven't looked."

"Where's that?"

"Deadwood." Fletcher tapped ash off the end of his smoke and said, "I plan to ride over there tomorrow and see if I can find her."

"I'll come with you."

"No, Matt, I need you at the cabin. Savannah might return here. Besides, somebody has to stay and look after the pup."

Baker thought for a few moments and obviously saw the logic in what Fletcher was saying. "You're right," he said. "Somebody has to stay. It might as well be me."

Fletcher saddled up at first light and headed northwest for Deadwood. Jeb's gold was in his saddlebags, and he rode alert and ready, prepared for trouble.

His big sorrel was eager for the trail and stepped out smartly as he rounded the peak of Lexington Hill, riding along a line of quaking aspen. With the coming of fall, their leaves had turned to bright yellow, splashed here and there with crimson, and among them grew tall green arrowheads of spruce and pine.

Fletcher rode past the hard-rock Chance Preston Mine, with its one-thousand-foot shafts tunneled deep into the bowels of the earth. Dozens of Chinese laborers in cone-shaped straw hats, speaking a language no one but they could understand, loaded quartz-lined ore into wagons under the watchful and intolerant eyes of bearded, cursing bullwhackers.

In the hierarchy of the West, the red-shirted, profane bullwhackers occupied society's lowest rung, lower by a notch or two than even the despised buffalo skinners. They toiled for twenty-five dollars a month, ten dollars a month less than the more respected mule skinners, yet it was their teams of eight oxen that made the Black Hills gold rush possible.

The big, ox-drawn freight wagons could cover ten miles a day, hauling essential supplies into Deadwood: everything from heavy drilling equipment and support timbers to calico, canned peaches and pins.

The bullwhacker's badge of office was his whip, a three-foot-long hickory stock attached to twenty feet of braided rawhide, a "popper" of buckskin at the end to make it crack. The lash weighed almost six pounds, was always wielded with two hands, and an experienced teamster could pick off a fly on the lead ox's ear without touching the skin.

Armed with his whip, a revolver buckled around his waist and a Bowie knife handy in his belt, the bullwhacker was feared by many on the plains even more than hostile Indians.

Just before noon, Fletcher crossed Spruce Gulch and rode into Deadwood. The town was roaring, bursting at the seams with thirty thousand miners and those who preyed on them: soft-handed gamblers, whores with bold, knowing eyes, and goldbrick artists of every stripe. Everywhere were hard-bitten horsemen in from the Plains: cowboys, drifting gunmen and soldiers, men who rode with the long winds in lonely places under a vast sky and had fought the Sioux and Cheyenne and sometimes each other.

In the months of June and July alone, a million dollars' worth of gold had been ripped out of the Black Hills, and Deadwood was booming.

The original tents and shanties had been replaced by more than two hundred buildings—houses, saw mills, saloons, brothels, hotels and restaurants, all climbing the steep walls of the gulch—and there was even talk of getting one of those newfangled telephone exchanges.

Fletcher rode along a narrow main street crowded with riders, belted and bearded miners on foot and freight wagons hauled by ox or mule teams. Men and occasionally women picked their way from one side of the street to the other across an oozing sea of churned-up black mud that was in places eighteen inches deep.

Saloons were everywhere, the grandest of which were the Bucket of Blood, the Montana, Nuttall and Mann's No. 10 and the Green Front Sporting House. Posters outside the Gem and Bella Union theaters advertised acts from as far away as New York and Chicago, and C. J. Allen's Gun Shop proclaimed it had the latest Winchester rifles for sale and, "back by the demand of the populace," brass-cased, factory-loaded ammunition in .44–40 and .45–75 caliber.

Fletcher rode his sorrel through the open doors of Patrick McGowan's livery stable and stepped out of the leather.

A small man in dungarees and a battered Confederate cavalry kepi came out of the office and patted the sorrel's neck. "Nice hoss you got there, mister," he said. "Haven't seen one quite like him since the war."

Fletcher nodded. "He'll do."

"I got a bait of oats," the man said. "And good, fresh hay."

"I'd be obliged," Fletcher said, stripping the saddle. "He hasn't had much by way of either recently."

The gunfighter pointed over his shoulder with his thumb. "Sign outside said Patrick McGowan's Livery. That you?"

The man nodded. "Came up from Texas last year.

Never struck it rich, but I panned me enough to build this place."

McGowan had a gentle, knowing way with horses, and Fletcher let him lead the sorrel to a stall.

When he came back, Fletcher said, "I'm looking for a woman—"

"Plenty of those in town." McGowan grinned.

"She's a blonde," Fletcher continued, ignoring the man's interruption. "About this tall. Her name is Savannah Jones, and she's riding a hammer-headed buckskin."

McGowan shook his head. "Sounds like nobody I've seen." He waved a hand around the stable. "There ain't a buckskin hoss in here."

"Is there another livery?"

"Yeah, there's another two, both of them on the other side of town, toward the top of the gulch."

Fletcher nodded. "Well, I'm obliged."

He stepped toward the door of the stable, then stopped. "Say, I have a friend in town, James Hickok. You know where I can find him?"

"Wild Bill, you mean? Why sure, he's down to the Ingleside Cemetery."

"Cemetery? What's he doing there?"

"Not much, mister. Bill's been dead more'n a month."

Fletcher was stunned. Bill Hickok dead? It was hard to believe.

"How did it happen?"

McGowan shook his head. "He was shot in the back by a no-good tramp whose name"—he spat—"it ain't fit for a man to mention."

Bill was dead. The realization was slow in coming to Fletcher. But why should it surprise him?

That's how men like Bill, like himself, were destined to die: face down in the sawdust of a saloon in some roaring, wide-open and doomed town that was just a small step removed from hell itself.

Once the West had needed men like Wild Bill Hickok, but that time was passing.

Despite their violence and arrogance and an uncompromising desire to walk their own path, gunfighters had played a vital part in taming a rough and turbulent land. But now, with talk of streetcars and telephone exchanges and schools and churches, their kind was writing the last chapter of a blazing, flamboyant history that had begun at the end of The War Between the States. They would soon be gone, like the buffalo fast disappearing from the Plains. Very soon it would be as if the Red Man and the gunfighter had never been.

And the land would be all the poorer for their passing.

Fletcher's melancholy thoughts were interrupted by McGowan, who had evidently been talking for some time.

". . . maybe the Bucket of Blood for starters."

Fletcher shook his head like a man coming out of a trance. "I'm sorry. What did you say?"

"I was saying," continued McGowan, unfazed, "that I would ask around the saloons about your woman. Me, I'd first try the Bucket of Blood. There's always a lot of danged loose talk in there."

Saloons were clearinghouses of information in the West, and often ranchers visited them more to talk cattle prices and Washington's policies toward the open range than to drink.

Fletcher nodded. "I'll do that. Thanks."

"One thing," McGowan said, his eyes running over Fletcher's well-worn guns. "If you visit the Bucket of Blood, stay clear of a man named William Buford. While Hickok was alive, this Buford pretty much stepped light around him and kept his mouth shut. But now Hickok's gone, he's claiming to be the new Wild Bill, and he's pizen mean and cutting a wide path. He plans to make his mark."

Fletcher smiled. "I've met his kind before. I'll be careful."

"Mind you do, pardner," McGowan said, his face concerned. "Last week Buford killed an old miner called Charlie Bell 'cause Charlie laughed at him when he spoke big and ordered him to call him Wild Bill. And a week before that, he killed a drifting cowboy who'd just come up the trail from Texas.

"That cowboy couldn't have been any more than eighteen, but Buford taunted him into drawing, bad-mouthing Texas and Texans alike, and then he killed him." McGowan's eyes were wide. "Mister, they say this Buford can draw faster than a striking rattler and then some. Every man he kills, he gets a little gold cross made up and has it inset into the handle of his gun. So far, he's got seven of them crosses." The little man shrugged. "Hell, what am I talking about? Maybe he is the new Wild Bill."

"There was only one Wild Bill, and there won't be another," Fletcher said mildly. "But thanks for the warning. I'll step real light and talk soft when I'm around that ranny. He sounds like a man best left alone."

As McGowan talked, Fletcher had been looking around the barn. Off in a corner, two tall mares stood in their stalls, now and again stomping away flies.

Fletcher strolled over to the stalls and studied the mares. They were both bays, with fine heads and long, clean limbs, standing around sixteen hands high. They looked to weigh better than one thousand pounds: big horses built for speed and endurance.

"Kentucky Thoroughbreds," McGowan said, stepping beside him. "They belong to a gambler named Whitcroft, runs the faro table at the Montana. He won them in a poker game from a feller who figured to race them."

Fletcher nodded. "Fine horses."

He picked up his saddlebags, bulging with Jeb's gold, and asked McGowan to recommend a bank.

"I'd say the Mercantile," the man replied. "It's owned by a former senator named Silas T. Pendleton. He's a solid citizen, and his bank has the reputation of being sound."

To Fletcher's relief, the bank was on the same side of the street as the livery barn, and he'd no need to cross that fetid swamp of mud.

By Deadwood standards, Fletcher's deposit was a small one, and the transaction was quickly handled by an efficient but low-level clerk.

"I make the total seven thousand, six hundred and fourteen dollars, Mr. Fletcher," the clerk said, visibly unimpressed.

But this was more money than Fletcher had ever seen in his life, and the total staggered him. "Give me two hundred cash and put the rest on deposit," he said, his voice a little unsteady. "I will draw on it later."

"Whatever you say."

Fletcher left the bank and stood outside for a few moments, stepping out of the way of the miners and townspeople crowding the boardwalk.

The Thoroughbreds were very much on Fletcher's mind. As brood mares mated to his big American stud, they would produce foals with plenty of size and bone, ideal mounts for the Dakota and Montana territories and their winter snowdrifts.

And he could buy more mares and maybe another stud.

But that would mean settling down on the Two-Bit. Was that what he really wanted?

Jeb had told him that the cabin on the creek was his home, the place he'd been searching for since he was a boy.

Could he settle down there, away from the roaring guns and the sudden, deadly violence of his calling? Or would his past always catch up to him, a dark shadow that never left him, making the dream of a normal life impossible?

Fletcher shook his head. Now was not the time to search for answers to those questions, he decided.

Mañana, the Mexicans said.

There is always tomorrow.

But still, he would buy the mares, if he could.

Chapter 11

When Fletcher stepped into the Bucket of Blood, it was still early in the day, and the place was almost empty. Miners who weren't working were nursing hangovers and wouldn't start drifting in with the rest of the good-time crowd until after dark.

A couple of drummers in broadcloth suits sat at a table, halfheartedly playing a penny-ante game of poker, and a plump man in greasy buckskins, a mule skinner by the look of him, sat at another table with a bottle of rye and a single glass.

The saloon's piano player was trying to tune his battered instrument, watched by a bored ten-cents-a-dance girl in a stained and faded dress of red silk.

When Fletcher stepped to the bar, the girl looked at him with interest and gave him an artificial smile, then quickly took in his guns and bruised face and immediately dismissed him as a potential partner. This big, solemn man didn't seem the good-time type. She shrugged her naked shoulders and went back to watching the piano player.

All this Fletcher took in at a glance.

Then, out of the corner of his eye, he studied the man standing at the bar close to him.

This could only be William Buford, the new Wild Bill.

He was tall and heavily built, only a little of it fat, and he wore the accepted uniform of the frontier gambler: a black frock coat to his knees and checked pants, the cuffs falling elegantly over highly polished, elastic-sided boots. The man sported a frilled shirt and black string tie, and, as Bill's had done, his long, perfumed hair hung in soft waves over his shoulders.

He wore two walnut-handled Colts butt forward in matching black holsters, and Fletcher noticed the row of little gold crosses on the right-hand gun. A bottle of Anderson's Little Brown Jug bourbon stood on the bar in front of him.

"What will it be?" The bartender, a red-faced man in a flowered vest, wiped the bar in front of Fletcher with a towel.

"Do you have beer?"

"Sure do, all the way from the Golden Brewery in Denver."

"Is it cold?"

"As a stepmother's breath."

Fletcher nodded. "Draw me one."

Buford turned his head and looked at Fletcher with contempt. "Beer," he said, like the very word was poison in his mouth. "He drinks beer."

The man's eyes were a hard blue in the florid red of his face, and they held a challenge. His cheeks were veined with red from alcohol and the harsh downstroke of the razor, and his lips were thin, framing a small, cruel mouth that was now twisted in a sneer.

Fletcher, knowing this man for what he was or aspired to be, let it go. Buford was a born killer who fervently wanted to build a reputation so that other—and as he saw them, lesser—mortals would step lightly around him.

He wished to be feared by all and thus never called to account.

It was a measure of the man's arrogance that he did not see in Fletcher a quiet potential for danger and sudden, shocking violence that the real Wild Bill had recognized instinctively years before—as he'd recognized it in John Wesley Hardin, another soft-spoken and deadly gunman of his acquaintance.

To gunfighters like Fletcher and Hardin, a Colt was a tool, a chunk of iron to be cleaned and oiled and kept in good working order.

Notching the handle—or, in Buford's case, decorating it with crosses so he could sit in his lonely room and gloat over the men he'd destroyed—was a tinhorn's trick. The true professional shunned it as he would the plague.

"Your beer, mister," the bartender said. The man's hand was shaking so bad that when he laid the glass on the bar, a little wave of foam spilled over the rim.

The man picked up Fletcher's nickel and whispered, "Watch yourself."

Fletcher nodded and put the glass to his lips, sipping appreciatively. The bartender had been right; the beer was fresh, and it was ice cold.

"What the hell happened to you?" Buford asked. It was a challenge, not a conversation opener.

Fletcher shrugged and sipped his beer. "Lost a fistfight," he said finally.

"Somebody cut you down to size, huh?" Buford said scornfully.

"Something like that," Fletcher said.

He picked up his glass from the bar and stepped toward a table in the corner. Behind him, Buford yelled, "Hey you! Don't walk away from me when I'm talking to you."

Fletcher ignored the gunman, and he heard the bartender say, "Take it easy, Wild Bill. You got no right to scare that man so bad."

As he took a chair at the table, Fletcher was followed by Buford's laugh. "By the lord Harry, I got the right. There's too many yellowbellies in Deadwood," he said loudly and pointedly. "I sure aim to cut me down a few."

That last remark lit Fletcher's fuse, and he felt sudden anger flare in him.

"Let it go, Buck. That son of a bitch isn't worth it."

Fletcher, surprised at hearing his name, looked up and saw the mule skinner in the greasy buckskins standing over him, his bottle and glass in his hand.

"Don't recognize me, do you, Buck?" the man said, his voice light and high. "Truth to tell, it took me a while to recognize you, all battered and beat up the way you are."

Fletcher looked more closely at the man's face. Then a grin lit up his face. This was no man!

"Martha Jane Canary, as I live and breathe." Fletcher rose to his feet and extended his hand. "Hell, I haven't seen you since Abilene."

The woman took Fletcher's hand. "That was in '71, Buck." She smiled, showing teeth stained brown from chewing tobacco. "Been a long time."

"Haw, haw, haw," Buford bellowed from the bar. "The yellowbelly climbed onto his feet for Calamity Jane!" He slapped his thigh. "I never seen the like in all my born days. Standing up like a perfect little gentleman for a two-dollar whore."

Fletcher stiffened, but Calamity shook her head. "Let it go, Buck. Tinhorns like that just ain't worth killing." She motioned to a chair. "Can I sit?"

"Sure," Fletcher said, still rankled. But he knew Calamity was right—a two-bit wanna-be like William Buford wasn't worth a bullet.

As Buford stood with an elbow on the bar, a slight smile on his face, intently watching them like he was

at a magic lantern show, Calamity poured herself a
drink and offered the bottle to Buck, who shook his
head.

"I'll stick with the beer," he said.

"So what brings you to Deadwood, Buck?"

Fletcher studied the woman for a few moments. Her
hair, showing gray at the temples, was cut short like
a man's, and her face was puffy and mottled. The
buckskins did nothing for her sagging, overweight
body, and Fletcher had to allow that Martha Jane was
a homely woman to say the least. But her blue eyes
were bright and showed both keen intelligence and a
degree of humanity not unmixed with a great deal
of humor.

Quickly Fletcher outlined the events of the last couple of weeks and then summed it all up by saying,
"And that's the reason I'm in Deadwood. I have to
find Savannah. Don't ask me why, but somehow I feel
responsible for her."

Calamity nodded. "Buck, do you think maybe she's
here working the line?"

That thought had lain unspoken at the back of
Fletcher's mind, and now that Calamity had brought
it into the open, he was forced to face it.

"It's possible," he said hesitantly. "She told the
hotel clerk she was in the Territory looking to buy a
ranch. But she must have realized pretty quick there
was a range war brewing, and there was no land for
sale." Fletcher looked puzzled. "She carried a Remington derringer. I thought it was odd for a young
lady to carry a stingy gun."

"That's a whore's weapon, an up close and personal
ace in the hole," Calamity said. "Buck, there's a lot
of money to be made here from the miners. A young
girl might figure to make her fortune on the line then
retire and get married and raise a family. It's happened before."

Fletcher nodded. "Maybe. But that doesn't explain why somebody was trying to kill her."

"A jealous customer maybe," Calamity suggested. "A spurned lover. That's also happened before."

"It just doesn't seem possible, Martha," Fletcher said. "I mean, Savannah is educated, beautiful, and she looks like she comes from a good family. If she wanted to get married, she could have any man she set her sights on."

Fletcher couldn't bring himself to believe that Savannah had come to the Territory to work as a whore in Deadwood. She just didn't seem the type. But what was the type? He'd seen plenty of soiled doves who were beautiful, well-educated and came from good families. Was it just that for the first time in a long time he'd found somebody he cared about, and now he couldn't bear the thought that she was selling her body to other men?

Or was he arguing against Savannah working as a whore because he was more concerned about his own bruised male ego than he was about her? That was very possible, and now Fletcher faced up to it.

"I'm going to talk to the girls on the line, see if any of them have seen or heard of Savannah Jones," he told Calamity. "I have to find her, no matter what she's doing."

The woman shook her head. "They won't talk to you, Buck. They'll figure you for some kind of johnny law and tell you nothing." Calamity poured herself another drink and downed it in one gulp. She wiped her mouth with the back of her hand, an oddly masculine gesture, and continued. "They'll talk to me. I've worked alongside most of those girls in the past, and they know and trust me. If your Savannah Jones is working the line in Deadwood, I'll find her."

Fletcher nodded. "I appreciate that, Martha. I surely do."

"There's a restaurant next to the Gem Theater called The Open Door," Calamity said. "Meet me there tomorrow morning just before sunup, and I'll tell you what I've learned."

"I'll be there," Fletcher said. He watched Calamity down another slug of rye. Then, as he built a smoke, his eyes on the makings, he said, "Heard about Bill. I took it hard."

Calamity hesitated only for a moment. "I loved him, Buck. I loved that man with every fiber of my being. To me, there was no other man in the entire world but Bill Hickok."

Fletcher put the cigarette between his bruised lips and thumbed a match into flame. "How does that feel?" he asked, lighting his cigarette. "I mean, how does it feel to love a man that much? Another human being that much?"

Calamity smiled, and a glow touched her features, making her look for a single fleeting moment like the pretty young girl she once had been. "It's part agony, part joy, Buck. But more than that, it's a feeling that you always want to be with a man, that you never want to be apart from him. When you boil it right down, that's what love is, I guess. It's just never wanting to be separated from a person for even a single day or a minute or a second."

Calamity poured herself another drink, but she left it untouched on the table. "We were married, you know," she said. "Bill wrote it down on the flyleaf of a Bible that we was hitched."

Fletcher nodded. "I heard that story. Couldn't quite believe it though. I didn't think Bill was the marrying kind."

The woman laughed. It wasn't the soft laugh of a woman, but the harsh roar of the mule skinner. "No wonder you couldn't believe it, Buck. It was a big joke! Bill made the whole thing up as a prank."

Calamity picked up her glass and drank the rye, then refilled it again.

"You know how Bill was with his practical jokes. He looked around and chose the most unlikely woman he could find to be his make-believe bride, and that woman was me. Bill figgered it was a real good flim-flam. He was so fastidious, remember? He took a bath every day and never wore the same shirt two days in a row. And me? Well, I know what I am. I'm ugly and dirty, and sometimes when I've been on a bender, I smell bad."

"Martha," Fletcher said, his voice soft. "You don't have to—"

"Yes, I do," Calamity said. "Now Bill is dead, I want to set the record straight." She drained her glass and shuddered. "Well, he marked that Bible, then put it about that he'd married Calamity Jane, and every-body laughed. And me, when people called me Mrs. Hickok, I laughed louder than all the rest."

Calamity tipped the bottle and filled her glass again. When she put the whiskey to her lips, her hand was unsteady. She drank the raw, amber rye and set the glass back on the table.

"But Bill hurt me, Buck. He hurt me awful bad. He hurt me right here"—she placed a hand over her heart between her slack breasts—"and it felt like he'd driven a knife into me. I loved him more than any-thing else in the world, and all he did was make a joke of it."

Fletcher placed his hand over Calamity's. Unlike Judith Tyrone's soft skin, the back of her hand felt rough, like old, dry saddle leather.

"Martha," he said softly, "I don't know what to say. I just can't find the words."

Calamity shook her head. "You don't have to say anything, Buck. Now Bill is in the grave, and what's done is done. It don't matter no more."

"For what it's worth, Martha, I knew Bill Hickok well, and I think he probably never realized how badly he could hurt you. It was a dumb joke, and if he'd thought it through, it would never have happened."

"Maybe," Calamity said. "Maybe not. But like I already said, Bill's gone, and now it don't matter a hill of beans."

She rose unsteadily to her feet. "I'll see you tomorrow morning." The woman took a few steps toward the saloon door, then stopped. "Buck," she said. "Bill writing a lie in the Bible like that: It had to be bad luck, didn't it?"

Fletcher shook his head. "I don't know, Martha. I guess maybe I'd have to study on it some and maybe talk to a preacher."

Calamity shrugged. "You don't have to, Buck. A man takes a pen and writes a lie in the Good Book, he's opening himself up to all kinds of bad trouble. That's what I think, an' that's what I know."

Calamity waved a hand in farewell and walked out of the saloon. Buford's eyes followed her with a look of burning contempt.

Fletcher drained his beer and stepped up to the bar.

"You know, Buford," he said, "you may call yourself the new Wild Bill, but Hickok was something you'll never be."

"What's that?" Buford asked belligerently, his eyes blazing.

"A gentleman," Fletcher said.

He didn't wait for a reply, but turned on his heel and walked out of the saloon.

When he'd walked a distance along the boardwalk, he glanced back and saw Buford standing outside the saloon looking after him.

The man's face was black with anger, and in his eyes was a naked desire to kill.

Chapter 12

Fletcher, the jinglebobs on his spurs chiming, made his way along the boardwalk and stepped into the Saracen's Head Hotel, a two-story, false-fronted building made of green lumber held together with a lick of paint and the cockeyed optimism of its owner.

He got a room on the second floor with a window overlooking the street. If Savannah was in Deadwood, this was an excellent vantage point to watch for her.

Fletcher brought a chair to the window and sat. He rolled himself a smoke and scanned the street. Below, heavily loaded wagons pulled by straining mules creaked and groaned through the mud, and horsemen picked their way through the traffic. Small knots of women gathered outside the general stores, taking the opportunity to talk with other members of their sex, no doubt discussing matters of domestic importance from babies to weddings to the latest styles in frilly bonnets all the way from Denver and New York.

But Savannah was not among them.

Fletcher was still there, patient as a cat on a window-sill, as the short day shaded into evening and oil lamps outside the saloons were lit, casting flickering orange circles on the boardwalk.

The tinny music of pianos reached him through the thin walls of his room, and thirsty, belted miners were already crowding into the saloons and gambling dens. Fletcher had seen no sign of Savannah. If she was in Deadwood, she was staying indoors.

His growling stomach suddenly reminded Fletcher how hungry he was. He rose, stretched and quickly made his way downstairs and out into the bustle of the street.

He had agreed to meet Calamity tomorrow morning at a restaurant called The Open Door, and this was as good a time as any to find the place.

A bearded miner, already half-drunk, directed him to the restaurant, which, to Fletcher's chagrin, lay clear on the other side of the street.

At intervals along both boardwalks, husky youngsters who called themselves ferrymen hustled for business, loudly advertising that they would carry anyone across the deep mud for two bits. But it was mostly women, careful of their long dresses, who took advantage of their services.

Fletcher decided being carried was an undignified way for a man to travel. Unbuckling his spurs, he stepped into the street.

By the time he hopped onto the boardwalk on the other side, his boots were covered in mud. He stomped the worst of it off before he walked into The Open Door, but since just about everyone in Deadwood had mud to their knees, the grimy trail he left behind him went unnoticed.

The restaurant's dozen tables were occupied by miners, drummers and a few women. A big miner with a red beard and hair, a broad-bladed Bowie knife in his belt, grinned and waved a friendly hand, directing Fletcher to an empty chair beside him and his two companions.

Fletcher ordered and was soon eating. The food was typical frontier fare, steak, onions and potatoes, but it was well-cooked. He spent a pleasant hour talking with the miners about the subject dearest to their hearts—gold and where it was and how to find it.

Afterward he recrossed the street and returned to his hotel. Within minutes he was in bed, sleeping soundly.

Just before sunup, Fletcher rose and dressed, strapping on his guns. He splashed ice cold water over his face, then ran a comb through his thick black hair. He rubbed a hand over his stubbly chin but decided shaving could wait. He walked downstairs and into the street. Even this early in the morning, Deadwood was buzzing.

The hard rock miners, most of them badly hung over, were crowding the boardwalks, getting ready for another day at the diggings, and heavy freight wagons again jammed the muddy street, the teamsters yelling, "Ho there, make way!" or cussing their big, recalcitrant Missouri mules.

Fletcher crossed the street again and walked into The Open Door. The restaurant was jammed with people, mostly miners, but several women sat with men in broadcloth suits, bankers by the look of them, and there were a couple of ink-stained newspapermen, weary after putting to bed the latest edition of the widely read *Black Hills Pioneer*.

Sam Hannon, the big, redheaded miner, was there and gave Fletcher a friendly wave, but this time there was no room at his table.

As he stood inside the door, a table in a corner cleared as four miners rose and left. Fletcher walked over and sat down, his back to the wall.

There was no sign yet of Calamity, so he asked for coffee and told the waiter he'd order later.

He was drinking coffee and smoking his first ciga-

rette of the day when Calamity came in, looking even
worse than she had the day before.

The woman was badly hung over, that much was
obvious by the way her trembling fingers kept straying
to her forehead and how she winced when someone
loudly clattered plates in the kitchen.

As she took a seat beside him, Fletcher poured Calamity coffee and waited. She'd talk when she was
ready.

It took a few minutes.

Finally, Calamity drained her cup and said slowly,
spacing out the words, "Your gal isn't in Deadwood."

"You sure, Martha?" Fletcher asked.

Calamity shook her head, then regretted it instantly.
She groaned and rubbed her forehead. "There's no
one called Savannah Jones working the line. All the
girls in town have been here for weeks. There are no
new faces. No one who even looks like your missing
gal. I don't think she's in Deadwood."

Fletcher felt vague disappointment mixed with relief. As he'd suspected, Savannah was no soiled dove.
But if she wasn't in Deadwood, where was she? Could
she be—he shuddered at the thought—already dead?

"I'm sorry, Buck," Calamity was saying, the words
coming after a hard struggle. "I just wish I could have
been more help."

Fletcher smiled. "You did your best, Martha, and
you discovered that Savannah isn't in Deadwood. I
thank you for that."

The waiter stepped to the table, and Fletcher ordered steak and eggs. Calamity, hurting, asked for a
raw egg in a glass of brandy, and if that wasn't avail-
able, would he please do her the kindness of just
shooting her.

"Buck," she whispered after the grinning waiter had
gone, "a miner struck it rich yesterday, and it was

Mumm's all round at the Montana. Drinking champagne seemed like a good idea last night, but it sure as hell don't seem like such a hot one this morning."

Fletcher smiled and shook his head at her. "It never does."

The restaurant door slammed open with a loud bang, and William Buford stepped belligerently inside. He had lost none of his arrogance; when he caught sight of Fletcher and Calamity, his mouth twisted into a gratified sneer.

The restaurant had been noisy, but now the talk slowly faded away into an expectant, uncomfortable silence, all eyes on the swaggering gunman. Buford, enjoying his moment, looked around, his cold eyes resting for a second or two on the newspapermen and then the influential bankers and their wives.

Fletcher recognized that the gunman was playing to the crowd, especially the *Black Hills Pioneer* men, who would eagerly record whatever happened.

Gun reputations were made in the newspaper columns, and, understanding that very well, William Buford, the new Wild Bill, was primed to kill a man for breakfast and earn a front-page story on how he'd added an eighth cross to the butt of his Colt.

Buck Fletcher knew he was targeted to be that man.

It took Buford a few moments to work out his next move. When he finally thought it through, a spiteful smile touched his mouth.

"You, yellowbelly," Buford snapped, jabbing a thick finger at Fletcher. "You're in my chair. Get the hell out of it."

The restaurant was suddenly so quiet that Fletcher could smell the stunned silence like an unpleasant odor.

He sat very still, but Calamity turned and said angrily, "Go away, Buford, and leave us the hell alone."

The man's face flushed. "Shut your mouth, you stinking tramp!" He jabbed a finger at Fletcher again, his right hand brushing aside his frock coat to clear his gun. "You, I've told you once. I won't repeat myself."

It had come.

Fletcher rose slowly to his feet. Buford, thinking he was vacating the chair for him, glanced over his shoulder at the expectant newspapermen, a triumphant grin on his face.

But the grin slipped a little as Fletcher strode purposefully toward him, his blue eyes now an icy, gunmetal gray.

When Fletcher stopped, just a single pace separated him from Buford.

"Mister," Fletcher said, "you've been pushing me mighty hard, and I think it's high time I read to you from the book. Up until now, you've stacked up pretty good against old timers and boys. Let's see how you do against a grown man."

In that moment of awful clarity, as Fletcher's eyes bored into his, Buford knew he'd made a terrible mistake. He'd picked on this man because he was a stranger who seemed unwilling, even afraid, to fight. But instead of the yellowbelly he'd expected, he realized with a sickening certainty that he now had a wild cougar by the tail. This man's eyes were the coldest he'd ever seen, and there was no give in them. And not even a trace of fear. It came to him then that the guns this man wore had been used often and weren't for show.

He'd made the wrong move. Now he had it to do, and everyone in The Open Door knew it.

Buford tried to save the situation by bluster, keenly aware that every eye in the restaurant was on him.

"When you talk to me, you call me Wild Bill," he said. The words clogged in his throat, and he knew with rising panic that his voice had sounded weak and uncertain, something that would be noted and commented on by the newspapermen.

To save himself, Buford had to do something dramatic and quick. He did it now. He went for his gun.

On a good day, William Buford was fast, very fast. And this was one of his better days.

When men talked of it later, they said he was so good, he was maybe half as quick as Buck Fletcher. "And mister," they'd say, eyes wide, "that's saying something!"

As Buford drew, Fletcher's gun flashed from the leather so fast that his hand blurred. But instead of shooting the gunman, Fletcher slammed the barrel of his Colt hard—but not too hard—against the side of the man's head.

Buford staggered and took a single step backward, blood pouring from the deep cut that Fletcher's gun barrel had opened on his head.

Buford's gun was still coming up, but Fletcher chopped the barrel of his Colt down violently on the man's wrist. Everyone in the restaurant heard the sharp crack of breaking bone.

The longhaired gunman screamed, and his Colt dropped to the floor from suddenly nerveless fingers. Fletcher grabbed him by the front of his fancy shirt and backhanded him viciously across the mouth, pulping Buford's lips against his teeth.

Fletcher kicked the Colt among the tables. "Get rid of that," he said to no one in particular.

Buford tried weakly to swing a left, but Fletcher easily brushed it aside and drove his fist hard into the man's nose, smashing it flat against his face.

Blood streaming from his shattered nose and mouth, Buford sank, moaning softly, to the floor. Fletcher, holding on to the collar of Buford's coat, stepped behind him and grabbed a hank of his long hair.

"Sam," he said to the red-bearded miner, a terrible, relentless rage in him, "give me your knife!"

"Hell, Buck, are you going to scalp him?"

"Give me your knife," Fletcher said again, the tone of his voice flat and hard, brooking no argument.

Sam Hannon, in common with the other miners, hated Buford's guts for killing one of their own, a harmless old man at that, so he pulled the knife and passed it hilt-first to Fletcher.

Then he sat back, grinning, prepared to enjoy whatever was going to happen next.

Fletcher took the hank of Buford's hair and slashed at it with the sharp blade of the Bowie. "You cheap, no-good tinhorn," he said as he tossed a thick handful of hair on the floor and grabbed for more. "Bill Hickok would have chewed you up and spit you out, and a dozen others just like you."

More hair, then more, spilled on the floor. Blood ran down Buford's scalp where the keen edge of the knife had bitten deep, and still the raging anger in Fletcher was a white-hot living thing that would not let him go.

The gunman moaned. Then, when all that remained of his flowing locks were a few long strands falling here and there from his gory, shaven scalp, Fletcher picked Buford up and slammed him bodily through the restaurant door.

The entire crowd spilled onto the boardwalk as Fletcher grabbed Buford and heaved the gunman into the deep, oozing mud of the street. Buford landed face down in the mud, tried to rise, then fell on his back.

After several tries, Buford finally managed to get to his feet, dripping black, odorous muck from head to toe. He looked up at the grinning crowd on the boardwalk like a strange primordial creature rising from a swamp.

The anger was still hot in Fletcher.

"Get your horse," he told Buford through gritted teeth. "If you're still in Deadwood an hour from now, I'll kill you." Fletcher took a step forward until he stood on the edge of the boardwalk. "And listen up, you two-bit backshooter. If I ever hear of you calling yourself Wild Bill again, I'll come after you. No matter where you are, this town or any other, I'll call you out, and I'll shoot you down. That I promise."

Buford's frightened eyes showed white against his thick coating of mud. The newspapermen were scribbling in their notepads, and the crowd that had gathered in the street, no longer intimidated by the neat row of crosses on Buford's gun, were ridiculing, pointing, yelling.

Buford knew he was finished in this or any other town. His days as Wild Bill, of walking a wide path and making his mark, were over. If he showed face in a Western town again, he'd be a laughingstock—the would-be Hickok who was cut down to size by a Texas toothpick haircut.

Buford looked up from the street at Fletcher. "Kill me!" he yelled. "Damn you, kill me and finish what you started!"

Fletcher, the rage draining out of him, felt cold and empty.

"Buford," he said, "Calamity Jane got it right. You're a cheap, two-bit tinhorn, and you just aren't worth a bullet."

Fletcher stepped back into The Open Door and poured himself a cup of coffee with a steady hand. He looked around at the customers as they filed back in, and he saw that the eyes of the banker's wives when they looked at him were bright with—what?

There was fear there, and something else. Maybe

the eyes of the Roman women who attended the combats in the Coliseum had held the same expression when they looked from under their lashes at the gladiators. It was a complex emotion, part revulsion, part fascination, part desire.

Fletcher didn't wish to arouse that kind of emotion in any woman. These respectable matrons were seeing him not as a man, but as some kind of wild animal. In their ordered, civilized lives, the violence they'd just seen was totally alien to them. They were repulsed and yet at the same time fascinated by it. Fletcher had crossed an invisible line into their world, a world of gingerbread houses, rose gardens and cream tea in the parlor, but now that the excitement was over, they badly wanted him to go back where he belonged.

The anger had left him, and Fletcher was tired, emotionally drained. Just where did he belong?

To his surprise, he found himself thinking longingly of the cabin on the Two-Bit and his place under the tree where he could sit quietly with his books and the speckled pup.

Perhaps Jeb had it right all along. Maybe it was time to turn his back on the violent, uncertain life he'd made for himself . . . and go home.

Calamity plumped down beside him, grinning, her hangover forgotten.

"Heeehaw!" she exclaimed. "I wouldn't have missed that for the world! Buck, you sure cut that tinhorn down to size. You should have seen the look on his face when you were giving him a Bowie knife haircut!"

Fletcher said, "Martha, let it go. It's over."

"Whatever you say, Buck," Calamity said, chastened. "But it was still a sight to see."

The waiter stepped up to the table and laid a plate in front of Fletcher. "Your steak and eggs."

The man's hand was trembling slightly, and Fletcher realized with a jolt of irritation that the waiter was afraid of him. He had gotten rid of Buford, but in the eyes of Deadwood, all he'd done was take his place.

Fletcher suddenly lost his appetite, and he pushed the plate away from him.

"You don't want that?" Calamity asked.

"It's all yours."

He watched the woman eat hungrily. Every now and again, Calamity would look at him, smiling, eager to talk about Buford. But Fletcher's set, grim face always held her back.

Sam Hannon stopped by the table, and Fletcher gave him back his knife.

"Buck," the miner said, sticking the Bowie in his belt, "you be careful. Bill Buford needed to be cut down to size, and you sure done it, but now he's going to be after you until he gets what he wants."

"And what's that?" Fletcher asked, puzzled.

"A bullet," Sam said.

Chapter 13

There was no reason for Fletcher to remain any longer in Deadwood, but he'd yet to speak to the gambler named Whitcroft at the Montana about the mares. Gamblers were as nocturnal as owls, and it was unlikely the man would be up and around much before noon, so Fletcher returned to the hotel, gave himself an all-over sponge bath, shaved and trimmed his mustache.

When he looked into the mirror above the dresser, he was pleased to see that his face had begun to heal. He'd never been long on good looks in the first place, but at least his normal homeliness was beginning to reemerge from the swollen mass of cuts and bruises Pike Prescott's fists had made of his features.

It was shortly after noon when Fletcher walked into the Montana. There were half a dozen men at the bar and others sitting at tables. Immediately a whisper of talk began, and interested eyes followed his every move, taking in his guns and the loose-limbed, confident way he walked.

In future, where men gathered, the talk would turn to Buck Fletcher and how he'd scalped Wild Bill Buford. With every retelling of the story, the truth would become less and less as the legend grew. After a few years, all the truth would be gone, and only the legend would remain. It was destined to become a wild and implausible tale, relating how Fletcher had rode up and down the main street of Deadwood on a white stallion, brandishing Buford's bloody scalp. But implausible or no, it would be eagerly taken as gospel by those who badly needed to believe.

All this Fletcher knew and accepted because there was no way to change it. The legend had been set in motion; now it would keep rolling and growing of its own unthinking momentum.

Whitcroft was already in the saloon, sitting at a table drinking coffee and his morning glass of bourbon. He was a tall, thin man with a black beard and mustache. He had the expressionless, shuttered eyes of the professional gambler, seemingly indolent but missing nothing.

"And you, by the cut of your jib, must be Buck Fletcher," Whitcroft said loudly as Fletcher stopped and looked around.

"I'm looking for a gambler named Whitcroft," Fletcher said.

"You've found him." Whitcroft rose and gave a little bow. "Nathan T. Whitcroft at your service."

Fletcher stepped up to Whitcroft's table. "Mind if I sit?"

"Please do."

Whitcroft lifted the china coffee pot, motioned with it in Fletcher's direction and raised a questioning eyebrow.

Fletcher nodded. "I could use some."

The gambler turned in his chair and called, "Bartender, another cup and saucer."

He turned again to Fletcher. "Oh, sorry. Bourbon?"

Fletcher shook his head. "Bit too early for me."

Whitcroft smiled. "Take my advice, Mr. Fletcher, always drink on an empty stomach. Nothing spoils the agreeable effects of bonded whiskey more than a full belly."

When Fletcher's cup arrived, Whitcroft poured coffee for him. "I heard you had a little, ah, unpleasantness this morning," he said obliquely, his eyes giving away nothing.

"Some," Fletcher admitted reluctantly.

Whitcroft nodded. "I briefly entertained the thought of putting a bullet into that Wild Bill Buford fellow myself," he said. "At first I thought him quite amusing, but then he began to irritate me." He shrugged. "But since he offered me no offense, I never found a reason. He chose his, ah, victims very carefully. Then he chose you, and that was a mistake."

The gambler sipped his whiskey, then laid his glass on the table. "But enough of Buford. What did you wish to talk to me about?"

Fletcher told the gambler that he wanted his Thoroughbred mares and asked him to name a price.

Whitcroft pondered this for a few moments, then said, "Since you've done the city of Deadwood a great service by ridding it of Wild Bill Buford, and since I have no interest in racing horses, the price to you, dear sir, is one hundred and eighty dollars the pair." The gambler smiled. "It was always thus with me. For those I like, I beggar myself."

"One-forty," Fletcher said with the air of a man who would brook no argument.

"Ah, you, sir, are a horse trader. I can tell that. One-seventy, and not a penny less."

"One-forty-five."

"For those fine animals, one-sixty-five. If you were my own sainted mother, I would go no lower."

Finally, Fletcher settled the price for the mares at one hundred and sixty dollars, and Whitcroft called on the bartender for pen, paper and ink and wrote out a bill of sale.

As Fletcher folded up the paper, Whitcroft studied him closely. Then, after the gunfighter made his farewells and stepped toward the door, he called out after him, "Mr. Fletcher!"

Fletcher turned. "Yes?"

"Good luck to you."

Fletcher waved a hand and walked outside.

At the livery stable, Fletcher saddled his sorrel and mounted, taking the lead ropes for the two mares in his hand.

He was about to leave, already ducking his head to get under the door, when Calamity entered. He stopped where he was as she stepped up to him and laid a hand on his thigh.

"Buck?"

"Yes?"

"Thank you for listening to me." Calamity's eyes glistened with tears. "Been a long time since a man listened to anything I had to say. I especially mean about Bill and me and the way things were between us."

Fletcher nodded, straightening up. "Anytime, Martha. You know that."

"Buck?"

"Yes?"

"Vaya con Dios."

Fletcher nodded and touched the brim of his hat, smiling. *"Hasta luego,* Martha."

Then he rode out of the livery stable and out of Deadwood, heading back to the Two-Bit.

Fletcher rode southeast. When he reached Dome Mountain, he headed north toward the cabin. Snow still lay inches thick on the ground, and he crossed the tracks of deer and antelope and once the prints of a lone wolf.

It was still a long way from nightfall, but shadows

were thickening among the pines on the hillsides, shading the canyons with blue, and the winter sun was low to the west, its slanting light pale and uncertain.

A careful man, Fletcher stopped when he was in sight of the cabin. A thin ribbon of smoke, straight as a string against a gray sky, rose from the chimney, but the place seemed deserted.

Fletcher slipped the rawhide thong off the hammer of his short-barreled crossdraw Colt and spurred the sorrel forward. The mares ponied willingly enough, eager to be in a barn out of the growing cold of the late afternoon.

His eyes alert for every movement, Fletcher rode across the stream next to the cabin, then stopped. He rose in the stirrups and yelled, "Hello the cabin!"

No answer.

Worried now, Fletcher rode up to the cabin, keeping his horse between himself and the door and windows as he dismounted.

He drew his gun and stepped up to the door before coming to a halt and listening for a few moments. There was no sound.

The gunfighter pushed the door open and stepped inside.

With a yip of delight, the pup hobbled up to him on three legs. Fletcher kneeled and patted the little animal's head. "You seem to be on the mend, boy," he said. "I'd say Matt Baker's been doing a good job."

But where was Matt?

A pot of beef and antelope stew simmered on the fire, and the coffee was still warm. The floors had been swept, and the old place looked neat and clean. Fletcher poured himself a cup and rolled a smoke.

Probably Matt Baker was out looking for Savannah. He glanced around. There was no sign the woman had been here, and only a single plate, fork and one coffee cup lay in the sink.

Fletcher finished his coffee and led the horses to the barn, where he forked them some hay and a little of the dwindling supply of oats.

The mares, close to the reassuring presence of Fletcher's stud, settled down immediately and began to eat. Fletcher left them and stepped back toward the cabin.

He stopped in his tracks as a faint, echoing rifle shot shattered the thin silence of the still afternoon. Then another.

The shots were maybe five or six miles distant, Fletcher guessed. They came from the southeast, in the direction of Bear Den Mountain, and that could only mean one thing—if Matt Baker was out there, he could be in trouble.

He would not be hunting, since a side of beef and a full deer carcass hung in the small smokehouse Fletcher's father had built behind the barn, and Baker was not a man to kill for the sake of killing.

Fletcher sprinted to the barn and saddled his sorrel. The big horse was less than happy to take the trail again away from the mares, and he humped his back and crow-hopped a few times in protest after Fletcher mounted.

The gunfighter quieted the sorrel and swung him in the direction of Bear Den Mountain. He rode past Pillar Peak, a craggy height rising well over five thousand feet into the darkening sky, then crossed Lost Gulch and saw the sprawling pine-and-spruce-covered mass of the Bear Den directly ahead of him.

Fletcher reined up the sorrel and listened. He had heard no more shots, and he could detect no movement among the pines now casting long shadows on the buffalo grass.

Warily, Fletcher urged his mount forward. Thick stands of aspen grew on the foothills of the mountain, and here and there weathered slabs of gray sandstone rock stood like still, silent ghosts among the trees.

A sickle moon was already beginning its climb into the sky, and a single bright star stood sentinel to the north, a lone picket heralding the end of the day.

Fletcher rode along the aspen line, his Winchester handy across his saddle horn. He crossed Lost Gulch and met up with Boulder Creek, following the creek for a mile before swinging west and then south, circling back toward the Two-Bit.

The sky was pale, with only that one star and the crescent moon. But a strange, transparent light illuminated the bottom of the draws and lay like fine silver mesh on the slopes of the hills, touching the ashy trunks of the aspens with blue.

The cabin came in sight, and Fletcher shoved his rifle back into the boot.

He had seen nothing.

It was full dark as he put up the sorrel and returned to the cabin. He shared a bowl of stew with the pup and drank the rest of the coffee, then stepped outside and rolled a smoke, worry nagging at him.

Matt had not returned, and Fletcher was sure those rifle shots had something to do with his disappearance. Yet he'd searched the Bear Den Mountain country and come up empty, though a man could vanish into that vast, rugged wilderness and leave not a trace.

Fletcher picked up the little dog and stroked his head. The pup, sharing a vitality common to all Western creatures, both men and animals, was recovering from his wounds rapidly, though his mangled hind leg would always be crippled.

Suddenly the pup jerked up his head and stared off into the darkness, his small black nose testing the wind.

"What do you see, boy?" Fletcher asked, smiling. "Is there a big ol' wolf out there, huh?"

The little dog growled deep in his throat, and

Fletcher felt the small body tense. The pup started to squirm, wanting to be put down, and Fletcher bent and stood him on the snow.

That movement saved Fletcher's life.

An instant later, he heard the deep-throated boom of a high-powered rifle, and a huge chunk of timber blasted from the cabin door, a shower of white splinters exploding in every direction.

The pup ran forward a few steps, raised his head and barked, a small, yipping sound that was drowned out by another booming shot.

But this time Fletcher was moving. He dove to his right, drawing his gun as he moved, then rolled behind the corner of the cabin. A bullet kicked up a vindictive V of snow where he'd been standing a split second earlier. Fletcher rose on one knee and thumbed off two quick shots into the darkness, waited a moment, then fired again.

There was no answering shot.

Rapid hoofbeats, muffled by the snow, died away and were soon lost in the thickening silence of the night.

The pup still stood his ground, yipping frantically at the fleeing horseman. Fletcher holstered his gun, picked up the little dog and carried him into the cabin.

Whoever had tried to kill him was no amateur. That much was certain.

The man had realized after his second miss that Fletcher was still alive and shooting back. He would not let himself be drawn into a gunfight. It was not his way. The man was a killer for hire, a sure-thing artist who would do his job coldly and efficiently but, if he figured the odds were stacked against him, be quite content to wait for another day.

Such men were professionals, and they had nothing to prove. They were for the most part quiet, taciturn men, and bragging was no part of their makeup. They went about their business without fuss, and when the job was done, moved on.

They did not speak of courage and honor as some men did, both concepts being totally alien to them. Money was their motivation, and in that respect they were as cold and unfeeling as any big city banker and just as practical.

Fletcher knew he'd meet this man again, but not face to face, since that was not the habit of the hired rifle killer. He would shoot from ambush. There would be no warning, no sense of fair play, no suggestion of an even break—and no mercy.

Whoever he was, this man was a dangerous and deadly enemy, and not one to be taken lightly.

Despite the warmth of the cabin, Fletcher shivered.

Who wanted him dead? And why?

He had no answers. And that troubled him.

Chapter 14

At daybreak, Fletcher saddled the sorrel and scouted the area around the cabin. He found where the mysterious gunman had lain in the snow, resting his rifle on a fallen log. The man's footprints, inches deep in the snow, told him nothing, nor had the man left anything behind that would provide a clue to his identity.

The shooter had ground-tied his horse beside a large pine, but again this revealed no clues, and Fletcher hadn't expected to find any. The man was a professional and would know how to cover his tracks well.

Fletcher headed back toward the Bear Den. Now that he had a full eight hours of daylight ahead of him, he planned to search the foothills for Matt Baker.

He passed scattered groups of cows, all wearing the Lazy R brand, with no PP Connected stuff mixed in with them. Pike Prescott had been murdered before he got a chance to move his herds, and it seemed that his daughter, for now at least, was not following in her father's footsteps.

Fletcher crossed Lost Gulch again and rode south. He planned to ride past Bear Den then swing around and head north again along Park Creek to check out the mountain's eastern slope. It was possible the shots had been fired from there.

A small herd of antelope scattered as Fletcher rode toward them, kicking up puffs of snow that caught the cold sunlight and glittered like diamond chips.

He saw some wolf tracks, but no horse prints. Near the spot where Strawberry Creek ran alongside the southern slope of the mountain, he came across the half-eaten carcass of a yearling steer. There were plenty of wolf tracks around the kill, and a large area of snow around the animal was stained red with its blood.

Fletcher reined up and studied the land around him.

The country was vast and magnificent, a breath-taking panorama of hills and jagged mountain peaks, the arrowheads of the pines dark green against the white of the snow. Ahead of him lay the shining arc of Strawberry Creek, thin sheets of ice already forming on the shallower water along its banks. Above, the sky was a magnificent pale blue arch, streaked here and there with narrow bands of white.

Fletcher's breath smoked in the cold air. Anxious to be going, the sorrel tossed his head, the bit jangling.

A shout behind him made Fletcher turn. He saw two riders approaching from the south. One of the men raised a hand in greeting, and as he grew closer, Fletcher recognized the rider and relaxed. It was Garnett, the Lazy R hand, and with him was the freckled towhead in the sheepskin coat Fletcher had met earlier.

The two men exchanged some friendly banter with Fletcher. Then the towhead looked at the dead steer and said bitterly, "That's the third dead cow we've seen since yesterday. Damn wolves."

"You boys hunting?" Fletcher asked.

"Yeah," the towhead said. "Wolves."

Fletcher understood the ranchers' attitude toward wolves, since they were the ones that suffered the livestock losses. But he believed nature had given the wolf a vital role to play, since he usually pulled down only the weak, sick or old and thus improved the health of the herds.

But this wasn't the time to reason with the punchers, especially standing over the carcass of a young Lazy R steer.

"Well, good luck," Fletcher said, touching his hat brim.

He stopped. "Have you boys seen Matt Baker by any chance?"

Garnett shook his head. "We haven't seen anybody since we left the ranch yesterday."

"Not even a damn wolf," the towhead added bitterly.

Fletcher nodded. "I'd like to stay and talk with you boys, but I got to be riding on."

Garnett began to raise a hand in farewell, but he never completed the gesture. He was blown backward off his saddle as the sound of a heavy rifle racketed around the surrounding hills.

"What the hell!" the towhead exclaimed, yanking the Winchester out of the boot under his left leg.

The rifle barked again, and the left side of the cowboy's head where it met his hat vanished in a thick, scarlet spray of blood and brain. Without a sound, the young puncher, his remaining eye wide and unbelieving, slowly toppled off the side of his horse and thudded onto the ground.

Fletcher saw a thin wisp of smoke rise from a stand of scattered lodgepole pine about a hundred yards away. He yanked his Winchester and put the spurs to the sorrel. He charged toward the spot, cranking the lever and shooting as he rode.

Fletcher fired at the smoke, then quickly dusted shots to the right and left. He was thirty yards away and closing fast when the hidden gunman's rifle slammed again.

The sorrel staggered like he had been hit by a massive sledgehammer, then pitched forward, his nose digging into the snow.

Fletcher went flying over the horse's head. He held on to his Winchester and met the ground rolling, ending up on his belly. He threw the rifle to his shoulder and fired into the lodgepoles, cranked the lever and fired again.

The echoes of his shots hammered around the hills then slowly faded into silence.

A few tense seconds ticked by as nothing stirred among the pines. Fletcher rose to his feet. Then, crouching low, he angled to his left and reached the tree line. He sprinted the last ten yards and threw himself into the sparse underbrush. Fletcher stood and treaded carefully, working his way toward the bushwhacker's position. The man could only be about twenty yards or so ahead, and Fletcher held his rifle at the ready, his finger on the trigger.

Jays quarreled in the branches above his head, and the acrid smell of powder smoke hung heavy in the air.

A twig cracked loudly under Fletcher's foot, and he stopped, every muscle of his body tensing for a rifle shot. It never came.

The rifleman, whoever he was, had escaped again, drifting silently through the trees to his waiting horse like a puff of smoke.

Fletcher cursed long and loud. He scouted the area for a few minutes, then walked out of the pines and back to where the two Lazy R hands lay staining the snow with their blood.

A quick glance told Fletcher that the towhead was dead. But Garnett, blood flecking his lips and mustache, still clung to life.

Fletcher kneeled beside the dying man. "How are you feeling, Garnett?" he asked.

The man managed a weak smile. "I don't feel a thing," he whispered. "What the hell hit me?"

"A bullet," Fletcher said. "A real big bullet."

Garnett strained to look down at his blood-splashed chest. "Hell, I'm all shot to pieces."

Fletcher nodded. "I won't try to fool you, Garnett," Fletcher said gently. "You're shot through and through, and your time is very short. Is there anyone I can tell? Family?"

Garnett shook his head. "No, no one. I was orphan born." He tried to look around him. "How is Lem?"

Fletcher glanced across at the young towhead. "He's dead."

When he looked back to Garnett, he too was gone.

Slowly, wearily, Fletcher rose to his feet. The attack on the Lazy R hands had been sudden, deadly and merciless. Who had ordered the killings? Was it the PP Connected, now owned by Pike Prescott's daughter? The apple doesn't fall far from the tree, he thought, and perhaps the girl shared her father's ambitions.

Fletcher shook his head. It was possible, but something about all this didn't add up, something he couldn't put his finger on . . . something as elusive and insubstantial as a will-o-the-wisp.

A single glance at the sorrel was enough to tell Fletcher that the big stud was dead. Part of his dream was gone, lying lifeless in the snow, and it was in Fletcher to wonder why he still remained in the Dakota Territory. What was holding him here? Was it really the falling-down cabin and one hundred and sixty hardscrabble acres on the Two-Bit?

He had no answer for that. Unless . . . could it be Savannah, if she was still alive? Or Judith Tyrone?

The gunfighter would not let himself admit that two beautiful women could have such a hold on him.

Fletcher loaded the two dead men onto Garnett's gray and mounted Lem's lineback dun. He led the gray and headed southwest, toward the Lazy R—and Judith Tyrone.

Windy Flats lay about a mile ahead of him when Fletcher saw a small figure alone on the buffalo grass. As he rode closer, he made out Bob, the English landscape painter, sitting on a fold-up stool at his easel and dabbing a brush on a large canvas. A leggy bay that looked like he could run was picketed close, and a loaded grulla packhorse grazed a distance away.

When Fletcher rode up, Bob pulled a piece of canvas over his picture and waved a hand in greeting, smiling. Then he saw the two dead men, and the smile changed to a look of horror.

"Oh my God, Buck, I heard the shooting. What happened?"

Briefly Fletcher described the bushwhacking and the deaths of the two Lazy R hands. "They didn't get any chance," he finished. "Lem was dead when he hit the ground, and Garnett didn't live but a couple of minutes."

Bob shook his head, clucking his tongue. "Buck, I fear this conflict between the PP Connected and the Lazy R is about to burst wide open. God knows, Judith Tyrone doesn't want a war, but when she sees this, well . . ."

"From what I'm told, Pike Prescott's daughter is only sixteen years old," Fletcher interrupted. "She's only a child."

Bob smiled. "Not in these parts. At sixteen there are girls around here already married with a couple of kids and a household to run. And she could be getting advice from that gunman Higgy Conroy. He's no child."

"It's possible," Fletcher admitted reluctantly. "Conroy is a snake, and he may have his own agenda."

He let his eyes wander briefly over the Englishman's rangy bay and then the packhorse. The grulla was loaded with a spare easel, rolled-up canvases, wooden boxes of paint, a picnic basket and a large rectangular leather case that Fletcher guessed must contain wood to make stretch frames for the canvases. Except for the Colt strapped around his waist that he'd seen Bob use so well in Buffalo City, Fletcher saw no other guns.

"Buck, where do you stand in all this?" Bob was asking.

Fletcher allowed himself a rare smile. "So far, I've been trying to keep out of it. But it seems somebody doesn't believe that and is trying his damndest to kill me."

"Conroy?"

"Maybe. But whoever it is, he uses a mighty big gun. He missed me but damn-near blew my cabin door apart. That just doesn't fit Conroy's style. He fancies himself a drawfighter, and he would want to get up close and personal."

"When this range war starts, you're going to have to choose a side, Buck," Bob said solemnly. "I think someone fears you'll sell your gun to Judith Tyrone, and the attempt was made on your life to force you out of the country."

The Englishman's face was small and pinched, the sunken, wrinkled cheeks as brown as saddle leather from exposure to all kinds of weather. His eyes were blue and mild, the eyes of an artist, a dreamer.

Yet, as Fletcher considered his answer, he recalled how well this man had used a Colt. But what was so peculiar about that? Plenty of the great Renaissance artists had been as handy with a rapier as they were with a paintbrush.

"I'm not selling my gun to anyone," Fletcher said finally. "I want to find Savannah Jones, wherever she is, and then I'll think about what I should do next."

The Englishman shook his head. "Buck, forget about Savannah. I believe she's already dead. I don't know who she was or what she was doing in the Dakota Territory, but I think she discovered something, something she wasn't supposed to discover. Pike Prescott tried to have her murdered, and when that failed, his daughter completed the job."

"It's thin, Bob," Fletcher said, shaking his head, his eyes bleak. "Mighty thin."

"The truth often is," Bob commented dryly.

"It seems to me Prescott's plans were pretty straightforward," Fletcher said. "Claim all the grass for miles around the Lazy R and box in Judith Tyrone so she'd be forced to sell. What could Savannah have discovered that was such a big secret?"

"I don't know," the Englishman admitted. "Unless Pike Prescott and now his daughter are fronting for somebody else. It's possible, I think."

Fletcher nodded. "All things are possible."

He touched the brim of his hat. "I have to be riding on."

"Buck," Bob said, "before you go."

"Yes?"

"Judith Tyrone needs you. She's a woman alone, and she needs a man like you now more than ever. That's something to think about."

Fletcher nodded. "It is indeed."

"First my husband, and now Lem Wilson and Hank Garnett," Judith Tyrone said, tears brimming in her eyes. "Buck, when is all this killing going to stop?"

Fletcher shook his head. "I don't know, Judith. I don't know what's behind it."

"I do," Judith said, dabbing her eyes with a small lace handkerchief as she poured coffee into Fletcher's cup. "I believe Amy Prescott, for all she's just a child, is as ruthless and ambitious as her father. She wants the Lazy R, and she'll do anything in her power to get it."

Fletcher's eyes wandered to the kitchen window. Outside, a dozen Lazy R hands were gently taking down the bodies of their two dead compadres. The men were muttering to each other: the hard, angry drone of war talk.

Judith's eyes followed Fletcher's, and she said, "My men are just ordinary punchers, Buck. They don't understand all this, and I can't send them against Higgy Conroy and the rest of Amy Prescott's hired guns. They'd be slaughtered."

Fetcher nodded absently. What Judith was telling him was true enough, but not quite accurate.

As he rode in, he'd recognized Tex Lando and the longhaired, buckskin-clad Tin Cup Kid hanging around the bunkhouse.

Lando had been a Texas Ranger for three years and had later run wild with John Wesley Hardin and that hard crowd in DeWitt County during the Sutton-Taylor feud. A few months ago, he'd killed Happy Tom Bear, the skilled Bodie gunfighter, and then a Mexican pistolero of known reputation in El Paso.

There was man down in the Nations who called himself the Tin Cup Kid, but this one was the genuine article: fast with a gun, and with four killings to his credit, one a deputy sheriff in Ellsworth.

Maybe Lando and Tin Cup wrangled cattle occasionally when times were hard, but they were no punchers. These two were men to be reckoned with. When Judith hired them on, did she know what she was getting?

Fletcher doubted it. Such men, confident of their gun skills, were not normally given to boasting. They usually kept their tracks well-covered.

He took out the makings of a smoke and gestured to Judith. "May I?"

"Of course." The woman studied Fletcher for a few moments, her eyes on his strong hands as he rolled his cigarette. Then she said, "Buck, I want you with me. I need you to stand with me."

Fletcher did not reply at once, thinking this thing through. Finally, he said slowly, "Judith, my gun is not for hire. I'm finished with all that." He lit his smoke and nodded toward the angry hands gathered on the other side of the kitchen window. "Did you know when you hired on Tex Lando and the Tin Cup Kid that they were gunfighters?"

Judith raised her head defensively. "Yes, I did, and I'm not ashamed of it. Amy Prescott has Higgy Conroy and other hired guns, so why shouldn't I?"

"Men like that," Fletcher said carefully, "are hard to control. They go their own way, and they'll step lightly from one side of the law to the other. I know, because up until very recently I was one of them."

"Men like that are what I need," Judith said, the defensive fire still in her eyes. "I'll do whatever it takes to save the Lazy R. I'll try to stay within the law to keep what's mine, but Amy Prescott's calling the tune, and I can't hold my men back any longer."

Fletcher sat bolt upright in his chair. "Judith, what are you planning?"

"In less than an hour from now, I'm leading my men to the PP Connected. We're going to burn Amy Prescott's place down around her ears. She and her father started this war; now I'm going to take it to her and finish it."

Judith's fingers lightly touched the back of Fletcher's hand. "Buck, she's already tried to kill you to stop you from taking my side. Please, ride with us."

The woman looked radiantly beautiful this morning, though there were fine lines at the corners of her eyes and at each side of her mouth. Fletcher realized with a vague pang of guilt that the strain was already beginning to tell on her.

"Judith," he said, "listen to me. I sense something here. I'm a man who's spent years relying on instinct to warn me of trouble, and now it's telling me that there's something very wrong here. I can't put my finger on it, but I sense . . . well, for want of a better word, I sense evil. I believe there's someone behind all this, playing both you and Amy Prescott like puppets. I don't know what his agenda is, but he badly wants this war. That I do know."

Fletcher took Judith's hand in his own and held it. "I don't think the man who killed your hands and maybe Savannah was carrying out orders from Amy Prescott. I think he's acting for someone else. But who that someone is, I just don't know."

Judith took Fletcher's hand and pressed it against her firm breasts. He felt a sudden hot jolt of desire run through him.

"Buck," she said, "ride at my side." She rubbed the back of his hand gently over her breasts; first one, then the other. "You won't ever regret it."

It was there. A promise. And now it lay between them.

Fletcher felt himself drift, the sweet, womanly smell of her filling his head. He moved closer to Judith across the small table. Her full lips parted, betraying her eagerness. His mouth met hers, and now there was no thought, no consciousness as he gave way to his overpowering passion, melting into her as they joined and became a single living entity.

Their lips parted, and Judith whispered huskily, "Take me to the bedroom, Buck. Now, before we leave."

Fletcher looked into Judith's eyes. What he saw there made him take a quick step back to reality. He'd expected to see a flaming passion to match his own; instead, there was only a dispassionate coolness and more than a hint of triumph.

Like a punch-drunk boxer, Fletcher shook his head. He said huskily, "No, Judith, not like this. You can't buy me with your body."

The woman rose and stood by Fletcher's chair, tall and breathtakingly beautiful, looking down at him. "I want you, Buck. I want you at my side always. My body is all yours, freely given. It's not a reward. There's no price on it."

Fletcher gently pushed Judith away and got to his feet. "Maybe later, when all this is settled. But not now, and not with dead men outside."

Anger flashed in the woman's eyes. "What do you want, Buck? Tell me, and it's yours."

"I want three days, Judith."

"What?"

"Give me three days to find out who's behind all this killing. Can you keep your men away from the PP Connected until then?"

Judith was silent for a few moments. Then she said, "Very well, Buck. I'll give you three days. You'll need a horse, so keep the dun. It's my gift."

"Thanks, Judith. Hold the hands back for three days. That's all I ask."

"You've got them. But when the three days are over, either ride with me or don't stand in my way."

Fletcher took the woman in his arms. "Judith, you have to trust me. I know you're scared, and I can understand that. All I need right now is a little time."

He kissed her then, but this time Judith's mouth was cool and unresponsive. Cold as ice.

As he rode away from the Lazy R, Fletcher turned in the saddle and saw Judith standing in the doorway of the ranch house. He waved. She didn't wave back.

He swung the dun toward the south.

It was time to talk to Amy Prescott.

Chapter 15

The PP Connected ranch lay thirty miles to the south, along Horsehead Creek. To the east, the ranch was bordered by the Badlands, hundreds of thousands of acres of sharply eroded buttes, pinnacles and spires. Here and there sparse, mixed grass prairie provided an unexpected green counterpoint to the weatherworn brown and rust red of the rock.

It was the Badlands that had forced Pike Prescott to graze his herd miles farther south, all the way to the Platte, and explained why he so badly wanted the Lazy R grass. Judith Tyrone's range was much closer to the Deadwood stockyards, and Prescott's beef would walk off little weight during the short drive.

The country Fletcher rode through was mostly hills covered in pine and spruce, with here and there aspen, now a riot of color in yellow and red. It was wild, beautiful country that had a way of making a man feel glad to be alive.

He passed small groups of cows, all wearing the PP Connected brand. Most of what he saw was young stuff, rangy longhorns brought up from Texas, with the notable exception of a single magnificent Hereford bull that glared at Fletcher belligerently out of red-rimmed eyes as he rode past. All the cattle seemed to be in excellent condition. Whatever else Pike Prescott might have been, Fletcher thought with grudging admiration, he was a rancher first and foremost. He'd known his business.

The PP Connected ranch house lay at a bend of the Horsehead. It was a low wooden building, its walls whitewashed, surrounded by several large corrals shaded by huge, spreading oaks. A barn with a steepled roof stood behind the house, and a dozen tall haystacks were neatly built against the coming of winter. A cookhouse, bunkhouse, blacksmith shop and some sheds completed the spread. To Fletcher's experienced eye, the whole place had the air of orderliness that comes only from careful planning and a lot of hard work.

Day was already shading into night as Fletcher reached the house and sat his horse outside the door. Several hands drifted over, some looking at him curiously, others with open hostility.

Looking around him, Fletcher recognized no gunhandlers of reputation, though the whole bunch looked pretty salty and didn't seem the kind to be easily stampeded.

The front door of the house opened, and a young, pretty woman stepped outside. She had black hair tied with a yellow ribbon at the back of her neck, and she wore a simple dress of blue gingham, a heart-shaped locket hanging on her breast. This could only be Amy Prescott—though, slender and delicately boned, she bore little resemblance to her huge, overbearing father.

Fletcher touched his hat brim. "Evening, ma'am. My name is Buck Fletcher, and I wonder if we could talk a spell." He smiled. "Maybe over supper on account of how I'm powerful hungry."

Before the woman could reply, Higgy Conroy, a red-checkered dinner napkin tied around his neck, stepped out of the house and said, "Amy, that's the man I told you about, the one who's squatting up on the Two-Bit. He's the saddle tramp who attacked your pa in Buffalo City. He's one of Judith Tyrone's hired guns, an' I suspect he knows who killed the boss, if he didn't do it his ownself."

"Conroy," Fletcher sighed, his contempt for this man obvious, "you're not wearing a gun, so I won't call you a liar. But go heel yourself, and I'll call you a liar then."

One of the hands giggled, and Conroy flushed. "Damn you," he snarled. "Wait right there."

"No!" Amy Prescott said. "There will be no shooting. Hig, go back inside and finish your dinner this minute."

Conroy stood his ground, glaring at Fletcher. Amy, iron in her voice, snapped, "Higgy Conroy, do as I say at once!"

The man threw a last, angry glance at Fletcher and stomped back into the house.

"Please step down, Mr. Fletcher," Amy Prescott said. "I'll turn no man away from my home hungry."

Fletcher stepped out of the leather, and a puncher led his horse toward the barn.

Amy waved a hand. "Please, come inside."

The interior of the cabin was warm and comfortable, its wood floor and furniture mellowed over the years to a deep honey color. A log fire burned in a huge stone fireplace, and Fletcher smelled the good smells of coffee and roasting beef.

The gunfighter removed his hat as Amy directed him to a chair at the table.

"Are you going to allow that saddle tramp to eat at your table?" Conroy asked, his snake eyes yellow and ugly.

"He's a guest, Hig," Amy said quietly. "Where else would I have him eat?"

"Hell," Conroy snapped, "he can eat with the hands. And even that's too good for him."

Amy Prescott shook her head. "As I said, Hig, Mr. Fletcher is a guest. I won't send him to eat with the hands."

"In that case," Conroy growled, jerking the napkin from around his neck and throwing it on the table, "you'll eat without me. I won't sit with saddle trash."

"Hig, please," Amy said plaintively.

But the gunman ignored her and brushed roughly past Fletcher, his eyes black with anger.

"I'm sorry," the girl said, her face flushed. "Hig is my foreman, and he can be very protective."

As Fletcher took his seat, he glanced at Amy. The girl was visibly upset. He realized that she regarded Higgy Conroy as much more than just her foreman. A friend maybe? Or did her feelings for the man go deeper?

It was something to study on later.

There was a roasted joint of beef on the table, along with gravy, potatoes, a bowl of onions and another of frijoles.

Fletcher poured himself a glass of buttermilk from a cool pitcher, then filled his plate. The food was good, and he ate heartily, aware that Amy Prescott only picked at the slice of beef on her plate.

After he'd eaten, Fletcher sighed contentedly and sat back in his chair. His hand absently strayed to his shirt pocket, and he quickly dropped it again.

Amy gave him a knowing smile. "Please smoke if you wish, Mr. Fletcher. I've lived all my life around men who use tobacco."

Gratefully, Fletcher rolled a smoke as the girl poured him coffee. He lit his cigarette, then, easing into what he had to say, declared matter-of-factly, "Two Lazy R hands were murdered this morning. Shot from ambush."

Through a cloud of blue smoke, his veiled eyes studied Amy Prescott's reaction. The girl was shocked, the blood suddenly draining from her pretty, heart-shaped face.

She was either a good actress, or this had come as a complete surprise to her.

"I exchanged shots with the killer," Fletcher pressed on, his voice flat, "but he got clean away."

"But . . . but that's so horrible," Amy said, a tangle of emotions breaking up her words. "I hope . . . I mean, Judith Tyrone doesn't think I had anything to do with it, does she? Or is that why you're here?"

Fletcher let the questions ride, saying only, "The PP Connected has been pushing her mighty hard."

Amy Prescott stiffened. "Aren't you forgetting something, Mr. Fletcher? My father was also murdered." Her downcast eyes looked at Fletcher from under long lashes. "Hig Conroy says you killed him or had a hand in it."

Stung, Fletcher shook his head at her. "I've killed men, Miss Prescott. I've never made a secret of that. But the men I killed were armed and facing me. I never in my life shot a man from ambush."

"Then, if you didn't kill my pa, who did?" Amy asked quietly.

"I don't know," Fletcher admitted. "That's why I rode out here to talk to you. I believe there's someone else behind all this, someone who wants to push you and Judith Tyrone into a range war. Then, when it's all over and the gunsmoke clears, he'll move in and pick up the pieces. It will be easy for him because most everybody will be dead or forced out of the country."

Outside, Fletcher heard Higgy Conroy's angry voice raised, trying to whip up the hands. He prayed silently that he wouldn't have to shoot his way out of here.

He'd die, that much was certain. But he'd take Conroy with him, and a few others besides.

But then nothing would be solved. He'd be dead, and the only person to gain would be the mystery man who was manipulating this range with all the skill of a ruthless and cold-blooded predator.

Did Amy know that Higgy Conroy had killed Jeb Coons? Somehow he thought that unlikely. When Fletcher had told her about the murder of the Lazy R hands, the girl had been genuinely shocked, even frightened.

He watched Amy Prescott as she gazed down at her plate for a few moments then pushed it angrily away from her.

"Mr. Fletcher, I don't wish to have a war with Judith Tyrone," she said. "I admit that my father wanted the Lazy R. He tried to buy it, but Deke Tyrone refused. Then, when the old man was murdered, there were plenty around who pointed the finger at Pa, Judith among them."

Amy's fingers strayed to the locket around her neck. "Mr. Fletcher, I loved my father, and that's why I wear his picture here. I know he was an ambitious, hard-driven man, and that there was no give in him, no room for compromise. This country breeds men like that. He was many things, not all of them admirable, but he wasn't a murderer."

"He ordered me off the Two-Bit," Fletcher pointed out reasonably. "Told me he'd hang me if I didn't leave."

Amy nodded. "That doesn't surprise me. In my father's eyes, hanging was not murder, but justice. I was just seven years old when he made me watch him hang a man, a young rustler who had come up out of the Nations.

"'Amy,' he told me, 'this is a hard land, occupied

by even harder men, and we must live by its code. It's a harsh code, and maybe it's not just, but it's all we have, and so we must honor it.' "

"And what about you, Amy?" Fletcher asked softly. "By what code do you live?"

The girl shook her head. "As of right now, I don't know. But I will tell you this: I believe the Lazy R and the PP Connected can live in peace. We can both sell beef to the miners and the army. Someday, when the gold runs out and the miners are gone, we can ship our herds together."

Amy looked Fletcher square in the eye. "Mr. Fletcher, I don't want to get rich. I just want enough to get by, to keep this ranch going. Please tell Judith that for me."

"I will," Fletcher said. "She's already promised me that she won't move against the PP Connected." He smiled slightly. "Well, she gave me three days to find whoever is behind all these murders. She won't do anything until then. But I think that you and her can be friends once I tell her how you feel."

The girl nodded. "I hope so. And I hope you find the person you're looking for. There's already been enough killing."

It was in Fletcher then to tell Amy Prescott how he felt about Higgy Conroy, that he planned to kill him for murdering Jeb Coons. But he let it pass. This was not the time or the place. Instead, he asked, "Amy, do you know a young woman named Savannah Jones?"

Amy shook her head. "No, I don't. Should I?"

"Not really," Fletcher said. Then, not wishing to go into it, he added only, "She's a friend of mine is all, and she's been missing for a while."

"I hope she's all right," Amy Prescott said, and Fletcher heard true sincerity in her voice.

"And so do I," he said.

As Western hospitality dictated, Amy offered Fletcher the spare bedroom in the ranch house, but he opted to bunk with the hands for fear the girl's reputation might be compromised.

The bunkhouse was typical of its kind at that time in the West, a long, low-roofed building made from cottonwood and pine logs. Inside, the walls were whitewashed, and a buffalo robe and some wolfskins covered the wood floor. Logs burned in a crude stone fireplace at one end of the room, providing warmth for the men who would sleep in the dozen or so bunks lining the walls.

When Fletcher stepped inside, his nose was assaulted by the familiar aroma of any bunkhouse: man sweat, dry cow manure, old work boots, the licorice in chewing tobacco plugs and the coal oil that burned in the lamps hanging from the ceiling.

Some of the hands were out on the range, and only six, Conroy among them, were in the bunkhouse. They made no effort to welcome him, and Fletcher had to step carefully over outstretched legs before finding an empty bunk.

Conroy wore his guns, and his face was a study in vindictiveness and hate as he watched Fletcher stretch out on the bunk.

"Don't get too comfortable," Conroy sneered. "At first light tomorrow you're riding out of here."

Fletcher, ignoring the man, tipped his hat over his eyes.

A hand sniggered, and Conroy snapped, "Did you hear what I said, saddle tramp?"

Slowly, Fletcher lifted his hat and studied Conroy with a single eye that had hardened to gunmetal. "Conroy," he said, deliberately spacing the words, "some day very soon you and I will have it out. But not tonight, and not here."

The hand sniggered again, and Conroy, full of impotent rage, snarled, "The sooner the better for me. I plan to kill you."

Fletcher nodded. "You can try."

Again the hand sniggered, but this time the sound died in his throat, cut off by the sound of roaring guns and the drum of hooves outside.

"What the hell!" Conroy yelled.

He pulled his guns and ran outside, followed by Fletcher and the rest of the hands.

There were at least a dozen men, some of them carrying blazing torches, galloping and yelling around the house and barn. The night was an orange-streaked hell of blazing guns and burning haystacks.

One stack went up in flames, then another and another.

Guns roared at fleeting targets illuminated by the flickering red and yellow glare of the burning stacks. Fletcher saw a rider fall. Then one of the PP Connected hands went down, doubled up by a belly wound.

Soon all the haystacks were ablaze. Torches were thrown through the open door of the bunkhouse, its dry timbers catching fire almost immediately.

Conroy stepped in front of a rider carrying a torch, and his guns spat flame. The man screamed, "No, Hig!" and plunged backward over his horse. Bullets kicked up angry Vs of snow and dirt around Conroy, and he sprinted for the cover of the blacksmith shop.

In the fire-and-bullet-streaked heat of the moment, Fletcher still noted that cry. The man had called out to Conroy as though surprised the gunman had shot him. The question was, why?

But he had no time to ponder the answer, because he saw Amy Prescott step out of the house wearing a long white nightdress. Fletcher yelled, "No!" He ran to the girl's side and pushed her back through the door.

"Leave me alone!" Amy protested angrily. "Fletcher, you brought this to us!"

The gunfighter shook his head. "No, Amy. I had nothing to do with this. You have to believe me."

There was only scorn in the girl's eyes. That and anger.

Fletcher grabbed the girl's shoulders and pulled her close to him. "Listen to me!" he yelled.

An instant later a bullet chipped the doorframe where Amy's head had been, and the girl opened her mouth to speak again. Fletcher didn't wait for what she had to say. He bundled her inside the house and slammed the door.

Fletcher looked around him in stunned disbelief. It seemed like the whole ranch was on fire. Only the main house was as yet untouched. But someone had tried to kill Amy Prescott. That shot had been no accident.

A man in buckskins, riding a black stud, its white eyes rolling, galloped up to the door. He saw Fletcher at the last minute and smiled. "Sorry, Buck," he said, "but business is business."

He leveled his gun, and Fletcher drew and shot him.

The man jerked in the saddle and tried to bring his Colt into play. Fletcher shot him again, this time square in the chest. The gunman went out of the saddle, landing on his back with a thud in the snow.

Fletcher stepped up to the man, his gun ready. He looked down and recognized the pain-twisted features of the Tin Cup Kid.

"Damn it all, Buck," the Kid whispered, shaking his head in admiration, "that was fast. I can hardly believe it my ownself."

"You didn't give me no choice, Kid," Fletcher said.

The Kid nodded. "I know that. But hell, Buck, you're the fastest I ever seen." Then he closed his eyes and died.

Now that the whole ranch was burning, the attacking riders galloped away. Three of their number, including the Tin Cup Kid, lay dead on the ground, and with them three of the PP Connected hands and another who was gut-shot and could not live.

It had been a devastating attack, perfectly planned, and it had accomplished its aim—to burn down Amy Prescott's ranch around her ears.

Chapter 16

Buck Fletcher stood amid the smoking ruins of the PP Connected, facing a hostile circle of the surviving punchers, the ranch cook, Higgy Conroy and Amy Prescott.

"He and Judith Tyrone set this up," Conroy snarled. "He came here with all his empty peace talk to lull us into a false sense of security so our guard would be down when the Lazy R gunmen attacked."

The cook, his eyes hard and unforgiving, held a sawed-off Remington 10-gauge shotgun, its barrels pointed directly at Fletcher's belly. "Just say the word, Miz Prescott, an' I'll cut this ranny in half," he said. The man's voice was level and calm, free of anger, and that made him all the more dangerous.

The girl shook her head. "No, Clem. I won't spill a man's blood on my doorstep after I've welcomed him into my home."

"Amy, please believe me. Judith Tyrone had nothing to do with this," Fletcher pleaded. "She gave me three days, and she would never go back on her word."

"It seems that she did," Amy Prescott said, apparently without malice. "My ranch is destroyed. All my winter feed is gone. Three of my men are dead, and another won't last until first light. I don't know about you, Mr. Fletcher, but I'd say she's very much gone back on her word."

"Enough of this empty talk," Conroy snapped. "Amy, do what your pa would have done. String this man up from the nearest oak."

"Amy," Fletcher began, ignoring Conroy, "I know in my heart this is none of Judith's doing . . ." He faltered into silence, looking around him at the circle of unfriendly eyes, realizing how lame his words sounded. He shook his head. "There's someone else behind this, Amy. You've got to trust me."

But the girl's clear hazel eyes revealed no trust, just an icy resolve.

"Mr. Fletcher, Clem wants to shoot you, and Hig wants to hang you, but I will permit neither. Not today at least. However, I want you to carry a message to Judith Tyrone."

Fletcher nodded silently. Whatever he was about to hear was not going to be good.

"Tell her these things, just as I now speak them. Tell her I come of a long line of Tennessee hill folk, and I was born and bred to the feud. Tell her that from this day forward, there can be no peace between us. Tell her that I will visit on her what she visited on me and the PP Connected. Tell her that the visitation will be of fire, destruction and death. Tell her I will take an eye for an eye, a tooth for a tooth."

The girl took a step closer to Fletcher, her eyes blazing. "That's a fairly short and uncomplicated message, Mr. Fletcher. Can I trust you to deliver it accurately?"

Again Fletcher nodded without speaking, knowing he had no words that would erase what had been done here.

Amy Prescott turned to one of the hands. "Bring Mr. Fletcher his horse."

She looked at Fletcher again. "The only reason you're riding out of here alive is that you were a guest in my home. When we meet again, that will no longer apply. From now until the ending of time, Mr. Fletcher, you are my sworn enemy."

The girl turned on her heel and walked into the ranch house, the only building left standing at the PP Connected.

The hand brought Fletcher his horse, and the gunfighter stepped into the leather.

Conroy looked up at him, his yellow eyes narrow and mean.

"If I see you around the Connected, I'll kill you," he said. "Fletcher, you're real good at hiding behind a woman's skirt, but next time, Amy Prescott or no, I'll draw down on you."

Fletcher nodded. "So be it," he said. "Conroy, you and I will meet again soon. You killed a harmless old man who was my friend, and you shot my dog, and now these things stand between us. There is a showdown to come."

Fletcher's cold eyes were bleak. "I tell you these things just so you know."

He rode away from the PP Connected without looking back, realizing that behind him were implacable enemies, people who lived by a harsh code that held little of forgiveness but much of vengeance and hate.

He would also have to deal with Higgy Conroy, and that would only make matters worse.

The war he'd tried to avoid was about to tear this country apart, gaining strength from its own headlong momentum. There could be no stopping it.

The time of the reckoning had come.

As the night gave way to morning, Buck Fletcher rode north, avoiding as much as he was able the open grassland where he could become a target for a hidden rifleman. He kept to the bases of the hills, riding close to the welcome cover of the tree lines.

The attack on the PP Connected had shaken Fletcher to the core. He couldn't let himself believe that Judith Tyrone had ordered it. But if it wasn't her, then who? And why had the Lazy R hands obeyed him?

One of the riders had recognized Higgy Conroy and had been surprised when the PP Connected foreman shot him. Could Conroy be the man behind all this? It was possible, but somehow Fletcher couldn't believe the snake-eyed gunman possessed the necessary brains and cunning.

No, it had to be someone else. But who?

And to top it all off, where was Savannah Jones, and why did the mystery man, whoever he was, want her dead?

Fletcher shook his head. As usual, there were plenty of questions running through his mind and mighty few answers.

Windy Flats and the Lazy R ranch still lay twenty miles to the north as Fletcher rode past a low, flat-topped butte, its slopes covered in spruce and thick brush. There were still several inches of snow on the ground, reflecting the pale light of the morning sun. A long wind, heavy with the scent of pine, stole softly across its glittering surface.

Something flashed on the slope of the butte, the sudden glimmer almost hidden by the trees. Fletcher caught the flash out of the corner of his eye, and he jerked his Winchester out of the boot.

Was it the sun reflecting off a gun barrel?

He kneed his horse toward the slope, his rifle ready. There it was again! But this time the light was steady, like a lamp flame burning. Puzzled now, but still wary, Fletcher rode to the base of the butte and dismounted.

He stepped into the pines, his eyes searching the slope of the butte. The pines grew thick here, and even though he was closer, he could no longer see the light. He walked carefully until he reached the base of the rise. Then he began to climb.

Over thousands of years, earth tremors had loosened rock that had tumbled down the slope accompanied by fans of tumulus, and Fletcher found it hard going, especially when his broken ribs began to pain him unmercifully from the unaccustomed exertion. He climbed upward from rock to rock until he was about five hundred feet above the ground.

Despite the morning chill, he was sweating heavily. He took off his hat and wiped the band with his fingers, looking around him.

About twenty feet above his head, where he'd mentally marked the spot of the light, there was an outcropping of rock shaped like the prow of a ship, its lower edge banded by a seam of quartz about a foot thick.

Fletcher settled his hat on his head and climbed up to the outcropping. He rested his rifle against a boulder and studied the quartz seam thoughtfully.

The quartz was rotten, and Fletcher was able to crumble off a small piece from the seam. It was the quartz that had glimmered from the slope. The light of the sun must have reflected on the snow and lit up the seam at exactly the right angle. A man could have ridden past this spot a thousand times and never seen the outcropping, let alone the wide seam of quartz.

Fletcher studied the piece in his hands closely. It was only about an inch in diameter, but even so he saw gold gleam within the quartz, looking like thin, spattered raindrops.

The seam rounded the outcropping and disappeared into the butte. To the right of the outcropping there was only about twenty yards or so of slope before it broke off abruptly, ending in a sheer cliff that dropped to the flat.

Could any trace of the seam be seen from the cliff face?

Fletcher picked up his Winchester and scrambled across the slope of the butte to the cliff, stepping carefully now that he was so close to an almost vertical five-hundred-foot drop.

He stepped close to the cliff face and looked around. The drop wasn't as sheer as he'd first thought because a ledge varying in width between three and six feet crossed the entire face of the cliff about twenty feet below where he stood.

Laying down his rifle again, Fletcher slid down the sandy rubble of the incline until he reached the ledge. He stepped onto the ledge and walked along it carefully, aware of the shattering fall that would result should he stumble or the soft rock of the ledge give way.

He'd only walked about ten yards or so when the ledge led past a narrow opening in the rock. Fletcher quickly realized this was a man-made opening, not a natural formation, and he could still make out the marks of a pick on the walls.

The opening was narrow, and Fletcher had to turn sideways to enter. Once inside, he discovered that the hole had been dug about ten feet into the rock, enough to expose the quartz seam that angled downward into the bluff.

Despite the dim light, Fletcher's unbelieving eyes saw that the seam was at least three feet thick. When he thumbed a match into flame, he caught the unmistakable glint of gold. The quartz was loaded with it, and although he was no miner, Fletcher knew he was looking at a mother lode.

There was a fortune waiting to be dug out of this butte—and someone already knew it.

The match burned Fletcher's fingers, and he dropped it, shaking his hand. He stepped back out onto the ledge.

The exploratory hole had been dug into the butte to check out the location and width of the quartz seam, and the lack of weathering suggested this had happened very recently.

Was this the reason someone wanted a war between the PP Connected and the Lazy R?

The butte was on PP Connected range, and what better way to get at its gold than to wait until the ranch had destroyed itself in a range war, then move in and take over by buying out Amy Prescott—or by force if necessary, an easy task against a weakened adversary.

The why of all this suddenly made sense to Fletcher, but he was still no further along in guessing the who.

Who was the mastermind behind all this? Who was playing Judith Tyrone and Amy Prescott like puppets for his own gain?

Fletcher had no answers and no guesses.

Maybe if he could find Savannah Jones, she could help him—if her memory had returned, but that was far from certain. He didn't even know if she was still alive.

Fletcher retrieved his rifle and climbed back up the slope. He chipped off a few more samples of quartz and placed them in the pocket of his shirt.

He turned away from the seam and walked through some thick underbrush. The toe of his right boot hit something hidden in the brush that clicked with a dry, rasping sound.

Fletcher pushed the brush aside with his foot and saw what he'd kicked—a skeletal hand outstretched from the rest of the body.

There were two complete skeletons lying close together. The dry, cracked leather of their belts had survived, as had the boots on their feet. They were lace-up boots, not the high-heeled boots of cattlemen but the rugged footwear of miners.

The dead men's story was not difficult to piece together.

Evidently the two miners had been hired by someone to dig the exploratory hole in the cliff face. Then, as soon as the quartz seam had been exposed, they'd been shot to keep them quiet.

Fletcher realized he was dealing here not only with a cold, calculating intelligence, but someone who was utterly ruthless and would kill—or order it done—without a moment's hesitation.

Whoever he was, this man had to be found and stopped. Soon, before it was too late.

After one last look at the outcropping, fixing the place in his mind, Fletcher made his way down the butte again and found his horse.

He had it in mind to talk to Judith Tyrone and find out who had ordered the attack on the PP Connected. That might give a clue to who was behind all this, and maybe he could end it once and for all.

Fletcher mounted and headed north, toward the Lazy R. It was still early, and the land smelled clean and fresh, the scent of the pines borne on the wind.

He continued to ride close to the tree lines, his eyes constantly scanning the country around him. But as far as he could see, it seemed empty of life.

Around him, stretching for miles, lay rich grassland and here and there the sudden, dramatic rise of craggy hills and buttes forested with pine. The deep canyons were great, narrow chasms of windswept rock, some of them brush-covered, others bare, worn smooth by the slow turning of countless centuries of severe weather made all the harsher by extremes of heat and cold.

The smell of raw iron mingled with the scent of the pines as the quiet afternoon whispered a forecast of snow. To the north, clouds were piling up in tall, mighty fortresses of black and gray.

Fletcher rode steadily, for now letting the buckskin set the pace as it eagerly homed toward the Lazy R and its warm barn.

He was in need of coffee but had none, hopefully something Judith would rectify when they met.

The topmost spires of the Badlands barrier had just risen into view to the east when Fletcher stopped and checked his back trail. Nothing was moving. The rising wind stirred some feathery white plumes from the surface of the snow, and the pines moved and whispered restlessly. But he saw no sign of life, animal or human.

He kicked his horse into motion again—and a giant fist struck him hard in the chest.

Fletcher was blown off his horse, crashing on his back into the snow. He heard the distant boom of a rifle, the sound finally catching up with the bullet. He'd been hit hard.

He rolled on his stomach and saw blood staining the side of his mackinaw, a dull red patch that was spreading as rapidly as his strength was draining.

The buckskin, startled, had run for a short distance and now stood, unconcerned, about a hundred yards away.

Fletcher drew his Colt and studied the country around him. That he'd been shot by the mysterious rifleman, he had no doubt. The question was, how badly was he hit?

Out in the open like this, he had no time to open his mackinaw and study the wound. The pain, like a hot fire, was low on his left side, but there was another, sharper pain high on his chest.

Had he been shot twice?

He'd heard only one rifle report, but there could have been two, very close together.

Fletcher transferred his gun to his left hand and shoved his right inside his mackinaw. His gloved fingers came away bloody, confirming a second wound. That fact filled him with concern not unmixed with fear.

He was miles from the Lazy R. This lovely but merciless country could kill a weakened man very quickly.

Within the limit of Fletcher's vision, nothing stirred. The rifleman, confident of his aim, had fired and seen him fall. He would figure his work was done and ride away.

Perhaps.

Fletcher had to get out of the open, where he was an easy target, and into the trees. He tried to rise, stumbled and stretched his length on the ground, the pain in his side spiking into him like a red-hot knife.

He rose again, and this time managed to stay on his feet. His Colt ready, he tried for his horse, staggering like a drunken man, the reeling horizon of hills, canyons and trees tilting this way and that as if he were on the heaving deck of a storm-tossed ship.

The buckskin, scenting blood, crow-hopped nervously away from him. Fletcher whispered reassuringly to the animal as he got closer. But the horse would have none of it. To remain in this place was to smell blood and endure more snow, the first flakes already falling. Beyond, across the grass, lay his warm barn. The buckskin made his choice and ran, stirrups flying, until he was lost from Fletcher's sight.

The gunfighter cursed horses in general and the buckskin in particular. He knew with terrible certainty that to be out here in this vast wilderness without a horse was a death sentence.

But it was not in Buck Fletcher to give up so easily.

The trees were close, growing thickly on a low hillside, and he painfully staggered across the snow, fell, picked himself up, then fell again. The pain of the wound in his side was a living thing, gnawing savagely at him, and his chest felt like it had been hit by a sixteen-pound sledgehammer.

He rose and stumbled forward for a few steps, then again pitched face first into the ground. Fletcher lay there for a few moments, stunned, gasping for breath, his teeth gritted against the pain in his side and chest. He glanced over at the aspen and the scattered pine. Not far. He could make it.

This time he did not attempt to walk. He crawled forward on his belly, leaving a long streak of blood to mark his path.

Closer now.

Fletcher reached the trees and crawled among them, burrowing through the slender trunks and underbrush like a wounded animal hunting a hole in which to die. He grabbed the trunk of an aspen and hauled himself painfully to his feet. Just a few yards to his right, a deep, narrow gorge had been carved by water runoffs from the hillside. A pine had fallen, and it lay across one rim of the gully, adding height to the shelter.

Staggering, holding on to the aspens for support, Fletcher reached the gully and half-fell, half-sat against the wall protected by the fallen pine. At least here he was out of the wind and could maybe start a small fire from the dry branches of the pine.

Fletcher reached up a hand and began to snap off small, brittle twigs. The movement flared the pain in his side, and now his broken ribs began to hurt badly. He dropped his arm, the few twigs he'd gathered falling from his fingers.

"Buck," he whispered to himself, "no doubt about

it, you're in a real fix." He lay his head against the wall of the gorge and closed his eyes. His chin slumped slowly onto his chest, and he let darkness overtake him.

Chapter 17

When Buck Fletcher woke, day had shaded into night. A few scattered flakes of snow were falling through the surrounding trees, and it had turned bitter cold.

Gritting his teeth against the pain, Fletcher struggled to his feet and again snapped off twigs and a few larger branches from the pine. Sheltered by the aspen, the branches were still dry, as were the brown pine needles that clung to them.

Fletcher gathered the twigs and pine needles together and thumbed a match to life. He cupped a shivering hand around the match, coaxing the needles into flame.

His first attempt produced nothing but a thin curl of smoke that died almost as soon as it was born.

He tried again.

This time the pine needles caught, and he quickly fed them tiny pieces of branch. Flames rose from the fire, and Fletcher laid on some more twigs and, when it seemed the fire was strong enough, some thicker branches.

He could have covered his campfire with his hat. Small as it was, it produced little heat, but it was enough to ward off at least some of the bone-numbing chill. But he would need more wood to keep the fire going—something that might prove an impossible task.

Gingerly, as he grew a little warmer, Fletcher shrugged out of his mackinaw. His side immediately began to bleed profusely as the coat pulled the blood-crusted shirt with it, tearing open the wound again.

Fletcher unbuttoned his shirt and looked down at the wound on his chest. He was puzzled for a few moments. Then it dawned on him what had happened.

The rifleman's bullet had hit the quartz in his shirt pocket, driving sharp fragments into his chest. But the gold-laden quartz had been tough and resilient enough to deflect the bullet. The heavy round had then ranged downward and torn his left side wide open, a deep gash that reached from just under his ribs to his belt.

The tremendous impact of the high-powered bullet hitting the quartz had knocked Fletcher from his horse and fooled the rifleman into thinking he was dead when he hit the ground.

It had been close, and he'd been incredibly lucky. But Fletcher knew that, weak as he was, there were still no guarantees. The bushwhacker's bullet could yet do its work—only more slowly.

He pulled on his mackinaw and fed more twigs to the fire, a small spark of comfort insignificant against a vast night of darkness and bitter cold.

Loss of blood made Fletcher drowsy. He dozed on and off, feeding the fire from his meager stock of twigs on the few occasions when he was awake.

Finally he fell into a deep sleep. He woke to a gray dawn, his fire burned down to a dismal circle of ash.

Fletcher was chilled and stiff, and the pain in his side had not lessened. He rose awkwardly to his feet and looked around. It had snowed a little during the night, adding maybe an inch to the white covering that stretched endlessly in all directions.

Tracks on the edge of the tree line showed where wolves had come close in the night then turned away, the fire and the man smell making them uneasy.

It didn't take much logic to convince Fletcher that he could not stay where he was. To do so was to die of cold and exposure. He would have to make it to the Lazy R on foot—if his fading strength could hold out that long.

He looked over the fallen pine and saw what he was looking for, a thick branch that had been one of the lower limbs of the tree. The branch was dry, but even so, it used up about all of his remaining strength to break it free of the trunk, the wood splintering as he worked it loose. He stripped off most of the smaller branches and ended up with a staff about six feet long and a couple of inches around. It would give him some support during his long walk.

Leaning heavily on the stick, Fletcher made it out of the trees and back onto the flat grassland. The snow was several inches thick underfoot. It was deep enough to slow him some, but not enough to cause a real problem.

Buttoning the mackinaw tight around his neck, Fletcher started out across the snow-covered buffalo grass, a tall man who many times stumbled and fell and was all but lost against the magnificent backdrop of mountains and sky. He knew very well that the glorious beauty of the land disguised its indifferent cruelty and unforgiving nature, and these things he accepted. He was the intruder here. Why should the land care if he lived or died?

Fletcher struggled on through most of the morning. He was fast reaching the limits of even his great endurance and calculated he had maybe a dozen miles yet to walk before he reached the Lazy R.

If the snow held off, he might make it. If he was lucky. Very lucky.

He walked on, staggering now with exhaustion, the blood from his side trickling down his leg all the way into his boot. Now and then he stopped and leaned on his staff to rest, and once he dozed off, wakening with a sudden jolt of pain when he crashed to the ground.

Above his head, the clouds had parted. The sun glared on the snow, burning into his eyes so that he could hardly open them wide enough to see where he was going.

Fletcher had no idea how far he'd come. The land stretched endlessly before him as if it had no beginning and no end.

He walked on.

He was dependent on the staff more and more, leaning most of his weight on the pine branch as his strength gave out. The sun was still far from its noon point in the sky when he stumbled into the shallow depression of an old buffalo wallow. He leaned even more heavily on the stick to climb up the other side, and suddenly the dry branch snapped in half with a loud crack, pitching him violently to the ground.

Fletcher lay there stunned for a few moments, unwilling to get to his feet again.

The pine branch had served him well, but now it was useless.

He wasn't going to make it.

When nightfall came, it would get much colder, and he'd be forced back into the trees. Did he have the strength to find wood and build another fire?

Fletcher shook his head. He knew he couldn't survive another night out here, not as weak as he was.

He lay on his back in the buffalo wallow as long minutes passed. He felt a drowsiness come over him, and with it a pleasant warmth. There was no longer pain. He was slipping away, easing gently into a welcoming slumber, drifting . . . drifting . . . drifting . . .

No!

Fletcher struggled to a sitting position, and immediately the pain in his chest and side hammered viciously at him again.

He would not allow himself to just give up and die on the prairie. That was a dog's death. If death came for him, he'd face it standing on his own two feet, fighting with every last ounce of his strength.

Groaning, Fletcher rose and stumbled forward. He climbed out of the wallow on his belly, then got to his feet again. Behind him, the snow was marked red with his blood, but he didn't notice, and he didn't care.

He walked on.

Noon came and went, and the morning slowly brightened into afternoon. Fletcher's eyes were red-rimmed from the glare of the sun on the snow. When he blinked, it felt like the lids were grinding on broken glass.

Walking, stumbling, falling, rising again. That became his pattern, and with it the pain gnawed constantly at him, devouring him from the inside, sapping his strength more and more.

He was not covering much ground because his pace was slow, and he dreaded the approaching night, knowing it would come all too soon, and with it the cold and the darkness.

Once again he stumbled, falling flat on his face. When he looked up, blinking against the sun, Colonel Jonathan Ward stood there, hands on his hips, glaring down at him angrily.

Fletcher's hand went to his h in a salute. "My guns are ready, sir," he said.

"Damn it all, Major Fletcher," Ward said, "I must admit I'm distressed and surprised to see you in this condition. The Rebs are pressing hard on my left flank, and I fear it will be turned unless you carry out my orders and get your horse battery to the heights. You must give the 83rd Pennsylvania some artillery support."

"I'm limbered up and ready to move out, Colonel," Fletcher said. "I've . . . I've been shot through and through, and I'm sore wounded, you see."

"No excuses, Major, please. Now get on your feet at once and see to your battery."

Fletcher struggled to his feet, his hand once again coming to his hat in a salute.

But this couldn't be happening. Colonel Ward was mortally wounded at Chickamauga. He'd been with him when he died. The colonel's arm and leg had been amputated, and he'd passed away in a field hospital an hour after the surgery.

Fletcher blinked again. There was no one there, just the prairie grass and the pine-covered hills. A few fat flakes of snow fell lazily from the sky, mocking his weakness and the unraveling of his mind.

His hand dropped from his hat brim. He pulled the collar of his mackinaw closer around his neck, holding it in place with his right hand. Snow rimmed his eyebrows and lay white and thick on his mustache so that he looked like a man made of frost.

His short, gasping breaths smoking in the air, he walked on.

An hour later, riders appeared in the distance. Fletcher's eyes were so sore and inflamed he almost didn't see them, and for a moment he believed they might be another hallucination. But then the riders stopped, standing on their stirrups, looking at him. The three men swung their horses around and rode toward him at a fast gallop.

As the men reined up, Fletcher lifted a hand in greeting, then dropped it again. One of the riders was the gunfighter Tex Lando, and the other was a Lazy R hand Fletcher didn't know. But there was no mistaking the man who led them.

It was Higgy Conroy.

Chapter 18

"Well, well, well, lookee here." Conroy smiled, his snake eyes ugly. "Boys, we caught ourselves a real prize. Mr. high-and-mighty Buck Fletcher his ownself."

Fletcher looked up at the man sitting the paint horse and tried to focus his thoughts.

Why was Conroy riding with the Lazy R? It didn't make sense. Unless Conroy was playing both sides. Or had he already moved in and taken over Judith's ranch and the PP Connected?

Had he been the mystery man behind the range war the whole time?

Fletcher didn't know, and he was too weak and hurting to think the thing through.

He shook his head. He'd study on it some other time. Maybe tomorrow, when he felt better.

Vaguely, he became aware of Conroy's voice.

"Now you don't have a woman's skirts to hide behind, Fletcher," he was saying. "But it don't hardly seem fair to draw down on you, seein' as how you're half-dead already."

Blinking, desperate to get a clear picture of the gunman, Fletcher whispered weakly, the words coming slow, "Don't let that stop you, Conroy."

Fletcher rubbed his eyes with the back of his gloved hand, trying to focus. But in that instant, Conroy pulled his gun, and Fletcher found himself looking into the muzzle of the gunman's Colt.

"Now, it don't seem hardly fair to kill a dead man," Conroy mused as though to himself, but Tex Lando laughed, and the other hand was grinning. "But then, I dearly want to be known as the man who put a bullet into the great gunfighting legend, Buck Fletcher."

Conroy rubbed his chin with the fingers of his left hand. "Mmm, what to do? What to do?"

Fletcher's mackinaw was buttoned shut, and he realized it would slow him if he went for his gun . . . as if he weren't slowed enough already from weakness and loss of blood. He was bucking a stacked deck, and he knew it.

Playing for time, he said, "Conroy, what have you done with Judith Tyrone?"

The gunman shrugged. "Me? Why, nothing. She was hale and hearty and happy as a pup with two tails when I saw her just this morning."

"You're a liar, Conroy," Fletcher snapped, swaying on his feet. The gunman, warm in a sheepskin coat and wool scarf, was an indistinct blur above him. "What did you do to her?"

Conroy shook his head. "There you go, calling me a liar—and in front of my friends an' all." The gunman, his snake eyes cold, sighed and said, "Well, Fletcher, I don't want to kill you right now. That would be way too quick. But I do want to put a bullet into you, so—"

Conroy fired, and Fletcher hit the ground as the gunman's bullet smashed into his right shoulder. Desperation growing in him, Fletcher sat up and clawed for his gun, but a loop snaked through the air and settled around his chest, pinioning his arms to his sides as it was drawn tight.

"Here, Hig!" Lando yelled, tossing the grinning

gunman the end of the rope. "Why don't you take this feller for an El Paso sleigh ride!"

Conroy yelled "Heeehaw!" and wrapped the rope around his saddle horn. He kicked his paint into a run, and Fletcher was dragged behind, bouncing over the uneven ground just a few feet from the pony's flashing, steel-shod hooves.

The gunman unmercifully rowelled his horse into a fast gallop, and Fletcher skidded, spinning wildly, across the snow-slicked grass. The ground was not as smooth as it appeared. Despite its covering of snow, there were plenty of ridges and furrows, and here and there sharp rocks tore viciously into Fletcher's sides and back as he was dragged, tumbling and bouncing, over them.

The mackinaw offered him some protection, but when Conroy galloped back to his grinning companions, it seemed he too had noticed that fact.

"Take that coat off him," he yelled. "And his boots and guns."

Lando dismounted and roughly tore off Fletcher's mackinaw and unbuckled his guns while the other Lazy R hand yanked off his boots.

"Yeeehaw!" Conroy yelled. He spurred his horse again, dragging Fletcher at the end of a tightly vibrating rope. This time, without the protection of the wool coat, Fletcher began to get torn up badly as he jerked and spun behind Conroy's galloping horse. His arms and hands were scraped raw and bloody, as were his back and chest, and the wound in his side had opened up, staining his entire shirt bright scarlet.

Conroy dragged Fletcher this way and that across the ground until he tired of the game. He rode back to the other two men and dropped the end of the rope onto Fletcher's torn body.

"He ain't going to bother anybody ever again," he grinned. "I'd say he's through."

"Want me to finish him off, Hig?" the Lazy R hand asked eagerly. "Should I put a bullet into him?"

"No, leave him, Eddie," the gunman replied. "Let him crawl off somewhere and find a hole where he can die like a dog."

Through swollen eyes, Fletcher saw them leave, Conroy whooping as he swung the bloody, tattered mackinaw around his head.

"You made a mistake, Conroy," he whispered, his breath coming in short, agonized gasps. "You should have killed me."

There was no question of walking now.

When Conroy and his gunmen were out of sight, Fletcher crawled forward on his belly. The Lazy R could not be that far away.

The shoulder wound made his right arm useless, and he used his left elbow to pull himself along, ignoring the savage pain in his side.

The snow where he crawled was stained by long rusty streaks of blood, a narrow, furrowed road leading to nowhere.

A hunting coyote trotted out of the trees, then stood stock still watching Fletcher. He tilted his nose, nostrils flaring, scenting blood in the wind. The little predator trotted closer, its normal fear of humans all but forgotten, instinctively recognizing this one as badly hurt and probably defenseless.

Fletcher lay on his right side and saw only a blurred shape carefully stalking him. Only when the animal got closer did he recognize it as a coyote. Was he hallucinating again? He'd heard of people being attacked by coyotes, but such attacks were very rare, if they ever really happened.

The coyote stopped, sniffed the air again, then ran forward quickly. The animal sank its teeth into Fletcher's left leg, then just as quickly sprang back again.

Fletcher yelled and kicked out with his foot, but the coyote was fast and crow-hopped out of reach.

The animal darted in to attack again, snapping at Fletcher's face. He swung at the animal and missed, and again it trotted out of reach.

"Get away from me, you stupid varmint!" he yelled.

This time, alarmed by the man's voice, the animal backed off a dozen yards, watching intently, head cocked, as Fletcher began to pull himself forward again. The coyote kept pace with him, biding his time, attacking, teeth bared, only when he saw an opening, then scampering quickly away.

The animal's hit-and-run tactics began to tell on Fletcher. His arms and legs, already torn up from being dragged behind Conroy's horse, were bleeding here and there from bite wounds.

There had been plenty of rocks around when he was being dragged, but now his hands frantically probed the snow around him and found nothing.

Again and again the coyote attacked, snarling in frustration, wanting to end this quickly. Unable to rip at Fletcher's belly as it did its natural prey, the animal bit whatever part of the man was closest to him: his arm, leg, back.

It began to snow harder, flakes falling from a sky that was rapidly darkening into night.

The coyote, anxious now to immobilize this human, attacked more frequently over the next two hours, hunger driving him to take greater and greater risks.

Dragging himself along painfully, bleeding from a dozen bites, Fletcher made for the trees.

Snarling and angry, the coyote followed, trotting alongside him, darting in to attack whenever he saw an opening.

Now that the sun had dropped, the night had turned cold. Fletcher shivered uncontrollably. His feet were numb in their wet socks, and his shirt and pants were sodden from the snow.

He had lost a lot of blood, and he was weakening fast.

Fletcher had always thought he'd die on a saloon floor, gun in hand following one hell-blazing moment of violence. But he'd been wrong. All along, he'd been destined to provide supper for a hungry coyote.

The irony of it all made him laugh out loud. He tilted his head back and roared, crazed peal after peal echoing among the silent hills.

Suddenly made wary by this new and unexpected development, the coyote drew off a few yards to consider its implications.

But, sensing that the man's strength was rapidly failing, it decided to grow bolder, attacking more and more often, its bites no longer mere nips but savage attacks by fangs that bit and held, trying to tear this obstinate victim apart.

Fletcher kept yelling at the animal, kicking out whenever he could, but his attempts were feeble, and the coyote instinctively knew that the time of the kill was close.

Crawling much slower now, Fletcher saw the tree line only a few yards away. He believed he must be among the Woodville Hills and that the Lazy R lay to the west. There was no chance of making it there tonight.

In fact, there was no chance of making it there at all.

Maybe he should just let the coyote take him. That was nature's way and the way of this land. The strong survived, and the weak perished. That had been long ago ordained, and there could be no changing of it.

But it was not in Fletcher to give up so easily. Hate was driving him now, the desire to avenge himself on

Higgy Conroy and the two who rode with him. And in Fletcher's world, hate, the most primitive of all emotions, was a powerful force. The three had tortured him and left him to die alone like a wounded animal.

He would not let that happen. He would not die this way.

He crawled forward, the coyote snapping at him, confident now. Fletcher's left hand, pushing through the snow, hit something hard. He dug the object out with frantic fingers. It was a rock, a piece of hard volcanic stone, heavy and jagged, tossed onto the plain eons ago when the smoking land was still forming, red hot with lava.

A man wounded and unarmed is prey. But a man armed, even with just a rock, is a different proposition entirely.

When the coyote darted in to attack, Fletcher swung the rock in his fist. He missed the animal, and it took only a single step backward before darting in again, going for Fletcher's face.

He swung the rock again, and this time connected. The heavy stone smashed into the coyote's shoulder blade just above the left front leg, and the animal yelped in pain and tumbled into the snow. It got to its feet quickly and drew back, teeth bared in a frustrated snarl.

There are clearly defined limits to coyote courage, and this animal had reached them. The human had gone from victim to aggressor. He had the capacity to inflict pain.

Fletcher pulled back his left arm and threw the rock, hitting the animal in the ribs. There was not much power behind the throw, but it was enough.

The coyote yelped and ran, its tail between its legs, and was soon lost in the trees, where perhaps there was easier prey.

Fletcher lifted his head and roared in triumph. It was a primordial sound, more animal than human, a ritual cry torn from his throat that had its origins in the darkest recesses of the human subconscious, its roots stretching back to the dawn of time and ancestors who hunted great tusked beasts using lances tipped with chipped stone.

Bleeding, hurting, drifting in and out of consciousness, Fletcher dragged himself into the trees.

The night was cold, the snow falling steadily. There were dead leaves lying among the aspens and loose underbrush, and Fletcher reached into his pocket for matches, thinking to start a fire. But he found only two, both of them wet and useless.

Shivering violently, he burrowed deep into the tangled underbrush, pulling leaves over him. Weak and badly wounded as he was, he managed to drag only a few leaves over his chest and belly, and they provided little warmth.

Snow drifted from the treetops, lying in thick patches here and there among the aspen roots, and frost was forming on their trunks.

Lying on his back, trying to control the uncontrollable shaking of his body, Fletcher calculated the temperature must be hovering at around zero. He was numb from the neck down, and frost was thick on his eyebrows and mustache.

Vainly he tried to drag more leaves over him, then gave up, the effort exhausting him even more. He was tormented by visions of the cabin on the Two-Bit, its warm fire, stew bubbling in the pot and the welcoming smell of coffee.

He closed his eyes, so used up he drifted off into a restless, pain-wracked sleep.

At some time during the long night, his parents came to him, asking him where were their graves, complaining that the markers were long gone.

"I don't know!" Fletcher called out aloud, a sound that startled the night animals as they scurried around the forest floor. "It was so long ago."

A Sioux without hands stood over him, holding up his bloody stumps, wailing for things lost, and then big, laughing Sergeant Shamus Mulrooney, killed at Shiloh, took his place. The sergeant saluted and told him that the battery was limbered up and ready to move out.

Colonel Jonathan Ward appeared at Mulrooney's elbow. "On your feet, Major Fletcher," he said. "The battle is won, and it is time we were moving on."

Fletcher tossed and turned under his thin blanket of leaves, his mouth moving in soundless whispers. Around him snowflakes drifted like white feathers, silent among the trees, and the night grew colder.

"Beggin' your pardon, Major, but you really must come with us," Sergeant Mulrooney pleaded. "You have suffered many wounds and grievous harm, but your battles are over, and the time of peace is at hand."

Slowly, painfully, Buck Fletcher struggled to his feet. "I am ready, Colonel," he said. And to Mulrooney: "Mount the men, Sergeant. Let us move out."

Wakefulness, driven by the cold, came to Fletcher as he stood among the aspen trees.

The night had gone, replaced by a gray dawn, and still the snow fell. Fletcher had no way of knowing how close to death he was, and, if he had known, he would have cared little. He was a man at the end of his strength, and he no longer had a grip on reality, drifting between hallucinations, wandering, stumbling, falling among the trees.

The land around him lay quiet and beautiful in its snowy mantle, uncaring of him, offering him nothing.

"Fletcher! Buck Fletcher!"

Fletcher heard the voice and peered out from the trees at the flatland. Two people sat their horses, standing in the stirrups and looking in his direction.

They had come for him! Higgy Conroy was back!

Panic and terror gripped Fletcher. He ran, falling, getting up, falling again among the trees, the fear growing in him. They would hurt him again, drag him behind a horse then feed him to the coyotes.

He lurched against an aspen, resting his fevered brow on the frosty bark. The battery wasn't limbered. The guns were scattered, the horses gone. Sergeant Mulrooney stood before him, his face white as chalk. "Our line is broken, Major! Flee for your life!"

Fletcher tried to run, stumbled and fell, then rose painfully to his feet again. He heard distant bugles as the Reb cavalry came on hard and fast.

The riders were almost upon him.

"Go away!" he screamed. "I don't want to be fed to the coyotes!"

He ran blindly through the trees. Then, when his strength could take him no farther, he fell headlong. The ground opened up under him, and he was plunging deep into a mine shaft lined with glittering quartz. Little Chinese men in cone-shaped hats laughed and prodded at him with sharp sticks, and then, looking down, he saw far below him a lake of fire.

He screamed. And screamed again.

Chapter 19

Buck Fletcher woke.

He was staring up at a ceiling familiar to him: rough pine planks nailed together in a shallow inverted V, other beams acting as crosswise supports.

He turned his head and saw Pa's stove warming him with its deep cherry-red glow. He smelled coffee and something else . . . the subtle fragrance of a woman's perfume.

He was in the cabin at Two-Bit, and he had no idea how he'd gotten here. A man's voice came to him then.

"Ah, our patient is awake."

Matt Baker's smiling face swam into view above the bunk where Fletcher lay. "How do you feel?"

"Like hell," Fletcher replied sincerely.

Baker nodded. "The bullet in your shoulder was deep," he said. Then, matter-of-factly: "I had to dig it out from the other side. Made the cut just above your shoulder blade. Then I spent the best part of a day picking little chunks of quartz out of your chest. Tricky," Baker added. "But I had some experience of doctoring when I rode with the Texas Rangers a spell back, and it all ended quite well, I think."

Baker was wearing his gun, and he looked tired. "That shot to the shoulder saved your life though," he said. "Savannah and I heard it while we were out searching for you. It led us to your hideout in the trees—eventually."

"Savannah? Is Savannah here?" Fletcher asked incredulously.

The woman, even more beautiful than Fletcher remembered, stepped beside Baker. "I'm here, Buck. And I don't plan to leave ever again."

Fletcher struggled to a sitting position. "Your . . . your memory?"

Savannah bit her lip. "Buck, I've something to tell you. But wait until you've had some food. It will help you regain your strength."

Fletcher ran a hand over the thick stubble on his chin. "How long . . ."

"Six days," Baker said. "Hell, man, I thought we'd lost you a time or two. It was mighty close."

"You mean I've been lying here, flat on my back, for six days?"

"On your back, sometimes on your side, but always flat, yes. And six days, yes."

Fletcher shook his head. "Hell, it seems all I've done since I came back to the Dakota Territory is sleep for days at a time." He glanced out the window, where lingering shadows clung to the surrounding pines. He had no idea if it was day or night.

"What time is it?" he asked Baker.

"Close to daybreak." The man pulled out his pocket watch. "Five-thirty, to be exact."

The pup jumped onto the bed and began to lick Fletcher's face. The big man rubbed the dog's head and said, "Hey, how are you, little feller?"

"You know," Baker said, smiling. "You ought to give that animal a name."

Fletcher shook his head. "He doesn't care what I name him. Probably has one for himself all made up already."

"I'd call him Lucky," Baker said. "Like you, he's lucky to be alive."

Savannah brought a bowl of thick soup and sat on the side of the bunk. "Open wide," she said. "I'm going to feed you."

"No need for that." Fletcher grinned weakly. "I think I can manage."

Baker and Savannah watched him eat. When the bowl was empty, the young woman refilled it. Fletcher ate that too.

Savannah brought him some coffee, and Baker dropped tobacco, papers and matches onto the bunk. "I know you're a smoking man," he said. "Never took to the habit myself."

He watched Fletcher build a smoke, then said, "Want to tell us what happened?"

Fletcher thumbed a match into flame, lit his cigarette, then, as briefly as he could, told Baker and Savannah about his visit to the Lazy R and the raid on the PP Connected. "On my way back, I found a quartz seam running right through a butte on Connected range," he said. "I figure there might be a million dollars worth of gold in that seam. Maybe a heap more."

Then, trying his best to understate it, he told how he'd been shot by the mysterious rifleman, then shot again by Higgy Conroy and dragged behind the gunman's horse.

"After Conroy left, I made it into the trees where you found me, I guess," he said. "Though I had to tangle with a hungry coyote before I got there."

Baker nodded. "Figured on something like that. In addition to your other miseries, and they're considerable, you've got bite marks all over you."

Fletcher finished his cigarette and looked around. "Use the soup bowl. I'll wash it out later," Savannah said.

He did as he was told, stubbing out the butt in the bowl, then said, "Okay, how come you two were searching for me?"

Weak and light-headed as he was, Fletcher noted the look that passed between Baker and Savannah. He got the impression that these two knew each other, not just from meeting here in the Territory, but going back a ways. That puzzled him and put him on guard.

"We'd ridden down to see Amy Prescott," Baker said finally. "I'm real surprised we didn't pass you on the trail."

"It's a big country," Fletcher said. "And I kept mostly to the trees."

"Well, when we got to the PP Connected, I guess I don't need to tell you what we found."

Fletcher nodded. "I know what you found: the ranch destroyed, the winter feed burned. But I don't believe that was any of Judith Tyrone's doing." The gunfighter struggled to a sitting position, wincing as the pain in his side and shoulder stung him mercilessly.

Again Baker and Savannah exchanged a darting look, and again Fletcher wondered at it.

"Amy told us you'd ridden out earlier that morning, but as it was getting on to dark, we spent the night and then took off after you at sunup," Baker said. He shook his head. "That little lady sure doesn't cotton to you, Buck. She blames you for what happened to her ranch— says you're in cahoots with Judith Tyrone."

"She's wrong about that, and I told her so," Fletcher said. "I was just as surprised as the rest of them by the attack."

Baker studied Fletcher's face intently for a few moments, reading something, then said, "Anyhow, I figured you'd ridden back here. But then we heard a shot and did some serious searching, quartering back and forth across the whole area. Didn't find anything though.

"We made camp and tried again at first light. An hour or so later we saw a wild man running half-nekkid in the trees, a ranny wide in the shoulders and downright homely, and I said to myself, 'That's just got to be ol' Buck.' And so it was. Savannah and I loaded you onto the back of her horse, and, well, here you are, and here we are."

"The wild man thanks you," Fletcher said dryly. Then, more sincerely: "You saved my life."

Baker nodded. "Strangely enough, like I said already, Higgy Conroy saved your life. If he hadn't plugged you, we may never have found you."

Savannah sat on the edge of the bunk. "Buck, are you sure that butte with the gold is on PP Connected land?"

Fletcher smiled. "Sure I'm sure. I was there."

"Then that explains a lot," Savannah said, her eyes bleak.

"What do you mean?" Fletcher asked.

Baker said, "Judith Tyrone is assembling tons of heavy mining equipment at the Lazy R: drills and scalers, support timbers and some mighty big wagons to haul them. Not only that, but she's been hiring miners, teamsters and Chinese laborers by the dozen.

"She means to have that gold, Buck. It will make her a lot richer a lot faster than selling tough range beef in Deadwood."

Fletcher shook his head. "No, that impossible. Judith Tyrone would never—"

"Buck, listen to me," Savannah interrupted urgently. "You asked me earlier about my memory, and the answer to that question is—I never really lost it." She reached out and touched Matt Baker lightly on the hand.

"Buck, Matt and I are Pinkerton agents. Matt's been an agent for six years, and as for me, well, this is my first case. Somehow or other, Judith Tyrone got wind of the fact that I was asking some highly personal questions around Buffalo City and set her hired killer on me, the man with the high-powered rifle. I don't know who gave her the information, but I suspect it was that English landscape painter. He and Judith are mighty close.

"When you found me in the snow that day, I was running from her hired killer, trying to make it to Deadwood, where there was law and I'd be safer."

Fletcher, his face stiff as his anger grew, asked roughly, "What about your memory?"

"After you saved my life out there, I put it around that I'd completely lost my memory. I thought it was the only way to get Judith Tyrone and her killer off my trail.

"Later, when I left you in Buffalo City, I was acting on orders from Matt. He told me I'd be safer if I got clear out of the Territory." She smiled. "I got as far as Cheyenne and then came back a week ago. Buck, I didn't feel right about leaving you here to face Judith Tyrone. She's more than a match for you, more than a match for any of us if we stand alone."

Fletcher shook his head. "I don't believe a word of this. I think you two are in cahoots, and maybe that butte full of gold is the reason."

"No, Buck," Savannah said. "It's not like that at all."

But Fletcher was beyond listening to reason. "Maybe it's you two who are behind the whole thing: the range war and all the killings."

"Right," Baker said, "and that's why we brought you all the way here and worked for days to save your ornery hide."

The logic of that hit Fletcher, and he looked from Baker to Savannah, his face puzzled, his anger easing.

"Listen, Buck," Baker said. "Judith Tyrone, sometimes known as Edith Wilson, Anna Grant, Mary Ann Branch and many others, is afraid of nothing and cares for no one except herself."

Fletcher opened his mouth to protest, but Baker held up a hand. "Listen to me until I'm through. Savannah and I have followed Judith's trail all the way from Boston. She's been married six times, and all of her husbands—men decades older than herself, with money in the bank—died under mysterious circumstances.

"Oh, the law investigated, of course, hinting darkly of poison and such, but nothing criminal could ever be proved. One thing Judith does very well is cover her tracks.

"But the son of her last victim wasn't willing to give up so easily. He asked the Pinkerton Detective Agency to investigate. The job was given to Savannah and me, and we tracked Judith to Richmond, Virginia, but then we lost her for a while. About a year ago, we learned from another Pinkerton agent that she'd met an elderly rancher named Deke Tyrone in Denver and that he'd asked her to marry him. We recognized Judith's old, familiar pattern, and we followed her here."

Savannah watched Fletcher build another smoke, his face frowning in thought, then said, "Matt and I believe Judith hired a killer to murder her husband so she could inherit his ranch. She knows her looks are fading, and this was her last chance to make it big.

"But the Lazy R wasn't enough for her. She wanted more. Judith is a lady who loves to travel—London, Paris, Rome—and she's a big spender. That takes money, a lot of money, so you can imagine her joy when Pike Prescott played right into her hands. When he tried to move in on the Lazy R, she had her husband shot down and blamed it on Prescott.

"That murder gave her free and clear title to old Deke's ranch.

"Later, she got rid of Prescott too, leaving the PP Connected in the hands of a girl who's not much more than a child. Judith figured to eliminate Amy Prescott then take over the Connected and own the whole shooting match.

"As far as the law is concerned, she'd be in the clear—just a poor young widow who stood up to a powerful rancher and decided to fight for what was hers. Can you imagine Judith up there on the stand, beautiful and grieving, sobbing into a bit of lace handkerchief as she tells why she'd been forced to kill Amy Prescott in self-defense and take over the PP Connected? There isn't a jury of twelve men in the Territory who would find against her."

Matt Baker poured himself some coffee. "But the stakes got a lot bigger when she heard about the gold on PP Connected land. I figure Higgy Conroy discovered that quartz seam in the butte when he was still working for Prescott. He got a couple of miners to help him explore the seam. Then, when he realized just how huge it was, he shot them both to shut their mouths for good.

"I believe Higgy brought the news of the gold to Judith and quickly found his way into her confidence—and, if the information I'm getting is correct, into her bed."

That last shook Fletcher, but he decided to not let it show. He shook his head. "But Judith had punchers killed. She wouldn't kill her own hands."

Baker smiled grimly. "Buck, in her own sweet way, Judith Tyrone is as cold-blooded a killer as Higgy Conroy and maybe more so. There's evil in her, a total lack of compassion and empathy for the suffering of others. Maybe she was born that way, maybe life made her that way. Who knows?"

Fletcher smoked in silence for a few moments, then said, "Judith wanted me to join her, sell her my gun. If you two are telling the truth, why would her hired killer shoot at me not once but three times, and the last time come mighty close to succeeding?"

"Buck, I don't think the rifleman, whoever he is, was trying to kill you, at least not at first," Savannah said. "He was trying to scare you into thinking he was working for Pike Prescott and that Prescott wanted you dead. It was Judith's way of forcing you to side with her against the PP Connected.

"But when you refused to join her, she ordered the killer to try again—but this time for real."

Fletcher shook his head. "This is a lot of talk. Can you prove any of it?"

"No," Baker said. "Not unless we can connect Judith Tyrone to the death of her husband and the other murders."

"Buck, we're not working for the law here," Savannah said. "We're working for a Pinkerton client. But bringing Judith Tyrone to justice is what he's paying for, and he doesn't expect anything less. Nor will we settle for less."

Fletcher was silent for a few moments, thinking. Then he said, "Where is Amy Prescott?"

Baker's face was grim. "Her ranch house was burned down a couple of days ago. Then Conroy outdrew and killed her cook in a saloon in Buffalo City when the man accused him of plotting against Amy. I guess that cook set store by her, and in the end it was the death of him.

"Now she and what's left of her punchers are hiding out in the hills, though Higgy Conroy has vowed to hunt them down and kill every last man of them."

"Where's the law in all this?"

"There's still no sheriff in Buffalo City, and as far as Deputy United States Marshal C. J. Graham is concerned, the Lazy R acted only in self-defense, especially after Higgy Conroy swore on a stack of Bibles that he changed sides after Amy Prescott ordered him to murder Judith Tyrone.

"Graham issued warrants for the arrest of Amy Prescott and her men, and she and her punchers are now hunted fugitives with a price on their heads. Unless Savannah and I can save them, I doubt that any of them, including Amy, will live much longer."

Fletcher was silent for a few moments. Then he said, "It's bad luck, to tell a lie on the Bible."

Savannah's face wore a puzzled expression. "Why, yes, I suppose it is."

Fletcher smiled. "Sorry, someone I know told me that. It just came into my head. I have no idea why."

Fletcher still had the tobacco hunger. He began to roll another smoke.

"Where are Conroy and Tex Lando? And there's another gun hand rides with them, a man called Eddie."

"As far as I know, they're in Buffalo City and walking a wide path," Baker said. "Conroy and the others seem well-supplied with money, and they've been talking about how they're about to strike it rich. Now, some folks think that strange since none of them is ever seen to do a lick of work, but they've got the town so cowed, nobody dares say it."

"I had around four hundred dollars in my money belt. They're probably spending that," Fletcher said ruefully. "What about the vigilantes?"

"They've got them buffaloed too," Baker replied. "They're all married men, and they don't want to face Higgy Conroy's guns. I can't say as I blame them."

Fletcher still couldn't bring himself to believe what he'd heard. Judith Tyrone was behind all this from the very start? It just didn't seem possible.

But then he recalled that day in the cabin when

he'd kissed her. After their mouths had parted, he'd
expected to see passion in her eyes. Instead, he'd seen
only calculating coldness and a hint of triumph.

Had she been using him, just as she had used her
husband and now Higgy Conroy?

He looked from Matt Baker to Savannah. If they
were indeed Pinkerton agents, there was no doubting
their word. Would Savannah lie to him? She'd lied
about losing her memory, and then she'd run away
and left him in Buffalo City. Yet when he looked at
her now, he saw only warmth and concern . . . and
something else, something very different from Judith's
cold stare.

Love, Martha Jane Canary had called it. Was he
seeing love in her eyes? Fletcher shook his head.

That was impossible.

"Buck," Matt Baker said, interrupting his thoughts,
"Savannah and I have talked it over, and we agree
that the best thing we can do right now is find Amy
Prescott and try to protect her."

"And me?" Fletcher asked.

"You're going to lie right there in that bunk and
get well." Savannah smiled. "Leave it all to Matt
and me."

"The hell I am. I'm going after Conroy and the
other two. We have a score to settle. Then I'm going
to talk to Judith Tyrone and get the straight of all
this."

Baker shook his head. "Buck, we gave you the
straight of it. Anyhow, you're going nowhere. You're
all shot to pieces. You can't face Conroy in this state.
He's lightning fast with a gun, and he'll kill you for
sure."

For the first time, Fletcher looked at the thick ban-
dages covering his side and shoulder. When he tried
to move, he felt only pain and stiffness.

As if reading his thoughts, Baker said, "I had to stitch up your side. Did it with a needle and thread while you were unconscious. If those stitches rip loose, you'll bleed again, and pretty soon you'll collapse. I don't know how you'd even get up on a horse."

Fletcher threw the blanket aside, only to discover with a shock that he was naked, his legs covered in angry red wheals from coyote bites.

He covered up quickly, feeling his face redden, and said to Savannah, "Woman, bring me my clothes."

Savannah looked helplessly at Baker. The man shrugged. "Do it. He won't get far."

Savannah left for the other room, then returned holding a bundle of clothing in her arms.

"Your own clothes were beyond hope," she said. "Matt bought you these. I think they'll fit."

The young woman laid underwear, shirt, pants, socks and a pair of store-bought boots on the bed. With these were canvas and leather suspenders and a new wool mackinaw of red-checkered plaid.

"We found your hat, but that was about all," Baker said, grinning.

"My guns?"

"Over there on the table. A new gunbelt, holster and .44–40 Colt and a used but serviceable Winchester in the same caliber."

Fletcher nodded, looking up at Baker. "I owe you."

Baker nodded. "You sure do. Around fifty dollars I'd say, give or take the odd penny or two."

"Like I told you," Fletcher said, unwilling to let it go, "I owe you, and not only for the clothes and guns."

"It was a pleasure, trust me," Baker said quickly, trying his best to end it.

Fletcher nodded. "Just so you know." He raised a quizzical eyebrow. "I don't suppose you bought me a horse?"

"I suppose I did," Baker said. "Not that you're fit to ride him." He waved toward the barn. "He's back there. An American stud a bit smaller than your old one, but he's game enough: got plenty of giddyup and not much whoa. I'm told he can jump a three-bar fence, but I haven't tried him."

"Where . . . where did you get him?" Fletcher asked incredulously.

"From a gambler by the name of Whitcroft. He has quite a sideline selling horses. 'Buy 'em cheap, sell 'em dear' is Mr. Whitcroft's motto."

Baker smiled. "While you were lying there refighting the War of Northern Aggression—on the wrong side, I might add—I rode into Buffalo City and talked to him." The man's smile widened. "Savannah feared for your life, fussing and fretting like womenfolk do, but I figured you were way too ornery to die and, when you woke up, you'd need a horse." He shrugged. "I guess I was right, and she was wrong."

"How much for the stud?"

"Well, he wanted two hundred dollars, but I got him down to one-fifty, and he threw in the saddle."

Fletcher shook his head. "And I thought I was a horse trader. Still, he didn't get the better of me. I only paid him one-sixty-five for the mares in the barn."

"I know," Baker smiled. "Whitcroft told me he was quite willing to go as low as one-thirty. But then he realized you were a pilgrim when it came to horse trading, and the price went up considerably. I'd say you was took."

"Seems like it," Fletcher agreed ruefully. "Maybe me and Mr. Whitcroft will have harsh words some day."

He pulled the clothes on the bunk closer to him. "Savannah, please, I need to get dressed," he said.

The woman smiled and turned her back to him. Fletcher swung his legs off the bed and stood. The entire room began to spin wildly, and he clutched desperately at the edge of the table, dizzy and suddenly nauseated.

He was weak, much weaker from loss of blood than he'd realized, and the pain in his side and shoulder, now that he was up and moving, hammered at him savagely, draining his strength even more.

Baker put an arm around Fletcher's waist, supporting him. "It's back into bed for you," he said gently.

"Leave me the hell alone!" Fletcher yelled angrily. He pushed Baker away and stood on his feet, swaying, until the room stopped reeling and finally came to a lurching halt.

Slowly, painfully, he dressed, each item of clothing its own separate ordeal that popped beads of sweat on his forehead and forced him to grind his teeth, fearful that he might cry out and disgrace himself.

Fletcher stomped into the boots. Then, guilty at how he'd yelled at Baker, he said, smiling, "Good fit."

He checked the loads in the Colt and buckled on the gunbelt, picking up the Winchester.

"It's loaded too," Baker said quietly.

Fletcher nodded. "Matt," he said, angry at himself for having to make the admission, "I don't think I can saddle my own horse."

Baker, an odd light in his eyes, said nothing. He merely nodded, then stepped outside.

Savannah and Fletcher followed a few moments later and stood in front of the cabin, waiting for Matt to bring the horse.

"I can't believe you're still determined to go after Conroy," Savannah said, her eyes blazing. "Don't you realize how weak you are?"

"I know how weak I am," Fletcher replied, struggling to smile. "I'm maybe about ten percent of the man I was when I first rode into the Territory. But that ten percent will have to be good enough."

"Let the law handle Conroy," Savannah persisted. "Matt and I will go with you and talk to Marshal Graham. We can get official documentation from Pinkerton's that he and I are who we say we are. Graham will listen to us."

Fletcher shook his head. "Savannah, Conroy and the two with him left me to die in the snow like a hurt animal, and they laughed at me while they were doing it. I can't let that pass, and I can't walk away from it. There's no place for the law in this. It's something I have to do myself."

His face set and grim, he added, "Much ill was done to me, and I must bring about the reckoning."

"Then go!" Savannah said, her eyes filling with tears. "See if I care."

She turned away from him. Fletcher reached a hand to her shoulder, but she shrugged it off, then ran into the cabin, slamming the door behind her.

"I got to hand it to you, Buck," Baker said. "You sure have a way with women."

His eyes bleak, Fletcher studied the horse Baker led. He wasn't as tall as his dead sorrel, but he had the same wide blaze on his face and the same four white stockings. He stepped light on his feet, eager for the trail.

"He'll do." Fletcher nodded approvingly.

Baker handed him the reins and then stepped back a half-dozen paces. Fletcher shoved the Winchester into the boot. He felt the ground under his feet move, and he pressed his fevered head against the cool leather of the saddle until the world righted itself again.

He was very weak, weaker than he'd first thought,

and for the first time that morning he began to have serious doubts if he could even make it to Buffalo City, let alone face Higgy Conroy.

But he had it to do, and Fletcher accepted that stark fact and all it implied.

He turned to say goodbye to Baker, but the man was watching him closely, a strange light in his eyes, his right hand very close to his gun.

"Fletcher!" he yelled.

And drew.

He was fast, very fast, and Fletcher didn't come close. His Colt hadn't even cleared the leather when he found himself looking into the muzzle of Baker's gun. A long, tense silence stretched between them. Then Baker spun the revolver, a flashing arc of silver, and let it thud back into the crossdraw holster.

"Higgy Conroy is faster than me," was all he said. "A lot faster."

Chapter 20

Buck Fletcher rode through gently rolling country past the 5,469-foot pinnacle of Pillar Peak, its rugged crest covered by a thick mantle of snow. Ahead lay Lost Gulch, and beyond, south of Bear Den Mountain, was Buffalo City.

He rode slumped in the saddle, dizzy from weakness. Once or twice he passed out, waking each time with a jolt. The stud kept walking steadily, as if sensing the dire straits of the man on his back.

The snow-covered land around him lay empty, trackless, with no sign of men, horses or cattle. The hills were lost in their own deep silence, touched by the light of the sun that had begun its long climb into a blue sky free of clouds.

Fletcher was wracked with pain, much worse now that he was riding, and only the irresistible urge to confront Higgy Conroy and the others drove him on. Matt Baker had proved to him how the weakness from his wounds had slowed his reactions. He could no longer consider himself a fast gun, yet he must face Conroy—and the snake-eyed gunman was faster than most.

So be it. What he could not do with speed, he must do with cunning. Though what the cunning might be, and where it would spring from, he had no idea.

At Lost Gulch, Fletcher stopped, dismounting heavily and awkwardly, and bathed his fevered face in a thin stream of ice-cold water splashing from the rocks. Then he drank deep and long and took time to roll and smoke a cigarette.

Later he rose and put a hand on the saddle horn, and again the world spun around him, trees, hills, sky and snow flashing past in a blur of green, blue and white.

Gradually, his brain cleared, and he got a foot into the stirrup and swung into the saddle, sudden jolts of pain a cruel reminder of just how badly shot up he was.

He turned the sorrel toward Bear Den and let him set his own pace for a while. The winter sun felt warm on Fletcher's face. He dozed off and on as he rode, finally waking when Buffalo City came in sight, the heights of the gorge around the town covered in snow.

He left his horse at the livery stable and stepped outside, the Winchester hanging loosely in his left hand.

Because of his weakened condition, he could no longer rely on the flashing speed of his draw. The rifle would have to provide the edge that would keep him alive.

And he couldn't afford to take bullets either.

Matt Baker had told him that before he left the Two-Bit.

"All shot to pieces the way you are, you can't trade hits with Conroy," Baker had said. "When you shoot, shoot straight, and make damn sure he's in no condition to shoot back."

That was a tall order, but Fletcher knew there was no other way.

The sun had climbed to its highest point in the sky, and Buffalo City was coming alive. People crowded the boardwalks, and wagons and riders crammed the muddy street. A stage pulled by six rangy mules stood outside the depot of the Black Hills Stage and Express Line, disgorging a few stiff and weary overnight travelers, their drawn, gray faces betraying the ordeal of their cramped, jolting journey.

All this Fletcher saw without interest. He'd seen similar scenes in a hundred different cow towns from Texas to Montana, and it no longer held any fascination for him.

He walked, stiff-legged and weary, toward the Hole in the Bucket Saloon. If Conroy and the others were in town, that was as good a place as any to start looking for them.

In that, Buck Fletcher was not disappointed.

When he stepped through the doors of the saloon, he saw the man called Eddie dancing in the middle of the rough, planked floor with a soft-bodied but hard-eyed blonde in a short red dress.

There was no music, but Eddie kept time by pounding his booted heels on the floor, yelling at the top of his lungs a song Fletcher had heard many times during The War Between the States.

> *Shoo fly, don't bother me,*
> *Shoo fly, don't bother me,*
> *Shoo fly, don't bother me,*
> *I belong to Company G.*

It was the saloon girl's painted smile suddenly changing to a shocked, scarlet O accompanied by a little gasp of alarm that finally drew Eddie's attention to Fletcher standing grim and terrible in the middle of the floor, his Winchester still hanging loose in his left hand.

The man's song faltered to a stop as the girl stepped warily away from him, her eyes frightened.

"Hi, Eddie," Fletcher said. "Remember me?"

Eddie's face was stricken. "You!" he gasped. "You're dead."

"Came close, Eddie," Fletcher said. "So close, I recollect you asking Conroy if you could finish me off. Well, here I am. Now's your chance."

Fletcher swayed slightly on his feet as dizziness took him again. Eddie, observant and sly as a bunkhouse rat, noted this and felt his flagging courage return. The gunman's eyes narrowed, his small-chinned face wrinkling as his mouth stretched in a sneer.

"I think maybe I'll just do that," he said. "I don't mind being known as the man who cut the great Buck Fletcher down to size. Why, I'm—"

"Are you going to talk me to death or haul your iron?" Fletcher asked grimly.

"Damn you!" Eddie yelled.

And he went for his gun.

Fletcher brought up the muzzle of the Winchester and fired. He cranked another round and fired again. Both shots hit Eddie square in the chest, the bullets clipping arcs out of the tobacco sack tag that hung from his shirt pocket. The man staggered backward, his Colt only now clearing leather. His face was stricken, unable to accept what was happening to him.

Fletcher fired again, and Eddie hit the wall of the saloon with a thud, rose on his toes, his eyes wild and afraid, and fell flat on his face.

The bartender, the man named Caleb Mills, stepped out from behind the bar and looked down at the dead gunman. This time there was no talk of vigilantes.

"That's Montana Eddie Sinclair," he said, providing the man with his only eulogy. "He's killed himself a few, though not a one of them had bullets in the front that I recall."

Fletcher felt the room spin. He stepped to the bar and leaned heavily on its polished mahogany, his breath coming in short, sharp gasps as he battled against the pain hammering at him.

After a few moments, as the world began to right itself, he looked at the bartender, the dance girl and a few idlers now clustering around Eddie Sinclair's body.

"A man rides with bad company, he reaps the whirlwind," Fletcher said. "He brought the reckoning on himself."

The bartender nodded, his normally florid face pale. "I'd say he did just that."

"Where's Higgy Conroy?" Fletcher asked.

Mills shrugged. "I don't know. He's around."

"There's another man, goes by the name of Tex Lando. Have you seen him?"

Mills' eyes flickered to the back door of the saloon. That scared, apprehensive glance lasted only an instant, but Fletcher noted it and guessed at what it implied.

"What's back there?" he asked, his voice hard and low.

"Nothing," Mills said. "Ain't nothing back there, 'cept the outhouse."

"There's a shack out there," the dance girl said, her face vindictive. "Lucy is back there with a feller. I think maybe it's your man."

"What's your stake in this?" Fletcher asked, surprised, as he fed shells into his rifle.

The girl shrugged. "I don't like Tex Lando. When he gets drunk, he likes to slap women around, and he's carved up a few in his time."

"Don't go back there, Fletcher," Mills said. "You're in no condition to draw against a gunman like Lando. He'll kill you for sure."

Fletcher ignored the man and walked to the back door of the saloon. He opened the door, then turned. "I'll take it right hard if someone comes out this door after I close it," he said.

Nobody moved.

Fletcher stepped outside and shut the door quietly behind him. A low timber-and-tarpaper shack stood about ten yards away, its single window to the front covered over with yellowing newspapers. He heard a man's raised voice, then a woman's giggle. There was a sharp slap, and the woman immediately hiccupped into silence.

Fletcher stepped softly to the door of the shack and stood listening.

"Now do like I told you and see what all the shooting was about. And while you're at it, bring me back another bottle."

It was Lando's voice.

Then the woman's again, the words slow, separated by sobs: "I'll go, Tex. You don't have to hit me again."

"Next time I tell you to do something, you jump right to it, you hear?" Lando said. "I don't take lip from no two-dollar whore."

"I'm going," the woman said. "I'll bring you back a bottle, Tex. You know I will."

"See you do." Lando laughed harshly. "Now git! Hell, maybe I missed all the fun. I bet ol' Hig has gunned him another pilgrim."

The door opened, and the girl started to step outside. Fletcher had time only to note the woman's wide, frightened eyes and the angry bruise on her right cheekbone before he grabbed her by the arm and hauled her out of the doorway.

He stepped inside and closed the door behind him.

Lando was lying on his back on an iron cot and smoking a thin cheroot, his arms behind his head.

"Do I have to slap you around again, bitch?" he snapped without looking up.

"You can try, Tex," Fletcher said quietly. "It won't be so easy with me."

The gunman sat bolt upright on the cot, his naked chest and shoulders stark white against the mahogany brown of his face and hands.

"What the hell!" Lando yelled. "We left you for dead, Fletcher."

"You made a bad mistake, Tex." Fletcher smiled without humor. "You should have killed me when you had the chance."

Lando's frantic eyes slid to the chair beside the bed where his gunbelt hung. Knowing he couldn't make it in time, he licked suddenly dry lips and decided not to try.

Fletcher nodded. "Good choice. I'd have killed you before you got halfway there, Tex."

The gunfighter stepped to the chair and lifted the gunbelt and its holstered Colt, hefting it in his hands.

"Where's Eddie?" Tex asked. "Did you kill him?"

Fletcher nodded. "Eddie paid the price for his sinful ways. He's at peace now."

Tex studied Fletcher closely, his finely honed gunfighter's instinct telling him that this man had reached the end of his rope, had tied a knot in it and was now barely hanging on.

In this he was right.

The cabin floor was lurching under Fletcher's feet, and Lando kept swimming in and out of his line of vision, now sharp and defined, now a hazy, indistinct blur. Aware of his growing weakness, Fletcher knew he must do what he'd come here to do. He was fast running out of time.

"Lando," he said, "it was your idea to drag me behind a horse. You gave Conroy the rope, and you laughed when you were doing it."

The gunman smiled. "Hell, Fletcher, that was just a prank."

"It was low down," Fletcher said, each word coming

slow and painful. "As pranks go, that one was the lowest."

Lando shook his head, grinning, playing for time. "Buck, Buck, let bygones be bygones. Hell, man, it was just a joke."

"It was no joke to me, Tex. I was the one being drug."

A few long moments of silence hung heavy and expectant between the two men. Then Fletcher said, "I'm going to give you more of a chance than you gave me, Tex." He threw the gunbelt on the cot. "Anytime you feeling like going for it, make your play."

Lando, a seasoned professional, knew every last grain of sand had run through the hourglass. The time for talk was over.

He clawed desperately for his holstered Colt.

Fletcher let him clear the leather, then shot him.

Unlike Eddie, he had no need to shoot again.

The heavy bullet took Lando square between the eyes, scarlet blood suddenly fanning high on the wall above his head. The gunman slammed back against the cot frame, its iron springs squealing shrilly in protest, then lay still.

Automatically, Fletcher ejected the spent round. The bright brass fell ringing to the wood floor of the shack, and he fed another round into the chamber.

He turned quickly, the rifle coming up fast as someone opened the door and stepped lightly inside. It was Lucy, the angry bruise on her cheek already turning a mottled black.

The whore looked at the dead man on the cot and spat. "Good riddance," she said. "Tex Lando, you weren't much."

Lucy looked at Fletcher, her eyes concerned. "Are you all right, mister?" she asked.

Fletcher nodded, swaying on his feet from exhaustion. "Two down," he whispered huskily. "One to go. Where can I find Higgy Conroy?"

The whore's eyes were hard and knowing. "Don't worry about that, mister," she said. "I got a feeling he'll find you."

Fletcher walked back into the saloon, ignoring the body of Montana Eddie Sinclair stretched out on the floor. The large crowd that had gathered parted quickly as he walked through them. Then men were running around him, dashing out the back door, anxious to see what had become of the fearsome Tex Lando.

He stopped at the bar and said to Mills, "Brandy."

The bartender nodded, brought out the bottle of Hennessy and poured Fletcher a generous shot. The gunfighter tilted the glass to his lips and drank it down in a single gulp.

The brandy hit his stomach, warming him, and immediately he felt a little better.

He was still very weak, and the pain from his wounds kept hammering at him, draining him. But at least the saloon was no longer reeling nauseatingly around him, and he could get his eyes in focus.

Matt Baker, who seemed to have thought of everything, had put money in the pockets of his pants, and Fletcher rang a dollar on the bar.

"For God's sakes, Fletcher, haven't you had enough?" Caleb Mills asked, picking up the coin. "Can't you just let it go?"

Fletcher shook his head at him. "This is a reckoning. Once it's begun, there's no ending of it. It won't be over until I kill Higgy Conroy. Or he kills me."

"Damn it all, man, you're already dead on your feet," Mills said. "You've been all shot to pieces."

This time Fletcher nodded. "I know that, but I still have it to do."

"Then do it outside," Mills snapped. "You're bad for business. There were only three big spenders in this town, and you've done shot two of them already."

Fletcher nodded, laid his glass on the counter, then stepped out of the saloon onto the boardwalk. The town was as he remembered it from the last occasion he was here, only this time, when the gunfight came, there would be no little English painter to help him and—

Wait!

Fletcher rubbed his fevered forehead, trying to dredge up something buried deep and impossibly vague from his past. Slowly, almost painfully, he remembered.

Suddenly he knew where he'd seen the little man before.

And he felt a chill run down his spine.

He was—

"Fletcher!"

Higgy Conroy stood straddle-legged across the street, his thumbs tucked into his gunbelts. The gunman was smiling confidently, relaxed and ready.

Fletcher stepped to the edge of the boardwalk. "I've come for you, Conroy," he said. "There's a reckoning to be paid."

As if by magic, frightened townspeople had cleared the busy street. Now Fletcher and Conroy stood alone, facing each other across twenty yards of mud and slushy snow.

An errant wind caught a piece of newspaper and tossed it high in the air. It hung there, fluttering, for a few moments before flapping to the street again like a wounded bird. A lean dog, his muzzle gray, lay outside the general store, head on his outstretched paws, watching what was happening with disinterested black eyes.

"Hell, I thought you'd be dead for sure by this time." Conroy smiled, his snake eyes ugly. "But I see you're only half-dead."

"You should have killed me when you had the chance," Fletcher said. "Now it's too late."

"It's never too late. I got plenty of time to do it now."

Conroy, moving easily, stepped lightly off the boardwalk onto the street.

"I'll always wonder who was faster," the gunman said. "But I guess now I'll never find out, all shot up the way you are. Must slow you some."

"I'm faster," Fletcher said. "A lot faster. On your best day you couldn't shade me, you cheap, no-good tinhorn."

"Then prove it," Conroy said, stung, his face livid. "Drop that Winchester and haul iron."

The rifle was hanging from Fletcher's left hand. He unbuttoned his mackinaw with his right and cleared the coat from his Colt. Then, slowly, he bent his knees and laid the Winchester at his feet.

A triumphant sneer stretched Conroy's thin mouth. This was going to be too easy.

But the gunman still needed an edge.

He reached for his gun first, his hand streaking downward in a blindingly fast, practiced motion.

Fletcher, in his weakened condition, was maybe half as fast that day as he'd been when he first rode into the Dakota Territory.

But it was enough.

He drew, and his gun hammered, bucking in his hand, as Conroy cleared leather. Fletcher saw two of his shots kick up little puffs of dust on the front of the gunman's shirt.

Conroy screamed in frustrated rage and staggered back. His face stiff and determined, he steadied himself and fired both guns at the same time. He fired again, and Fletcher felt a bullet burn across the outside of his right thigh.

He couldn't take hits like that!

Fletcher consciously slowed down and fired again. This time he saw blood blossom like an opening flower just above Conroy's belt buckle.

The gunman doubled over, his left arm instinctively covering his stomach as a gut-shot man will do. But he was still in the fight, firing unsteadily with the Colt in his right fist. A shot slammed into the front of the saloon, then two more splintered the boardwalk to the right and then the left of Fletcher.

Conroy tried to raise both his revolvers, but they suddenly seemed like anvils in his hands, and he pitched forward on his belly into the mud, his eyes wide and unbelieving.

He was dying and he knew it, and the man who'd killed him was still standing.

It wasn't supposed to be happening this way. He'd wanted to be known as the man who'd killed Buck Fletcher, and now that chance was slipping away and would soon be gone forever.

Driven by the instinct for revenge, Conroy raised his arm, attempting to lift his gun again, trying for one last shot.

He never squeezed the trigger. Death stilled his finger, and Higgy Conroy was no more, his arm frozen forever in its last shooting position.

The next day, they buried Higgy that way, the undertaker unable to get the stiff, outstretched arm back to his side despite breaking it with a ball peen hammer in three places.

He couldn't do anything with the look of fear and

anger on the dead man's face either; but then, no family or friends came to view the dear departed, and so in the end it didn't matter.

As for the people of Buffalo City, they came and saw and didn't care. They were building a church and a city hall and would soon have a telephone exchange and maybe streetcars.

Higgy Conroy, the feared gunman who once strutted a wide path in their town, would very soon become just a minor footnote in Buffalo City history.

Chapter 21

Buck Fletcher thumbed shells into his gun. He glanced briefly and coldly at the contorted body of Higgy Conroy lying in the street, then holstered his Colt and began to walk along the boardwalk in the direction of the hotel.

"Fletcher, wait!"

The gunfighter turned and saw Mills walking hurriedly toward him, his face flushed and determined, eyes blazing.

But this was no longer the Buck Fletcher who had ridden into Buffalo City a few short weeks before, confused and uncertain about his place in the world. He had reverted to what he once had been, a professional gunfighter, rigid and unbending, a man who must go his own way. There was no longer any give in him; nor, he told himself, would there ever be again.

That realization had come quick and unbidden in the moments before the gunfight with Conroy, and hard and uncompromising though it was, Fletcher knew there could be no turning away from what life and circumstance had made of him.

He had killed as an act of vengeance, true to his harsh code, and now he could not go forward. He could only go back.

Like a gambler desperately trying to outrun a losing

streak, Fletcher had attempted to flee his past. It had not worked. The years that lay behind a man had a way of catching up to him the moment he stopped to take a breath. And once caught, the past took a firm hold and would not let him go.

This Fletcher accepted, and he vowed that he would never again permit himself to think it through and perhaps dare to hope otherwise.

"Mills," he said, his voice flat and icy, "I will not be run out of town, and I will not be laid hands on. If you call your vigilantes, I swear to God, there will be more dead men in the street today."

The bartender, shrewd in the ways of those who wore guns, read the warning signs and backed off, suddenly fearful. In the space of less than an hour this man had visited death on Buffalo City, and now, as the clock continued to tick, he was perhaps best left alone.

"Hell, man," Mills stumbled, trying hard to reach some safe middle ground, "you're all shot to pieces. You better go see Doc Hawthorne and get patched up. You're dead on your feet your ownself."

Fletcher nodded. "That thought had occurred to me."

Hawthorne studied the wound on Fletcher's side and made an annoyed tut-tutting sound with the tip of his tongue. He probed the gunfighter's shoulder wound and the cut Conroy's bullet had opened on his right thigh.

"Been through the wars, haven't you, son?" the old doctor said.

Fletcher nodded. "Some."

"Heard the shooting; but then, since Higgy Conroy and the other two got here, gunfire hasn't been all that unusual." Hawthorne studied Fletcher's face, his faded eyes shrewd. "Ran into him, did you?"

Again Fletcher nodded. "The three of them aren't around anymore," he said.

"Figured that," Hawthorne said, smiling slightly.

He looked again at the wound on Fletcher's side. "What ham-handed quack masquerading as a physician stitched this up for you?"

Despite his desperate tiredness, a grin touched Fletcher's lips. "It's worse than that, Doc. This was done by a Pinkerton agent masquerading as a ham-handed quack."

Hawthorne shook his head. "I'm going to pull these sutures out and do the job right." He looked at Fletcher. "At least he'd the good sense to keep the entry and exit wounds on your shoulder open. Those must heal from the inside."

"How about my leg, Doc?" Fletcher asked. "It's paining me some."

"A scratch. I'll bandage it up for you."

The old man rose to his feet and opened a glass cupboard. He selected a small blue bottle from the shelf and handed it to Fletcher.

"What's this?"

"It's laudanum. It will ease the pain when I start to suture you up again."

Fletcher shook his head. "I've never been much of a one for taking medications and stuff like that. If it's all the same to you, I'll do without."

Hawthorne shrugged, his smile cold as a tomb. "Your funeral. It will hurt."

The gunfighter nodded and said grimly, "Sew away, Doc."

As the old man had predicted, the process was painful. Fletcher gritted his teeth, trying hard not to cry out.

At one point, Hawthorne looked up from his work and said, "You're very brave, you know. I mean, you don't yell and holler like some of my patients."

"Yeeeouch!" Fletcher cried loudly. He smiled. "See, Doc? I'm not that brave."

After it was over and Fletcher was bandaged up again, Hawthorne asked, "Have you ever gone to a museum and seen one of those ancient Egyptian mummies?"

Fletcher shook his head. "Can't say as I have."

"Well, believe me, you look like one," Hawthorne chuckled.

His face suddenly sober, the old physician said, "You know, by rights you should be dead. Do you know why you aren't?"

"No. Luck, I guess."

"Luck's got nothing to do with it. You're alive because you're not civilized. If you were from Back East, a banker or stockbroker or a member of some other civilized profession, right now you'd already be pushing up daisies or at least lying flat on a hospital bed earnestly talking to a preacher."

Fletcher forced another smile, knowing how insincere it must look. "Never thought of myself as being uncivilized."

"Well, you are. I've heard about you, Fletcher, and the things you've done. Sure, you might read Goethe or Cervantes or ponder the deeper meanings of the *Meditations* of Marcus Aurelius, but at heart you're as wild and uncivilized as any Apache or painted Cheyenne Dog Soldier."

Hawthorne grinned, trying to soften the criticism. "Paradoxically, it's uncivilized men like you who brought civilization to the West. Once the land needed your kind: violent, tough, enduring and unbending. But now"—the doctor shrugged—"we're real close to being thoroughly civilized, and we don't need your help or your guns anymore."

Fletcher's mouth hardened to a bitter line under

his mustache. "What are you trying to tell me, Doc?"

"Just this: In the end, the civilization you helped create will kill you, Mr. Fletcher. Like the wild Indians out there on the plains, you've become an embarrassment, a very visible, living anachronism, and that's why you can no longer be tolerated, even in a backwoods burg like Buffalo City. You're a constant reminder of a past the more civilized among us would rather forget.

"Oh, civilization may not kill you with a rope or a bullet, but it will destroy you by indifference, neglect and contempt. Like the Indians, that's something your touchy pride will be unable to accept. Eventually you'll just curl up and die, maybe in bed, eaten up by a sense of grief and loss, or more quickly, by whiskey or your own hand. In the end it won't matter. Either way, you'll be just as dead."

"There's still a lot of civilizing to be done," Fletcher said, an impotent anger rising in him. "It's not all over yet, not by a long shot."

Hawthorne nodded. "You're correct, of course. But the time for you and your kind is fast running out. This is 1876. I believe in less than ten years, it will be all over. Buffalo City is already talking about streetcars, street lamps, a telephone exchange and a nice, civilized police force in smart blue uniforms."

"Ten years is all the time I need, Doc," Fletcher said. "I don't aim to live forever."

Hawthorne shook his head, his voice exasperated. "As your doctor, I'm giving you some advice, young man. Stay in that cabin up on the Two-Bit and settle down. Find yourself a good, steady woman who can bear you tall sons and will never want to leave your side. Do it now before it's too late."

"Doc," Fletcher said quietly, "I reckon it's already too late."

The old physician sighed. "Well, maybe it is. Only you know that." He shook his head thoughtfully. Then, suddenly all business, said, "Come back in two weeks, and I'll take those stitches out." He stretched out his palm. "That will be two dollars."

Buck Fletcher walked to the hotel, where the desk clerk, his eyes wide and frightened, quickly handed him a key to a room. The three killings had obviously made the man wary and more than a little tense.

"I'm afraid your friend, Doc Holliday, is no longer in residence," he said, trying to demonstrate his helpfulness. "I believe he's now in Deadwood."

Fletcher nodded. "Doc is a wanderer." Then he took the stairs to his room. It was not yet evening, but the gunfighter was bone tired, and his side and shoulder hurt where Hawthorne had poked and probed and stitched.

Quickly, he undressed and lay on the bed; within minutes he was asleep. Fletcher slumbered on as the afternoon passed and day shaded into evening. Along the street, oil lamps were lit. The saloons began to fill up with revelers, and the talk was all of Buck Fletcher and the gunmen he had killed.

Just down the street, the three dead men lay naked in the undertaker's embalming room, dollar coins on their eyes, their skins tinted blue by the moonlight streaming through a skylight window. They would be buried next morning at city expense, and there was none to grieve for them.

Night came, and one by one the saloon patrons dispersed to their homes, bending their heads against a wind that blew long and cold from the Black Hills and warned of a hard winter.

Gradually, Buffalo City grew quiet. A teamster,

taken with consumption, coughed up blood in his tormented sleep, and once, close to midnight, a damp-haired woman tilted back her head and cried out her pleasure from an open mouth, uncaring of who heard.

Full darkness shrouded the heights and plains surrounding the town, and the slow, slumbering hours passed. Only the restless wind stayed awake, prowling among the wooden buildings, stirring the fallen leaves into swirling, rustling circles as it whispered pine-scented secrets it had learned long ago from the hills.

Dawn came, a dark blue sky streaked with fingers of red. A rooster strutted along the roof of a chicken coop and proudly proclaimed the start of a new day.

Fletcher slept on.

He did not wake until the sun climbed to its highest point above Buffalo City. Then he returned to consciousness slowly and painfully.

He rose stiffly and dressed. Despite the constant pain in his shoulder and side, the long sleep had restored him, and he felt a little stronger and more alert.

Fletcher strapped on his gunbelt and picked up his Winchester. He made his way downstairs, paid the clerk and walked along the boardwalk to a restaurant he'd seen earlier.

The restaurant was warm and cozy and smelled of frying steak and coffee. Only a few townspeople sat at other tables, surreptitiously glancing at him now and then, a strange mixture of fear, apprehension and fascination in their eyes.

Fletcher ignored them, concentrating on his plate. The coffee was good and the food was better. After he'd eaten, he paid his bill and walked to the livery stable. He saddled his horse without too much difficulty and rode out of Buffalo City, heading southwest toward the Lazy R and Judith Tyrone.

The day was fresh and clear but bitter cold, and

Fletcher's breath fogged in the air as he reached Bear Den Mountain and then swung south.

Since his arrival in the Dakota Territory, he'd been dealt a hand from a stacked deck, and the thought came to him that he should just keep on riding and leave this whole sorry mess far behind him.

But almost as soon as the idea entered his mind, he impatiently dismissed it. He had done enough running. He would not allow himself to throw in his cards but would play out this hand to the bitter end.

He wanted to hear from her own lips Judith deny the allegations made against her by Savannah Jones and Matt Baker. He wanted to see those wagons and the gold miners they said she'd gathered at the ranch. Even if Savannah and Matt were indeed Pinkertons, the whole thing could still be a setup, with Judith playing the scapegoat while the real brains behind all this remained free to plot and scheme.

He had little doubt in his own mind that Judith was innocent, but he needed to talk to her and hear her say it. He must know where things stood, not only with her ranch, but with him.

Especially with him.

Would she leave with him if he asked her? Would she turn her back on the Lazy R and ride away from all this turmoil? If she loved him she would.

But did she love him?

Fletcher shook his head. He had no certain answer to that question.

In his present weak condition, riding was tiring. After crossing Strawberry Creek, Fletcher stepped out of the saddle and staked his horse on some good grass near the creek bank, where the ground was mostly free of snow. He laid his back against the trunk of an ancient cottonwood and rolled a smoke, lit it and held it between tight lips.

A jackrabbit loped through the snow about twenty feet from where he sat, then settled on its haunches and tested the wind, sensitive nose twitching. The little animal turned its head, watching Fletcher out of one bright eye, then ran back the way it had come, its curiosity satisfied.

The jackrabbit's tracks pointed south, toward Strawberry Ridge and its rolling, pine-covered hills, and idly Fletcher smoked and marked their progress.

His eyes, accustomed to long distances, caught something: a dark object against the snow. The rabbit's tracks had veered around whatever the thing was, then even wider around a nearby outcropping of tumbled sandstone rock crested by a few stunted spruce.

Puzzled, Fletcher stood and ground out his cigarette butt under his heel. He swung into the saddle and rode at a walk toward the object in the snow. The sorrel tossed his head, bit jangling, liking the trail and the coolness of the sun-splashed winter afternoon.

When he was about fifty yards from the object, Fletcher made out what it was. It was the English painter's easel. His pack donkey and long-legged horse stood nearby, nosing under the snow cover to get at the grass.

Fletcher rode up to the easel and swung stiffly out of the saddle. He looked around at the surrounding hills and trees, but saw nothing. Warily now, he pushed his mackinaw away from his gun and stepped up to the inverted V of the easel and the canvas propped against it. The canvas was covered by a dirty white cloth, and Fletcher lifted it. What he saw made him smile tightly and nod. He'd suspected as much.

The painting, such as it was, was just a tangled mess of color, splotches of red, green and black daubed here and there with random, artless brushstrokes.

Bob was an artist all right, Fletcher thought grimly. But of a very different kind.

The rectangular leather case he'd earlier thought might contain dismantled frames lay near the easel. But this was no artist's case. The inside was lined with green velvet, expertly compartmentalized to take the stock, barrel and forearm of a takedown rifle. Fletcher tipped down the lid with the toe of his boot. An oval brass plaque set into the expensive leather read:

> *Alexander Henry & Co.*
> *Gunmakers*
> Edinburgh,
> Scotland.

Fletcher glanced at the canvas again. It seemed Bob had fooled everybody.

"Not very good, is it?"

Fletcher froze, cursing his carelessness. He'd walked into a carefully prepared ambush like any pilgrim.

He turned slowly, keeping his hand away from his gun. The little Englishman was walking toward him out of the rocks, smiling, a beautiful double-barreled hunting rifle with a sighting scope in his hands. His fingers were steady on the gun's triggers.

"But then I'm not much of an artist, am I, Buck?"

"How did you know I'd be here?" Fletcher asked, puzzled despite the very real danger he was facing.

Could he draw and fire before Bob pulled those triggers? He doubted it, and that realization chilled him to the bone.

"I didn't, actually. I've just been scouting around, searching for that young Amy Prescott person and her lads. But then I saw you in the distance—riding another of those big sorrel horses you love so much. There's just no mistaking you, Buck. You're such a distinctive figure. And, well, you know the rest. Shall we just say you walked right into my little trap? Just a small lapse of concentration that will be your death."

"You've tried to kill me before, Bob, and I'm still here," Fletcher said, desperately playing for time. "I think the first time was in the blizzard when I found Savannah Jones. You were lucky that day, Bob. My pup nudged my rifle and threw off my aim."

"Miss Jones is a Pinkerton agent, did you know that?" Bob asked. "How very unusual. I mean, her being a woman and all." He shook his head. "I would have had her that day if you hadn't shown up at the wrong time."

"You shot at me that day and missed, and a few times after that. You were trying your best to kill me."

"My best? Not really. All the shots I fired at you, except for the last one, of course, were just warnings. An attempt to drive you into the camp—and, might I add, into the arms—of my employer, Judith Tyrone."

"Birmingham Bob Spooner," Fletcher said, "the sure-thing contract killer. I don't believe Judith would have anything to do with a snake like you."

The little man shrugged. "Believe what you like. But I killed her husband and then that lout Pike Prescott on her orders. And a few others: cowboys mostly, men of little account."

"You've always had the reputation of being a methodical man, Bob," Fletcher said, trying to spin this out.

There were only he and Bob and the empty land around them. And one of them would die here on the snow. Very soon now.

"Methodical, yes. I have that reputation. But I must admit, when we first met in Buffalo City, I feared for a moment that you'd recognized me, and my cover would be blown—so much so that I seriously considered putting a bullet in your back during our scrape with those two hillbillies."

"It took me a while, Bob," Fletcher said. "Then I recalled seeing you one time when you were hunting Comanche scalps for a bounty down along the Rio Grande in the Neuces Plains country. As I recollect, you were selling Mexican scalps—men, women and children—and passing them off as Comanche. Seems Mexicans were a lot easier to kill."

If Bob was annoyed, he didn't let it show. He shrugged his thin shoulders. "A man makes a living any way he can."

"Heard of you again a couple of years back, only this time you were up on the Cimarron killing nesters for one of the big English cattle companies. They say you weren't any too particular who you shot with that rifle of yours then either. Men, women, children: They were all the same to you."

Bob nodded. "Did my job. Cleared those nesters out. That's what I was paid to do, and I did it. Over the years, I believe I've killed around sixty people, all of them for money. You will be number sixty-one, and no doubt Mrs. Tyrone will pay handsomely for your— dare I say it?—singularly unhandsome head."

"You're pretty low down, Bob," Fletcher said. "A contract killer who shoots from ambush isn't much."

The little man's smile slipped. "This grows tiresome." His washed-out blue eyes were ugly. "By the by, I'm going to kill you very, very soon, you know."

Bob's face wrinkled into a thoughtful scowl. "One thing before you . . . ah . . . leave. I don't understand how you survived when I shot you off your horse as you were riding back from the PP Connected. I laid the sights of the scope right on your chest. I didn't miss, did I? That's impossible."

"Quartz," Fletcher said.

"Pardon?"

"I had a pocketful of quartz, and it deflected the bullet."

"Impossible! This weapon is an Alexander Henry big game rifle. It fires a steel-jacketed .500 caliber nitro express round that can kill an elephant at a hundred yards. Nothing deflects that bullet. Nothing."

"The quartz did."

Fletcher was thinking fast. The little man seemed shook, his confidence in his weapon undermined. Like any craftsman, Bob took great pride in the tools of his trade, and he obviously set store by his rifle. Was this the time to draw before he could pull those triggers? Fletcher knew his chance of success was thin, but it was the only chance he had.

"I believe you're lying to me, Buck," Bob said. "And for that, as a little punishment, I'm going to give you both rounds in the belly. It will take you hours to die, and for most of that time you'll scream like a woman. Believe me, death will come as a welcome release."

The little man's knuckles were white on the rifle. Desperately, Fletcher said, "Bob, during the war I saw thirty-pound cannonballs deflected by tree branches no bigger around than your little finger. One time I saw a rifled ball from my own battery fly half a mile straight up in the air after hitting a chestnut tree twig. It happens."

Birmingham Bob scowled. "This is all very interesting, but now I really must shoot you."

"You're a methodical man, Bob," Fletcher said quickly, forcing a grin. "But not so methodical that you remembered to ear back the hammers on that rifle of yours."

Birmingham Bob experienced only a minute fraction of a second of doubt, and the tiny, almost imperceptible downward shift of his eyes toward his gun took even less. But it was all Fletcher needed.

He drew and fired.

Despite his wounds and his weakness, everything was on the line, and he had never in his life pulled a Colt faster. The flashing speed of the draw caught Birmingham Bob completely by surprise.

The bullet crashed into the little man's chest and slammed him back on his heels. Both barrels of the double rifle went off at the same instant, but the muzzle of the gun was slightly high, and the rounds whined through the air inches above Fletcher's head.

Fletcher fired again, and this time his bullet ricocheted off the rifle's engraved sidelock and ranged upward, slamming into Bob's face just under his right cheekbone.

The Englishman gasped and fell on his back in the snow, his eyes wild.

His gun cocked and ready, Fletcher stood over the fallen man, swaying slightly on his feet as pain from his side beat at him mercilessly.

Birmingham Bob was looking up at him, blood running down his cheek and chin from his shattered face, but the eyes remained mean and defiant.

"You're fast, Buck," he said. "Very fast with a Colt. But I tell you something, Higgy Conroy will kill you. You're nowhere as fast as he is."

"As it happens, he wasn't," Fletcher said. "He didn't even come close."

Bob's eyes widened as he took this in. Then his mouth twisted, and he snarled, "Fletcher, for all your high-and-mighty talk and uppity ways, you're no better than me. Now, go to hell."

Fletcher nodded, a slight smile touching his lips. "Keep a spot warm for me, Bob."

But Birmingham Bob was beyond replying.

He was dead.

Fletcher nodded. "For a methodical man, Bob, you sure played hob."

He reloaded his Colt and shoved it back into the leather. Then, systematically, Fletcher went through the packs on the donkey. He found nothing of interest. Kneeling in the snow, he searched Bob's pockets and then discovered what he'd hoped to find.

A letter.

Bob, as was his style, had kept the letter. For him, it was what amounted to a contract, and, as Fletcher had expected, he would not part with it.

It was addressed to the little Englishman in care of a hotel in Denver. Written in a fine, copperplate hand, it read:

Dear Mr. Spooner,

As per our conversation at your hotel on the 23rd of June, please hasten with all possible speed to Buffalo City in the Dakota Territory.

Check into the Cattleman's Hotel, and let me know of your arrival. I will arrange for a good horse to be brought to you.

The agreement we made in Denver still stands. I will pay you $500 on the death of my husband, then $200 a head for others I may name.

Your request for $5 a day expenses is quite agreeable.

I wish this matter to be settled quickly, efficiently and methodically, and my name to be kept out of it. It is for all these reasons that I have chosen you.

The PP Connected foreman, Mr. Higman Conroy (I believe you two are acquainted),

*told me you are the very best there is, and,
after meeting you in person, I have no reason to doubt his word or, indeed, the veracity
of my own judgment.*

*In closing, let me say that your chosen dis-
guise as an eccentric landscape painter is just
too deliciously droll.*

*Warmest regards,
Judith Tyrone (Mrs.)*

P.S. Please destroy this letter after reading.

For a few moments, Fletcher was too stunned to
move. The woman he'd dared to think loved him,
whom perhaps he could love in return, was a cold-
blooded killer. The proof was right here in his hands.

A gusting wind blew cold across the snow and fluttered a corner of the letter as Fletcher read it again.
He shook his head. This was no forgery. Birmingham
Bob, a methodical man, should have destroyed the
letter, but he'd kept it with him, maybe as insurance,
maybe as a future source of blackmail.

Savannah and Matt Baker had told him they had
no proof that Judith was behind all this killing. Now
they would have all the proof they needed.

For an instant, Fletcher thought about tearing the
letter into a hundred pieces and letting the wind scatter it forever. But he knew he could not.

In a certain way, Birmingham Bob had been right.
Like the Englishman, he was indeed a man who hired
his gun to the highest bidder.

But there was a big difference.

Unlike Bob, the men he'd killed had been named
gunmen, belted, armed and ready, and their wounds
had all been in the front.

What Judith and this man had planned was not a contest between armed men, but murder.

Fletcher stared at the letter for a long time. Then he folded it up carefully and placed it in the pocket of his mackinaw.

There was no question of burying Birmingham Bob in the frozen ground. In any case, Fletcher had no shovel.

He dragged the little Englishman to the rocks and found enough loose boulders to cover him and keep the coyotes away from his body.

The Alexander Henry rifle was a fine weapon, but in Bob's hands it had done more than its share of killing. Fletcher smashed it against the rocks again and again until it was just a mess of tangled metal and splintered walnut. These pieces he laid on the grave.

Quickly, gasping now and then as waves of pain hit him, Fletcher unstaked the grulla gelding and let him loose. He would probably find his way back to the Lazy R. If he did, it would be a message Judith Tyrone would understand.

He did the same for the donkey, but, unlike the grulla, the animal stubbornly refused to budge from where it stood.

Fletcher nodded. "So be it, burro. Stay right here and freeze to death for all I care."

He swung into the saddle and headed north, toward the Two-Bit. The burro fell in behind, his short legs working fast to keep up with Fletcher's big sorrel.

Fletcher reined in, turned in the saddle and waved at the donkey irritably. "Go home. Get lost."

The burro ignored him, standing splaylegged a few yards behind Fletcher's horse. As burros invariably do, the little animal sought to impress him by making a great display of his fine manners and good breeding— but he steadfastly refused to move away.

The gunfighter shook his head. "For some reason, it seems like every stray critter in the territory wants to attach itself to me."

Behind him the burro nodded his long, homely head.

And Fletcher grinned.

Chapter 22

The cabin on Two-Bit was a hive of activity when Fletcher rode up and stepped out of the leather. Matt Baker and a couple of men, punchers by the look of them, were carrying armfuls of firewood, and Savannah stood earnestly talking to a dark-haired young woman.

The girl was Amy Prescott.

Savannah ran to Fletcher and threw her arms around his neck. "Buck," she said, "thank God you're safe."

"It was close," Fletcher said, smiling. "I was lucky."

Savannah's eyes suddenly reddened. She sobbed softly, and then her lips sought his. Surprised, Fletcher returned her kiss, confused and more than a little embarrassed.

"I missed you, Buck," Savannah whispered, her lips still clinging to his. "I missed you so much."

Fletcher stood there feeling big and clumsy and awkward, trying hard for words he couldn't find.

He was saved by the speckled pup. The little dog charged toward him on three legs, yipping his happiness, and Fletcher gently disentangled himself from Savannah and kneeled and rubbed the pup's ears.

Matt Baker dropped the firewood he was carrying and stuck out his hand. "Welcome back, Buck. I'm

glad you made it." He studied Fletcher shrewdly.
"Want to tell us about it?"

"Not much to tell. I—"

"Oh, Buck!"

Savannah, looking fresh and lovely in a white shirt
and split canvas riding skirt, ran to the burro and
hugged the little animal's head close. "He's beautiful."
She looked up at Fletcher. "Oh, Buck, can we keep
him?"

Fletcher heard that "we" and wondered at it.

"Sure you can keep him," he said, shifting the em-
phasis as he tried to keep the exasperation out of his
voice. "He's pretty much made up his mind that he's
not going anyplace."

He glanced at Amy Prescott. The girl was looking
at him with eyes that were not hostile but not welcoming either.

"Nice to see you again, Mr. Fletcher," she said, her
voice cool.

Fletcher touched the brim of his hat, matching her
formality. "You too, Miss Prescott."

It seemed the girl still didn't trust him. He really
couldn't blame her.

The gunfighter looked around him. The two punchers he'd seen earlier were PP Connected hands, and
now another stepped around the side of the cabin, his
head swathed in a thick bandage. It seemed like Amy
Prescott and the surviving men of her outfit had been
through the wars.

But the three cowboys still looked salty and tough,
and Fletcher knew they were no pushovers.

He turned to Baker. "Matt, mind telling me what's
going on here?"

"It's simple enough, I reckon," Baker replied. "We
found Amy and her men in the hills. There was another one, but we buried him yesterday. With Judith

Tyrone's gunmen on the prowl, we figured this would be the safest place."

Baker looked at Fletcher quizzically. "Now, you going to tell us what happened to you, or are you going to keep it all to yourself?"

Fletcher nodded. "You others gather around," he said. "You should all hear this."

Briefly, without embellishment, Fletcher told of his showdown with Higgy Conroy and his gunmen and his run-in with Birmingham Bob Spooner.

"After it was over, I found this in Bob's pocket," he said, his eyes bleak, handing Judith Tyrone's letter to Baker. "I guess it will interest you."

Baker read the letter and handed it to Savannah without comment. The girl read it and in turn handed it to Amy Prescott.

"It's proof of a sort," Savannah said. "But it may not stand up in court. Letters can be forged. I think a good lawyer could shred this to pieces, especially since the two men who could testify to the authenticity of this letter are dead."

Baker nodded. "Maybe so. But I believe this is something we should let Deputy Marshal Graham decide."

"Where is Graham?" Fletcher asked, his confidence in the man's ability slight.

"Probably in Deadwood, and probably right now in Nuttall and Mann's Number 10 Saloon. It's his unofficial headquarters."

Baker glanced up at the sky, noting the sun's position. "I'm going to ride into Deadwood and get him. I'll bring him here before nightfall."

"Suppose he doesn't want to come?" Fletcher suggested mildly.

Baker grinned. "Like I said, I'll bring him here before nightfall, even if I have to hogtie him."

Fletcher's shoulders slumped, defeat hanging heavy on him. "After what Savannah said about the letter, it may not do any good. But I guess it's worth a try."

Baker left to saddle his horse, and Fletcher took Savannah's arm and pulled her aside. "I just want you to know that when this is all over, I'm riding on out of here," he said harshly, trying to end the girl's all-too-apparent interest in him.

Savannah's expression did not change. "Fine. Then I'm going with you."

Fletcher shook his head. "You don't understand. I'll be riding far and fast, and where I'm going is no place for a woman."

"And where are you going?" Savannah asked, her determined eyes revealing that she would not give an inch.

"Somewhere," Fletcher said, faltering. God, she was beautiful! "I mean, a place where there's work for a man like me." He thought for a few moments, then smiled slightly. "A place an uncivilized hombre like me can civilize with his gun."

Savannah nodded. "So be it. I'm still coming with you. We'll civilize together."

"You're not, Savannah. This is something I have to do alone. There's no place for you in my life."

The girl shook her head. "We'll just have to see about that, won't we, Mr. Fletcher?"

She turned on her heel and stalked away from him, leaving Fletcher openmouthed and flatfooted . . . and feeling more than a little foolish.

His frustrated male helplessness in the face of a strong and determined woman grew even worse when he saw Savannah and Amy, their heads together, whispering earnestly as they smiled and stole knowing glances at him.

"Women," Fletcher said to himself, shaking his head. They were a mystery.

*   *   *

After Matt Baker rode out, Buck Fletcher led his horse around the back of the cabin to the barn. The three PP Connected hands were stacking firewood against the coming of the heavy winter snows and generally making themselves useful around the place. Savannah and Amy had finally whispered their way inside, taking the pup with them.

The day was bright and cold, the sky clear of cloud, and the breeze had stilled. Inside the cabin, Fletcher heard Savannah singing softly. One of the PP Connected hands said something, and another laughed.

It was a peaceful scene, yet he felt uneasy. It was the feeling a man has when he's being intently watched by someone at a distance.

Fletcher shook his head. It was all in his overwrought imagination. Yet the uneasiness persisted, refusing to let him go, and it was a worrisome thing. At last he gave in to it, unable to step away from his troubled instincts.

The ache in Fletcher's side was unrelenting, and he was tiring fast. But he swung into the saddle and rode around the cabin, passing the tree where he'd once sat and read his books.

He skirted along the bottom of the ridge towering behind the cabin and rode west and then south in a wide arc. The pines on the hills around him were still, and the land was hushed under its white mantle of snow.

Fletcher rode into a narrow stream, its bubbling water still unfrozen, and briefly let his horse drink as he looked around at the surrounding hills. He rode out of the stream and up a shallow rise crested by a stand of aspen, broken up here and there by the darker green of spruce and juniper.

As the sorrel picked his way through the trees, Fletcher heard only the soft footfalls of the horse, muffled by pine needles, and the creak of his saddle leather.

He cleared the trees and rode down the other side of the rise, his horse kicking through some deeper snow, and then swung east, back toward the cabin. So far he'd seen nothing.

The day had grown colder, and Fletcher's breath steamed in the air. He reined up in the shade of a large pine and pulled off his gloves, blowing on his cupped hands to keep the circulation going. Slowly and awkwardly, he built himself a smoke and lit his cigarette. Annoyed at being halted, the sorrel tossed his head and snorted, crow-hopping a little, anxious to be going again.

Fletcher finished his smoke and dropped the cold butt into the snow. He kneed the horse into a walk and rode through the gap between a pair of saddleback hills and then took the slope of another, higher rise, its craggy incline broken up here and there by deep, V-shaped citadels of gray rock.

Tall lodgepole pines marched along the entire length of the hill, and Fletcher rode into them, his mountain-bred horse carefully picking his way among the slender gray trunks. Beyond the downward slope of the hill there lay a wide stretch of open grassland, now snow-covered, and then the cabin and, close behind it, the ridge.

Nothing moved up here. The branches of the lodgepoles were still, as though the trees were dozing in the watery sunlight.

Fletcher reined up the sorrel and tested the air. He smelled smoke. Cigarette smoke. Its sharp, musky aroma hung on the hill now that there was no wind to disperse it.

Stiffly, Fletcher stepped out of the saddle and pulled his Winchester from the boot. He cranked a round into the chamber, then walked forward on cat feet, farther into the pines.

The smell was stronger now. Closer.

Being fond of tobacco himself, Fletcher was aware that cigarette smoking was a recent import from Mexico, where the vaqueros were much addicted to it. So far, at a time when most men chewed or smoked a pipe or cigars, the habit hadn't traveled much beyond the Canadian. That could mean that the man who'd smoked among these pines was a Texan. And if he was, he was a long way from home, and up here for no honest reason.

Fletcher stopped and studied some horse droppings at the base of a pine. He pushed them with his toe. They were still fresh. The man who'd ridden this horse was gone, and not long before.

A few minutes searching, and Fletcher found the place where the man had stood. Several cigarette butts littered the ground, telling Fletcher that he'd lingered up here, hidden by the trees, for a long while. From this high vantage spot, the spy had enjoyed an unobstructed view of the cabin, and he must know that Amy Prescott and her hands were there.

Fletcher swore. He'd also seen Matt Baker ride away. But Matt would have to look out for himself.

Unless his hunch was wrong, Fletcher figured an attack would be made on the cabin very soon, just as soon as the Texan, if that's what he was, rode back and reported to Judith Tyrone.

Judith was smart. She would figure that, with all of her enemies gathered together in one place, now was the time to strike and get rid of them once and for all.

Fletcher found his horse, swung into the saddle and rode down to the cabin. He was hurting bad, and the ride had tired him.

But there could be no rest. Not now.

Unless his instinct for danger was wrong, and it had rarely failed him before, the attack would come before nightfall.

Judith Tyrone was hunting trouble.

Chapter 23

Fletcher put up his horse, slid his Winchester from the boot, then quickly told the others what he'd seen on the hill.

"I believe we'll be attacked very soon," he concluded. "And right now I'm not inclined to give favorable odds on our chances."

"How many men does Judith Tyrone have?" asked one of the punchers, the skinny youngster with the bandaged head.

"Enough," Fletcher replied. "Somehow we've got to even the numbers."

"We could ride out now and lay for them someplace," another Connected puncher, a man named Walker, suggested. "They won't expect to be bushwhacked."

Fletcher shook his head at the man. "There are too few of us. Judith's men are experienced gun hands. They won't be stampeded easily, and they're not the kind to ride into an ambush. If they catch us out there in the open, we'll be in a world of trouble." Fletcher's worried expression suddenly cleared. "Unless . . ."

He took the three Connected hands aside and spoke to them briefly and urgently. Walker, a wide-shouldered, blue-eyed man with a thick dragoon mustache and sandy eyebrows, grinned widely and nodded. "It might just work."

Fletcher smiled grimly. "It's got to work, or we'll all be dead as hell in a preacher's backyard before the moon spikes itself on a pine tonight."

Despite the man's protests, Fletcher kept the wounded youngster at the cabin while Walker and the other puncher saddled up and rode out. They retraced the route Fletcher had taken earlier and were soon lost among the pines.

"Buck, do you really think we're in danger?" Savannah asked, her face pale and frightened.

They were inside the cabin. Gates, the young puncher, stood at a window, his Winchester in his hands, alertly gazing out at the surrounding country, where a few flakes of snow were falling, unhurriedly drifting to earth.

"Savannah," Fletcher said, "I've got to give it to you straight. I believe by this time Judith knows you and Amy are here and that there's no better time to get rid of you both. That Texas gunman up on the hill must have seen Matt ride out, but Judith probably figures she can deal with him later. Right now her concern is with you and Amy . . . and maybe," he finished grimly, "me."

Savannah was scared, but now she demonstrated that she had backbone. "She'll have to work for it," she said, her eyes blazing and determined. "I won't go without a fight."

"Me neither," Amy said. The girl had her own rifle, and Fletcher figured that, like most ranch-born girls, she knew how to use it.

Fletcher smiled at Savannah. "You'll need more than that derringer stingy gun."

The girl nodded. "I've got Jeb's Henry, and there's plenty of shells for it."

"I ain't no slouch with this here rifle gun either," Gates said from the window, grinning. "I fit Comanches when I were just a younker, and I've used it some since."

"You know," Fletcher said, "I was feeling pretty bad about this earlier. But now I got the notion that maybe Judith Tyrone is about to bite off more than she can chew."

He didn't really. But he knew this was something the others would like to hear him say. "Bolstering morale," they'd called it in the army.

He had two girls and a wounded man in the cabin, and if the plan he'd earlier hatched with Walker failed, he didn't give much for their chances against Judith's skilled gun hands.

Fletcher was tired, worn out by the constant pain in his side and now his worry for Savannah and the others. He swayed slightly on his feet and sat down heavily on the bunk.

"Buck," Savannah said, her face concerned, "you're all in. Why don't you catch some sleep while you have a chance?"

Fletcher shook his head. "I'm not tired. I can make it."

"You're not going to be much good to us in a gun battle if you're completely exhausted," Savannah persisted. "Now just lie down and get some rest."

"Okay, you win." Fletcher smiled. He stretched out on the bunk. "See, I'm lying down. Does that make you happy?"

Savannah nodded. "Yes, it does."

But Fletcher didn't hear.

He was already asleep.

Fletcher woke with a start. The light had changed in the cabin, fading from bright daylight to the transparent, cobalt blue of early evening.

An oil lamp flickered on the table, surrounding itself with an orange and yellow halo, and the fire glowed cherry-red in the stove.

Savannah stepped to his side. "You're awake, I see."

"Douse that damn lamp!" Fletcher yelled sharply, swinging his legs off the bed. He rose to his feet, feeling the room spin around him. "If the Lazy R is going to attack us, it will be now, before it gets any darker," he snapped. "I don't want us outlined against a lamp as easy targets for a rifleman."

Savannah blew out the lamp. "Sorry," she said, "but I'm new to this kind of thing."

"New or not, any damn fool knows not to light—"

Fletcher saw the sudden hurt in Savannah's eyes and checked himself. "I mean . . ." He shook his head, annoyed and ashamed of his outburst. "Hell, I don't know what I mean. Just . . . just don't light that lamp again, okay?"

He was groggy with pain, and the nap had not refreshed him. He was tense, uneasy and teetering right on the edge of exhaustion.

"Anything you say, Major Fletcher," Savannah returned stiffly, snapping off a smart salute. She sniffed, tilted her nose on the air, then stalked away, heels clacking as she took her place by the window and studiously ignored him.

Fletcher shook his head. Thank heaven they'll never allow women in the army! he thought.

He picked up his Winchester and strolled over to Gates. "See anything?"

The man shook his head. "Not a thing."

"They'll come," Fletcher said. Then, almost as if reassuring himself: "I know they'll come."

The attack came ten minutes later, just as the day was slowly fading into night and the moon began its climb into a pale, starless sky.

There were eight of them, and they charged the cabin at a fast gallop, trusting to the word of Judith Tyrone's spy that they would take Fletcher and the others by surprise.

The horses of the Lazy R gunmen kicked up high flurries of snow from their churning hooves, the breath from their flared nostrils smoking in the cold air.

Fletcher, seeing the horsemen come fast, realized it was their plan to charge right up to the cabin and force their way inside, shooting down everyone they found before the occupants had a chance to react.

In that, they were sorely disappointed.

Gates was firing from the window, Savannah shooting beside him. Amy, firing her rifle steadily and well, stood beside Fletcher.

Fletcher saw one rider throw his arms in the air and fall from his horse. Then another went down, his terrified mount crashing on top of him. The man's shrill scream cut across the night above the roar of the guns. Then he was silent.

Fletcher, by training and inclination a revolver fighter, laid down his rifle and stepped to the cabin door. He threw the door open wide and stepped outside, the Colt in his right fist hammering as soon as he located a target.

A rider fired at him, a gout of orange flame flaring from the muzzle of his rifle, and Fletcher fired back, emptying the man's saddle.

Another rider swung his gray horse around and charged at Fletcher, the man letting his mount have its head as he fired his two Colts. Bullets kicked up angry Vs of snow around Fletcher's feet and split the air around his head as he thumbed off two quick shots at the oncoming gunman. Both missed.

Fletcher fired again, and the rider went down with his horse, an explosion of snow scattering into the air as man and animal crashed heavily to the ground.

Knowing that they had lost the element of surprise, the surviving riders drew off a hundred yards or so and bunched together, getting themselves in a frame of mind to charge again. But there was to be no rest for them.

Walker and the other puncher opened up from the hillside where Fletcher had sent them. Quickly, two riders went down. The others, seeing they were caught in a lethal crossfire, swung their horses around and galloped away, a few of them firing some last defiant but futile shots in the direction of the cabin.

The attack had ended as suddenly as it had begun.

And for the Lazy R gunmen, it had been a disaster.

Six men were down, staining the snow around them with their blood. A horse kicked and screamed, its back broken. Fletcher put the horse out of its misery with a well-aimed shot to the head, then looked around him at the catastrophe that had befallen Judith Tyrone's gunmen.

The others came from the cabin. Walker and the puncher with him were riding slowly down the hill toward them, their rifles at the ready.

"Oh my God," Savannah whispered. "They're all dead."

Fletcher nodded, his face set and grim. "Most of them. I shot one ranny over there who's still breathing, but I doubt he'll last much longer."

Amy's eyes were huge in her pale face. "This isn't worth it," she gasped. "All the money in the world isn't worth so much death."

"It is to Judith Tyrone," Savannah said bitterly. "She doesn't care how many die just so long as she gets rich."

Fletcher stepped up to the dying gunman and

looked down at him without sympathy. "Been a long time, Mickey."

The man managed a wan smile. "Down to Colfax County that time when you and me was runnin' wild with Clay Allison and that bunch." The gunman's face took on a puzzled frown. "Though I don't rightly recollect what side you was on in that war."

"The losing side," Fletcher said. "I had to light a shuck out of Texas pretty fast."

Blood stained the gunman's lips as he chuckled. "Ol' Clay Allison, he's something, ain't he, Buck?"

Fletcher nodded. "I'd say he is."

"Well, you've done for me, Buck, but that happens in our business. One day a ranny's your friend, another day your enemy. I got no hard feelings."

"No hard feelings," Fletcher said, unbending enough to give a dying man a little comfort.

Mickey nodded. "That's how it ought to be."

Then death rattled in the gunman's throat, and his open eyes looked out on nothing but darkness.

"Was he a friend of yours?" Gates asked, glancing at the dead man as he stepped beside Fletcher.

Fletcher shook his head. "Our paths crossed a few times. His name was Mickey Foster. He liked gray horses, and he was good with a gun."

Gates was silent for a few moments. Then he said, "Not much to say about a man, is it?"

An emptiness inside him, Fletcher nodded. "No, Gates. I guess it isn't."

He looked at Savannah. She was staring at him, her eyes troubled, trying hard to reach out to him.

Fletcher looked away quickly, his face flushing.

"We got some burying to do," he said to Walker and the other puncher as they reined up beside him. "Up there on the hillside, away from the cabin."

"Never knew what hit them," Walker said, grinning.

"I mean, your idea to catch them in a crossfire threw them for a loop."

"It ain't something that makes me real proud," Fletcher said.

Chapter 24

The dead were buried shallow in ground too hard for graves, and it was almost midnight when the difficult and melancholy task was completed.

Matt Baker and Graham rode in an hour later, the Deputy United States Marshal obviously irritated at being forced to ride so far from the delights of Deadwood.

But after a bowl of hot stew and coffee sweetened with good bourbon, Graham visibly relaxed and lit a cigar, the closeness of pretty female company also helping to mellow him.

"Matt here showed me the letter allegedly written by Judith Tyrone," he said from behind a cloud of smoke. "You know it's not going to stand up in court." Graham shook his head, his face puzzled. "I just find it hard to believe that Miz Tyrone would have a hand in murder."

"Tell that to the six dead men buried up there on the hill," Fletcher said bitterly.

Graham took the letter from the inside pocket of his coat and studied it. "The paper is of excellent quality, but typical of the stuff the better hotels supply for their guests. If this had been written on paper you could prove was exclusively used by Judith Tyrone— imported from abroad, say—then maybe we'd have a slight case."

Graham sighed, his long face unhappy. "But as it stands, this letter is worthless. It's just too easy to forge somebody's handwriting. I've seen it done."

"I took that letter off the body of Birmingham Bob Spooner," Fletcher said. "You heard of him, Graham?"

The lawman nodded. "Contract rifle killer, an' a good one by all accounts. Got his start down along the Rio Grande as a scalp hunter as I recollect." Graham shrugged. "But the fact that Bob was carrying it still doesn't prove the letter is genuine."

"I sent his horse back to the Lazy R," Fletcher said. "Judith knows something happened to her hired killer, but she doesn't know if he's dead or alive. That gives us an advantage."

"What kind of advantage?" Graham asked warily.

"Advantage enough to get her to confess to the murder of her husband, Pike Prescott, and many others."

Graham shook his head. "I don't get your drift."

Fletcher smiled. "I have a plan."

Quickly he outlined his scheme to Graham, and the expression on the man's face grew more and more shocked, his chin dropping lower to his chest with each of Fletcher's words, until finally he exploded. "Hell, no! I won't do it! That's highly irregular." He looked around at the circle of faces in the cabin and spread his arms wide. "You folks understand, don't you? Suppose it doesn't work? It's more than my job is worth."

Savannah's eyes were blazing and merciless. "You've got to do it, Marshal. It will be more than your job is worth if you let a cold-blooded killer like Judith Tyrone go free."

Matt Baker smiled without humor. "One of the perks of being a Pinkerton agent is that you get to make some powerful friends in Washington. Graham, if I have to, I'll call in some favors from mighty high places and get you busted down to swamper in the county jail."

Graham looked like a trapped animal. For a few tense moments, he thought the thing through. Then, his long, homely face gloomy, he admitted defeat and said slowly, "Okay, I'll do it, but only under protest." He looked around at the people surrounding him. "You folks sure know how to gang up on a man."

Fletcher and the others saddled up just as dawn was washing the blue shadows out of the ravines and coulees among the surrounding hills.

Graham, grouchy and ill-tempered, stood a little apart from the rest, tightening the girth on his balky dun, muttering to himself, now and then looking up at a lemon-colored sky streaked with narrow bands of red.

But the lawman carefully checked his shotgun before sliding it into the boot, and he removed the thong from the hammer of his Colt, easing the gun in its holster.

Whatever else he was, Fletcher decided, Graham was a professional. When the chips were down, there would be backup in him. Maybe, after all, he was a man to ride the river with.

Fletcher was about to swing into the saddle when Savannah and Amy appeared from the direction of the barn, leading their horses.

Both women wore long skirts split for riding, and they had donned short sheepskin jackets, scarves and gloves.

"You two aren't going," Fletcher said, shaking his head. The morning sky touched his face with red, making him look as hard and impassive as a cigar store Indian. "If shooting starts, it will be too dangerous."

"How come you didn't say that last night, Major?" Savannah asked, her eyes bright with mischief.

"Last night we were all fighting for our lives," Fletcher replied. "This is different. There's no need for you and Amy to risk your lives." He laid a hand on the saddle horn, his left foot on the stirrup, preparing to swing into the saddle. "And please stop calling me Major. The war ended a long time ago."

"This one hasn't," Savannah said. "And that's why we're coming with you."

"Oh no you're not," Fletcher said, stepping into the saddle.

"Oh yes we are."

Fletcher looked at Matt Baker and spread his hands helplessly. "Matt, talk some sense into your fellow Pinkerton."

Baker grinned. "Can't be done, Buck. Savannah has resigned from the Pinkertons as of a couple of weeks ago."

Surprised, Fletcher turned to the girl. "Why did you do that?"

Savannah smiled. "Because I plan to spend the rest of my life with you."

"Oh no, you're not. I won't be tied down by a woman."

Savannah swung gracefully into the saddle. "That's what you think." A pause, then: "Major."

Fletcher looked around him. The Connected hands were grinning, and even Graham's gloomy face was lit up with a smile.

The gunfighter made a little yelp of frustration in his throat and said, "All right. Boots and saddles." He turned to Savannah. "Just stay out of my way."

The girl snapped off another smart salute. "Yes, sir!"

Fletcher groaned.

The eight riders, Fletcher and Graham in the lead, followed Two-Bit Creek as it curved to the southwest, passing Dome Mountain and then Anchor Hill, where they caught their first sight of the rising sun. Water still splashed free in the creek despite the coldness of the season, and along its banks the snow sparkled in the sun. The surrounding pines, lit up by the bright morning, looked green instead of black and stirred restlessly in the wind that had again started to blow long and chill from the north.

Soon, when the big snows came, the Two-Bit would freeze hard as iron, and the land would be locked in tight. But right now the going across the plain was easy, and Fletcher set a brisk pace.

At noon they stopped south of Strawberry Ridge and sheltered in a grove of aspen to boil coffee and eat cold bacon sandwiches Savannah and Amy had prepared the night before.

Graham spiked his coffee with a generous splash of bourbon, declaring it to be "a heart starter," and offered the bottle to the others.

The Connected hands took the marshal up on his offer, but Fletcher and Matt Baker declined.

"Here," Graham said, looking at Fletcher suspiciously, "you ain't one o' them temperance fellers, are you?"

Fletcher smiled and shook his head. "Just never much took to whiskey, especially this early in the morning."

"Always do your drinking on an empty stomach," Graham said. "Them's words of wisdom, and I give them to you freely."

Fletcher nodded. "A gambler feller told me the same thing not too long ago."

"Wise man," Graham said approvingly.

They mounted again. Now that the Lazy R was getting closer, Fletcher and the others rode warily, their heads turning this way and that as they constantly scanned the surrounding hills.

There were the tracks of cattle everywhere, but Fletcher saw just one small herd in the distance, moving like gray ghosts in single file along the aspen line at the base of a hill.

When they were a couple of miles from the Lazy R, Matt Baker rode up alongside Fletcher and Graham. He nodded to the west and then the east. "We got company," he said.

Fletcher turned and saw riders flanking them, rifles drawn. Two rode on their left, a single rider to the right. They kept the same pace as Fletcher and the others, making no attempt to close the distance.

"I guess Judith Tyrone's taking no chances," Fletcher said grimly. "She wants to keep an eye on us."

He leaned down in the saddle and slid the Winchester from the boot under his knee. One by one, Baker and the PP Connected hands did the same.

If the Lazy R riders were impressed by all this firepower, they didn't let it show. They kept their distance but still matched the pace of Fletcher's party.

The outriders stayed with them until they rode up to the Lazy R ranch house—and into a scene of roaring chaos.

Six huge freight wagons, five of them hitched to eight-ox teams, the other to mules, crowded the front of the house, their springs creaking under the weight of mining equipment, great, steel-rimmed wheels scarring the earth into deep, corrugated ridges of mud and slush.

The wagons were loaded with massive drills and more mundane tools like picks and shovels, sluice boxes and wheeled ore carriers. But what caught

Fletcher's attention were the iron barrels of high-powered water cannon, called in these parts hydraulic monitors, some of them twenty feet long, their gaping muzzles a foot or more across. These would be attached to nozzles of a smaller diameter, forcing out jets of water at tremendous pressure.

Not for Judith Tyrone the slow, laborious and expensive process of digging gold from a tough quartz seam. She was planning to use water cannon to blast the mesa apart—and time was running out on her. She had to do it now, before the creeks and ditches around the mesa that would supply the water froze.

Bitterly, Fletcher realized that hydraulic mining on such a massive scale would scar and poison the land for generations. But that obviously meant nothing to Judith.

She wanted the gold, and she didn't care how she got it.

Scores of yammering Chinese coolies in their cone-shaped straw hats and pigtails were already climbing onto the wagons. The cursing, profane bullwhackers were uncoiling their bullwhips, getting ready to move out.

Fletcher saw three of Judith's riders sitting their horses among the wagons, watching him and the others, and he caught the small movement of a curtain at a window in the ranch house. Judith had lost heavily on the attack on the cabin, but evidently she still had men enough to put up a fight if it came to that.

Graham reined up alongside Fletcher. Matt Baker, tense and wary, rode up on his left. The PP Connected hands fanned out behind them, Savannah and Amy in the middle of them.

One of the Lazy R riders, a tall man in a black hat and black and white cowskin vest, rode up to the door of the ranch house. He leaned from the saddle and rapped on the door sharply. A few moments later, Judith appeared, and Fletcher saw her nod and say a few urgent words to the man.

Then she walked from the house toward Fletcher and the others, settling a shawl around her slim shoulders.

To Fletcher, she looked breathtakingly lovely this morning. Her auburn hair was piled on top of her head, kept in place by green ribbons that matched her velvet riding outfit.

He experienced a few seconds of doubt as the woman walked, smiling, toward him.

Could this beautiful creature really be a cold-blooded killer?

The doubt passed as quickly as it had come. The evidence was all around him.

Judith stopped about ten paces from where Fletcher sat his horse. Her beautiful smile grew even more dazzling. "Why, Buck, how nice to see you again. And you too, Marshal Graham."

Graham was flustered. He touched his hat brim and said, "And it's real nice to see you again, Miz Tyrone." The man opened his mouth to speak further, but couldn't find the words. He let it go, glancing over at Fletcher helplessly.

"What brings you here, Marshal?" Judith smiled, pressing home her advantage. "As you see, you caught me at an inopportune moment." She waved a hand toward the waiting wagons. "As you can see, I'm about to do a little gold mining."

"No, you're not!"

Amy Prescott kneed her horse forward, her eyes blazing. "That gold-bearing mesa is on PP Connected range, and you've no right to be there."

"Well, I do declare." Judith gasped, putting a slender hand to the base of her throat. "You bold-faced thing, coming here of all places after you ordered my husband killed and tried to take over my ranch!" Judith turned to Graham, her eyes just as angry as Amy's. "Marshal, do your duty and arrest that woman."

Graham was confused, and it showed. "Well, ma'am," he faltered, "Miz Prescott has a point. I mean, if the mesa is on her land."

"Of course it's on land she once claimed," Judith flared. "But after she attacked the Lazy R and we retaliated in self-defense, she abandoned her ranch. She has no legal right to the mesa or to anywhere else in the Territory, for that matter."

Delicately, Judith touched a lace handkerchief to suddenly reddened eyes. "Marshal Graham, sometimes I think they're all ganging up on me to take my ranch." She looked at the marshal pleadingly. "You're the law in this country. Can't you do something?"

"Miz Tyrone," Graham said, suddenly drawing on a hitherto hidden reserve of strength and resolve, "I must ask you this. Did your hands attack Mr. Fletcher's cabin last night?"

Judith was shocked. "Why, no, of course not. My men were all here at the ranch getting our mining equipment ready." She looked up at Fletcher. "Buck, who would do such a thing?"

Fletcher, unimpressed by Judith's acting skills, let it go. But Matt Baker quickly stepped into the waiting silence. "Show her the letter, Graham."

The lawman's reluctance made him hesitate. His hand went to the inside of his coat and then dropped. "I—I—don't know," he stammered.

"Show her the letter!" Baker snapped, his face livid.

Slowly, Graham took the letter from his pocket. "We . . . we found this letter, Miz Tyrone. It appears to be written by you to one Birmingham Bob Spooner, promising him five hundred dollars to kill your husband."

There was a limit to even Judith's acting, and her face paled. "Let me see that," she said unsteadily.

"You can read it just fine from there," Baker said. "Hell, it's your writing."

Judith took a couple of steps toward Graham and quickly scanned the letter that the lawman held up for her. "That's a blatant forgery," she said. "I would never write a letter like that." She looked at Graham, her eyes pleading. "Don't you understand, Marshal? I loved my husband very much."

Again Graham was flustered, his confidence shredding under the melting gaze of this beautiful and apparently devastated woman.

He wasn't going to carry out the plan!

Fletcher stepped in, his voice harsh, determined to succeed where Graham had failed. "That's not what Birmingham Bob says, Judith. He confessed to everything: killing Deke Tyrone on your orders and the murder of Pike Prescott and many others." He smiled tightly. "Bob is quite eager to sacrifice you to save his own worthless neck."

"That's a lie!" Judith screamed. "He's dead. His horse came back and—" She stopped, realizing what she'd said, her face stricken.

The teamsters on the wagons were watching Judith intently, unsure of exactly what was happening. Even the normally talkative Chinese had fallen silent.

"What about his horse, Judith?" Fletcher prompted, his words dropping like chunks of ice into the sudden pool of quiet.

Judith took several steps backward, toward the house. "That fool!" she screeched. "That idiot! I told him to destroy the letter."

Matt Baker turned to Graham, who was sitting his

horse, his long, melancholy face stunned. "Arrest that woman, Marshal."

Graham, rooted to the spot, eyes wide and unbelieving, didn't move.

Then Fletcher saw it.

Judith made a single, all but imperceptible motion with her left hand, a slight wave that the others did not see. "Watch out!" he yelled.

It was too late.

The man in the cowskin vest cut loose with his rifle, and Fletcher heard the bullet slam into Graham. The marshal gasped and toppled to his left, falling against Fletcher's arm as he tried to bring up his Winchester.

Fletcher pushed the lawman away, and Graham went over the other side of his saddle and hit the ground.

The firing had become general, and one of the Connected hands went down. Aiming quickly, Fletcher fired at the man in the cowskin vest. The bullet hit home, and the Lazy R rider reeled in the saddle. Fletcher cranked another round and fired again. This time the man threw up his arms and fell backward over his horse.

A Chinese coolie was hit by a stray round. He stood up in the back of a wagon and clutched at his bloody chest, screaming. A moment later, a bearded bullwhacker was burned across the arm, and he immediately made the air around him sulphurous with profanity.

The Chinese and the teamsters had signed up to be gold prospectors. It was no part of their agreement with Judith Tyrone to get involved in a gunfight.

The lone mule skinner whipped his team into motion, and one by one the big ox wagons followed suit and started to creak and sway across the muddy ground, hell-bent on getting out of the line of fire.

Beside him, Fletcher heard Matt Baker's rifle bark and saw a Lazy R hand go down. Gates, cranking and shooting his Winchester like an expert, cut down the remaining rider, then slammed shots into the ranch house, where men were firing from the windows.

As the battle raged, Judith Tyrone had not moved. But now, as she saw her men fall, she turned and ran for the house.

She didn't see the mule-drawn wagon that killed her.

The mules were cantering fast across the mud, the heavy drill on their wagon bouncing high as the wheels hit the rutted ground. The teamster up on the seat was cracking his whip, yelling at the mules, urging them into an even faster gallop.

Judith, intent only on reaching her men inside the house, ran blindly in front of the straining mules and was knocked down by their flying hooves. She fell heavily, screaming in terror, as the mules pounded her into the ground. Then the wagon wheels, shod with steel and each as tall as a man, rolled over her. The screams became an agonized screech that ended in an abrupt, echoing silence.

The wagon rolled on, leaving behind a crushed, broken and bloody thing in the mud. A single glance over his shoulder convinced the mule skinner that it would be a bad idea to stop, and his wagon rolled across the level ground without slowing, snow flaring from its spinning wheels.

The woman's horrible death had shocked everyone into stunned immobility.

It was Baker who was the first to recover. He cupped a hand to his mouth and yelled, "You in the house! It's all over. Your boss is dead. No point in continuing the fight. No point in more of you dying." He paused for effect, then added, "But if you're hell-bent on dying, we can accommodate you."

A few tense moments passed. Then the door of the house opened, and four men walked outside, their hands in the air, apparently impressed by Baker's harsh logic.

Savannah walked past Fletcher's horse and ran to where Judith's body lay in the churned-up mud. She glanced at it and turned away quickly, her hand going to her mouth in horror.

While Baker and the two surviving Connected hands covered the Lazy R riders with their guns, Fletcher went to Savannah and took her in his arms.

The woman buried her face in his chest and sobbed. "It's so terrible," she whispered. "Even Judith Tyrone didn't deserve a death like that."

"It's over, Savannah," Fletcher said. "It's all over now."

He was almost out on his feet, his side hurting like a red-hot brand. But he knew that at this moment Savannah needed strong arms around her more than anything else in the world, and so he held her close.

"Buck," she said, "why did she have to die like that?"

The gunfighter shook his head. "I don't know, Savannah. I once read a book about a universal force called karma. The Buddhists believe that if you do evil things in life, you put out such bad karma that it will eventually come back on you, only ten times worse."

He smiled, tilting up her chin, his big, hard hand thumbing away tears from her eyes. "Now, I don't know if all that's true. But I guess it's one explanation for why Judith died that way."

Fletcher paused, his face thoughtful. "It was a reckoning," he said finally.

"Buck, over here!"

The gunfighter turned and saw Matt Baker beckoning to him as he kneeled beside the prone form of Marshal Graham.

"Will you be all right?" Fletcher asked Savannah. The woman nodded. "I'll be fine now."

Fletcher left her and stood over Graham. The lawman was still alive, and he indicated that Fletcher should come closer. The gunfighter kneeled beside him, quickly assessing Graham's wound.

The man had been hit low in the right shoulder. There was no exit wound, so the bullet was still in there.

"Will I live?" Graham asked, smiling weakly.

"You've been hit hard," Fletcher said. "But I reckon it will take more than a shoulder wound to kill an old warhorse like you."

Graham nodded. "I didn't expect something like this, Buck. Miz Tyrone could have walked away from it. We had no evidence, just a pack of lies."

Fletcher shrugged. "We had a bum hand all right, but all we could do was play the cards we were dealt. It was her own guilty conscience that killed her in the end."

"We have to get Graham to a doctor," Baker said urgently. "And there's a Lazy R gunman still alive, though he's in a bad way."

"I may be all shot to pieces," Graham protested, "but I'm still able to conduct my affairs. This ranch"—he waved weakly toward the house—"and all the assets pertaining there to, is now the property of the federal government until I can establish whether or not Deke Tyrone had any heirs."

Graham looked at Fletcher, his sagging eyes determined. "Buck, I also declare the horses, saddles and guns of the men killed at your cabin to be the property of the United States government."

Fletcher smiled. "Exceeding your authority some, aren't you, Graham?"

The marshal's long face was sly. "Maybe so, but I'm the federal law around here, and what I say goes."

Fletcher didn't feel like arguing the point, so he nodded. "You tell them United States government fellers to pick those horses up right quick, because I'll be riding on pretty soon."

One ox-drawn wagon still remained in front of the house, the driver either braver, or more likely slower, than the others.

Baker ordered the man to clear a space in the back for Graham and the wounded Lazy R gunman and to carry them to the doctor in Buffalo City.

Later, Fletcher watched the wagon leave, Graham waving a limp hand as he lurched away across the snow.

"What are we going to do with them?" Baker asked, nodding toward the four captive gunmen.

"I'll deal with them," Fletcher said, his face set and grim.

The four men stood tense and wary, covered by the rifles of Walker and the other Connected hand.

These were hired guns, working for wages, with no stake in Judith Tyrone's scheming. Fletcher, being a member of the same fraternity, was inclined to be charitable.

"You four get your horses and ride on out of here," he said. "You can clear the Territory by nightfall. If you don't, I swear I'll hunt down each and every one of you and kill you."

One of the four, a tall man with quiet eyes, nodded and said, "You can't say it fairer than that. All we want to do is put distance between us and this country, and we don't ever want to come back here. It just ain't healthy for a man."

The four gunmen rode out a few minutes later, and Fletcher and Baker watched them go.

"Think they'll be true to their word?" Baker asked.

Fletcher nodded. "They've got no other choice. There's no one around anymore to pay their wages."

The gunfighter smiled. "And besides, they know I'll keep my word."

Later, just as night was falling, they buried Judith Tyrone and her two gunmen in a patch of open ground behind the ranch house.

As Gates held up a guttering oil lamp against the growing darkness, Baker turned to the others and asked, "Anyone want to say anything?"

The orange glow of the lamp reflected on the stony faces of Fletcher and the PP Connected hands. Savannah and Amy stood off to one side, their long skirts flattened against their legs by the keening wind, their hair tossing around their shoulders.

"Anybody?" Baker asked again in quiet desperation.

Finally, Fletcher said, "Let it rest, Matt. None of us feels much inclined to say the words."

"So be it," Baker said.

And one by one, they turned away from Judith Tyrone's grave and walked back to the ranch house.

It began to snow, and within a very short while the graves were covered over, looking no different from the white and silent land around them.

Chapter 25

They saddled up at dawn and prepared to leave the Lazy R.

Amy Prescott, Gates and Walker were headed back to the PP Connected to rebuild what had been destroyed.

"You're a rich woman now," Fletcher told Amy as she stood by her horse. "There's enough gold in the mesa to rebuild the Connected even better than it was before."

Amy Prescott shook her head at him. "There's·been enough dying over that gold," she said. "From now on, I plan to call it Dead Man Mesa because I believe it's cursed." Her eyes determined, she added, "The gold will stay right where it is. My father left me enough money to rebuild the Connected, and I'll go right on selling beef to the Deadwood miners and the army."

The girl smiled. "I'll get by. I don't want to get rich. I just want to stay on my ranch and run it the way my father would have wanted me to."

She stepped lightly into the saddle. "I'm going home, Mr. Fletcher."

Fletcher, Savannah and Baker watched Amy and her riders leave. Then they mounted up and headed for the cabin on the Two-Bit.

It took Fletcher and Baker several days to round up the horses that had belonged to the riders who had attacked the cabin. The animals had wandered far, foraging for grass in the coulees and ravines among the hills that were still relatively free of drifting snow.

"Since, according to Graham, these horses are now government property, I guess we should build some kind of corral," Baker suggested once the animals were herded close to the cabin. "Otherwise they'll just up and scatter to hell and gone."

While Savannah busied herself in the cabin, the men spent two days constructing a crude pole corral among the aspens at the bottom of the ridge. There was plenty of shelter here from the wind, and the trees would keep out most of the snow.

Drawing on his account at the bank, Fletcher had wagonloads of oats and baled hay brought from a big outfit near Cheyenne Crossing, paying top dollar for everything. But the supplies would keep the horses alive through the winter, and even if he wasn't there himself, he could hire a man to live at the cabin and see to their needs.

A week after the corral was finished and the horses penned up, Fletcher, Savannah and Baker sat at supper. It was warm and welcoming inside the cabin, sheltered from the cold wind outside that gusted and sighed among the aspen and drove tattered black clouds across the wide face of the full moon.

Baker sat back in his chair and patted his stomach. "An elegant meal, as always, Savannah. I'm going to miss your cooking."

"You're leaving, Matt?" Savannah asked, surprised.

The man nodded. "Pulling out tomorrow morning. I'm heading back to Washington to be reassigned."

Fletcher smiled. "Hard to think of you not being here, Matt. I've come to regard you as a fixture around the place."

"I can't stay any longer, Buck. I believe I might be in enough trouble as it is." Baker grinned. "I think my boss could consider that I've tarried here for no good reason."

"We'll miss you, Matt," Savannah said. "I really mean that."

Fletcher rolled a smoke, and, not looking up from the makings, said, "I'm pulling out too. There's nothing for me here."

If Savannah was concerned, she didn't let it show.

"We're both pulling out, you mean."

Fletcher nodded. "I guess so, Savannah, but only as far as Cheyenne. Then we go our separate ways."

Savannah shook her head. "That's not going to happen."

Startled, Fletcher looked at her. "What do you mean? Riding together to Cheyenne?"

"No," Savannah answered. "I mean what you said about us going our separate ways."

Fletcher, his face stiff, said, "Well, we'll just have to see about that."

"Yes, we will." Savannah smiled.

Fletcher opened his mouth to say something, then closed it again. Sometimes there was just no reasoning with a determined woman.

Matt Baker saddled up and prepared to ride out at daybreak the next morning.

Savannah said her good-byes. Then, her tears getting the better of her, she ran back into the cabin.

Baker watched her go with sympathetic eyes, then swung into the saddle. He looked down at Fletcher and stuck out his hand.

Fletcher shook Baker's hand and said, "Ride careful, Matt. And thanks. I mean, thanks for everything."

Baker nodded. "It was a privilege knowing you, Buck." He studied the gunfighter's face carefully for a few moments, then said, "I realize you're not a man who sets much store on advice from others, but what old Jeb Coons told you was right on the money."

"What was that?" Fletcher asked warily.

"That this is your home, here on Two-Bit Creek, and here you should stay. Besides"—Baker looked to the cabin—"there's a woman inside there who loves you more than life itself. A man shouldn't ride away from something like that."

Fletcher's face hardened. "You're right, Matt. I don't take advice easily, and I don't intend to start now."

Baker nodded. "Figured you to say something like that, so I only have one more thing to tell you."

"What's that?"

"Buck Fletcher," Baker said, unsmiling, "you're the biggest damn fool in God's creation."

The Pinkerton touched his hat. "See you around."

Then he touched spurs to his horse and was soon lost among the tall hills and the snow and the pines.

Later that day, a strange restlessness in him, Fletcher let the two Thoroughbred mares and his stud loose on the flat around the cabin, trusting them to stay close to the barn and their supply of food.

He shrugged into his mackinaw and took a book, clearing snow away from under the tree where he liked to sit and read. The speckled pup, gamely following on three legs, curled up next to him and promptly fell asleep.

From inside the cabin, Fletcher heard Savannah sing "Brennan on the Moor," just as his mother had once done back in that misty, forgotten time.

He laid down his book, testing the breeze. The scent of biscuits and stew teased his nose.

He knew he should already be riding on, but something was holding him back. Was it this place? Savannah? Or both?

Fletcher shook his head. He didn't have the answers. But somehow he felt at ease, suddenly perfectly content. He had a cabin, money in the bank and the love of a good woman. Did he really want or need anything else?

Then, as the wind stirred the pine branches above his head, the answer came to him.

What Matt Baker had said was true. There was nothing better than right here.

He was home. And here he should stay.

Still, the restlessness had not left him.

He rose, the pup trailing after him, walked to the cabin and stepped inside. Savannah, her hands white with flour, smiled. "I thought you were going to read for a while," she said.

Fletcher shook his head. "Just couldn't settle to it."

He reached for a biscuit, golden brown and hot from the stove, but Savannah slapped his hand. "Those are for dinner. You'll spoil your appetite."

"Just one?"

Savannah smiled. "I guess one won't do you any harm."

As he ate, Fletcher studied the woman as she kneaded more biscuit dough, a stray strand of blond hair falling over her forehead.

"I kind of like having you around here," he said, trying to reach out to her. "You . . . I don't quite know how to say it. You please me, I guess is what I'm trying to tell you."

"And it pleases me to be here," Savannah said, smiling. "I like being around you, Buck Fletcher."

"You don't worry about your reputation being compromised? I mean, an unmarried lady being up here in a cabin alone with a man and all."

"What people say has never bothered me much," Savannah said, her face suddenly serious. "Anyway, you'll be my husband real soon."

Taken aback, Fletcher choked on a biscuit crumb. When his fit of coughing had passed, he managed: "Who said anything about marriage?"

"I just did," Savannah said.

"But I'm not up for taking a wife. I mean, not now."

Savannah bent her head to the bowl of dough in front of her and smiled. "We'll just have to see about that, won't we?"

The days passed slowly, and, thanks in no small measure to Savannah's cooking and her constant fussing, Fletcher's strength grew. The wounds in his side and shoulder healed rapidly.

"Buck, it's time you went to see Doc Hawthorne and got those stitches removed," Savannah said one evening after supper. "Maybe we should ride over there tomorrow."

Fletcher laid down his book and nodded. "Suits me fine. I have to buy some tobacco anyway."

They saddled up next morning under a threatening sky, the black clouds so low they misted the tops of the higher hills. The air was filled with the raw iron smell of snow, and it was bitter cold.

Fletcher let his sorrel stay with the mares and rode a rangy hammerhead black that had belonged to one of the Lazy R riders.

They had just crossed Strawberry Creek when the snow started to fall thickly, driven by a relentless wind blowing from the north. Heads down, their faces muffled by woolen scarves, Fletcher and Savannah rode in silence. Around them the hills were hidden behind a constantly shifting curtain of snow, and their horses were beginning to kick through shallow drifts.

Fletcher turned in the saddle and leaned close to Savannah. "You going to make it?"

The woman nodded, only her eyes appearing above her scarf. "Nice day for a ride," she said.

Fletcher's grin widened. "Amazing what a man will do when he's out of tobacco."

The main street of Buffalo City was almost deserted when they rode in and left their horses at the livery stable.

Like Deadwood, the town was built in a gulch, and the high rock walls protected the rickety wood buildings from the worst of the wind. But the snow still gusted in ragged sheets twenty feet high over the parapets of the gulch, falling on the street like goose down from a gigantic burst pillow.

It wasn't yet noon, but the day was so dark that some of the oil lamps along the boardwalk had already been lit, their flickering flames setting circles of orange and yellow light to dancing on the front of the buildings.

After Fletcher and Savannah left the comparative warmth of the livery stable, they walked to Doc Hawthorne's office, heads bent against the blizzard, and were ushered by the old man into his waiting room.

"I have a miner with a case of the rheumatisms to see to, and then I'll be right with you," Hawthorne said.

Fletcher sat in a chair beside a cherry-red potbellied stove and picked up a three-day-old copy of the *Buffalo City Times,* idly flicking through the pages. Savannah, shapeless in a mackinaw, long skirt and boots, studied the pictures on the wall, faded prints of gallant three-masted clipper ships battling through stormy seas.

Hawthorne appeared after ten minutes and beckoned Fletcher into his surgery, his eyes lingering for a moment on Savannah. "I'm glad to see you took my advice, young man," he said when they were alone.

"What was that?" Fletcher asked. "As I recollect, you gave me a lot of advice."

"About finding yourself a good woman."

Fletcher grinned. "I think she found me."

"No matter," Hawthorne said, unsmiling. "The effect is the same." He nodded at Fletcher. "Now pull up your shirt, and let me check on my handiwork."

After a great deal of tut-tutting, Hawthorne overcame the traditional medical reluctance to pronounce a clean bill of health and was forced to concede that the wound had indeed healed well and that the stitches should come out at once.

"They won't smart quite as much coming out as they did going in," he said.

"That fills me with reassurance," Fletcher said.

The shoulder wound had also healed, though it had left a deep, puckered scar on Fletcher's shoulder, joining several others just like it he carried on his body.

As Fletcher was leaving, Doc Hawthorne laid a hand on his arm.

"Do you recall what I said about uncivilized men civilizing the West with their guns?" he asked.

Fletcher nodded. "I won't forget that particular lecture anytime soon, Doc."

"Nor should you. Well, now it's time for you to move on to other things. I believe, in ten years or so, this Territory will achieve statehood. We'll need men like you, Mr. Fletcher. Oh, not for your guns—that time will have passed—but for your courage and determination and refusal to bend." He opened the door, allowing a gust of cold air and scattered snowflakes to find their way inside.

"When statehood comes, we'll need senators to

send to Washington. I'm not stooping to base flattery when I tell you this, but I think you could well be one of them." He turned to Savannah and smiled. "I predict this man of yours will make his mark one day, but in a way he never imagined."

Savannah returned the old physician's smile. "Doctor, I have no doubt about that. No doubt about that at all."

The snow was falling steadily as Fletcher and Savannah left the doctor's office and stepped onto the boardwalk. There were still few people braving the weather, but a single ox-drawn freight wagon lurched along the almost-deserted street.

Not for the bullwhacker the comfort of a seat on the wagon box like that provided for mule skinners; he either sat on the tongue or walked alongside his oxen. This man was walking, head bent against the wind, and he looked neither to the right nor the left as his team made their slow, plodding way along the street. Soon they were lost in the swirling white shroud of the snow.

Fletcher bought a couple of sacks of tobacco at the general store, then suggested to Savannah that they get something to eat before making the long trip back to the Two-Bit.

The woman nodded. "Hot coffee would taste real good about now."

As they walked along the boardwalk, Fletcher noticed two horses tied to the hitching rail outside the bank, and he considered briefly that this was not a day to be doing banking business.

He soon dismissed the thought and walked past the bank toward the restaurant.

Suddenly a shot shattered the silence of the morning, then another. From somewhere close by, a man's voice yelled, "The bank's being robbed!"

Fletcher turned and saw two men wearing long dusters and fur hats run from the bank, a sack in each of their hands.

The men mounted quickly and swung their horses away from the hitching rail, but the taller of the two suddenly reined up and for a moment studied Fletcher closely.

"You!" he yelled.

His gun came up very fast as Fletcher drew and fired. The man threw up his hands and tumbled from his horse. The second man was aiming his Colt right at Fletcher, and the gunfighter knew he was going to be a split second late getting his own gun into play.

Blam!

A shot sounded close to Fletcher's ear, and he heard the man yelp and drop his gun into the snow, clutching at his arm. Booted feet sounded on the boardwalk, and several vigilantes appeared, shotguns quickly covering the wounded robber.

Fletcher turned. Savannah stood close to him, her right arm still outstretched, a smoking derringer in her hand.

"Thanks," he said. "I figured I was going to be a shade late."

Savannah nodded. "I figured that too."

Fletcher stepped onto the street. The wounded man on the horse was a youngster he didn't know. But he recognized the man he'd shot. The robber's hat had fallen off, exposing close-cropped hair. He looked older and maybe thinner than the last time Fletcher had seen him, but there was no mistaking the blue eyes and the hard gash of a mouth.

It was Bill Buford, a scarlet circle of blood slowly growing in the middle of his chest, the driving snow already settling over his body.

"I figured I had you cold, Fletcher," he said, his face defiant. "Didn't work out that way."

"It seldom does, Buford."

It came to Fletcher then that he'd stripped this man of his dignity and now his life, and it was in him to give something back. He smiled and said, "You came close, Wild Bill."

The dying man grinned. "Wild Bill . . . I like the sound of that."

He was still grinning, his eyes gazing blankly at an iron sky, when death took him.

Fletcher and Savannah shrugged off the thanks of the beaming bank manager, who told them over and over again that they'd saved him from ruination.

"If you ever need anything in the banking line, don't hesitate to call on me," the man said. "My door will always be open."

"Right nice feller, wasn't he?" Fletcher said as he and Savannah stepped into the livery stable.

The woman smiled. "Try asking him for an unsecured loan. See how nice he is then."

Fletcher stood at the door of the stable, glumly studying the worsening blizzard.

"Maybe we should get rooms at the hotel," he said, "until this thing blows itself out."

Savannah shook her head at him. "No, Buck. I want to go home, home to our cabin on the Two-Bit."

She threw her arms around his neck. "Buck Fletcher, from now until the day I die, I never want to be apart from you—not for a day, an hour or a single minute." Her lips met his, and when she drew away, she whispered, "I love you."

Fletcher nodded. "I love you too, Savannah."

It was a lie.

Right then.

But it was a lie that would grow less of a lie with every passing year of the long, happy and eventful life they were destined to spend together.